Praise for *The Wakes*

'*The Wakes* is a truly delightful debut novel about life, death . . . and chicken sandwiches. Funny, moving, tender and wise, I ate up every delicious word' Liane Moriarty

'I adored this novel. It's charming, poignant and moving but also very funny and left me full of the joys of this hard yet beautiful business of being alive' Cathy Rentzenbrink

'Some books grab hold of you and won't let you go until the last page – and far beyond that. *The Wakes* is just such a book, an unforgettable story of hope and regret, of love lost and friendship found, and of understanding how the past and present are always intertwined' Sophie Green

'An absolute delight . . . immensely human and warm and satisfying' Shelley Burr

'I devoured it in two sittings – utterly wonderful! The kind of book where you want to stay in that world long after it's finished. Such a brilliant mix of gentle humour and devastating sadness. My favourite kind of poignant read' Kayte Nunn

'*The Wakes* is an utter delight – warm, funny and profound. I can't wait for everyone to read it. I couldn't believe it was a debut' Sally Hepworth

'Far from a book about mourning, *The Wakes* is a celebration of what it means to be alive, and the joy of finding friendship where you least expect it. Dianne Yarwood explores the messiness of middle age with warmth, humanity and wry humour, as well as fiction's most delicious lemon tarts! I'd eat this book if I could'

Joanna Nell

'*The Wakes* is a truly exceptional novel. Dianne Yarwood skilfully illuminates the breadth of the human experience through a suite of perfectly imperfect characters. This novel is rich with wisdom, love, humour and a sparkling joy – that unique kind of story that can make you sob and chuckle in the very same scene. I flew through this book in just a few sittings and have been gushing about it ever since!'

Kelly Rimmer

'I loved it. So warm and poignant and sweetly funny'

Jacqueline Maley

'It's hard to believe Dianne Yarwood is a debut novelist because *The Wakes* proves that she has the heart of a writer. This is a glorious book that will make you simultaneously want to eat Louisa and Clare's lemon tarts as well as forge a friendship like theirs. It reminded me that life is the most precious gift of all and every day is a treat meant to be enjoyed to its fullest' Natasha Lester

The
Wakes

DIANNE
YARWOOD

PHOENIX

First published in Great Britain in 2023 by Phoenix Books,
an imprint of The Orion Publishing Group Ltd
Carmelite House, 50 Victoria Embankment
London EC4Y 0DZ

An Hachette UK Company

1 3 5 7 9 10 8 6 4 2

A CIP catalogue record for this book is
available from the British Library.

ISBN (Hardback) 978 1 3996 0055 2
ISBN (Export Trade Paperback) 978 1 3996 0056 9
ISBN (eBook) 978 1 3996 0058 3
ISBN (Audio) 978 1 3996 0059 0

Prin

For my husband, Tony

I meant to write about death,
only life came breaking in as usual.

Virginia Woolf

SYDNEY, 2018

1

Three days after his sister-in-law's death, Paul rang Clare. He called in the afternoon as she was walking her dog, and for a few hesitant seconds she considered not answering. It was a late-spring day and as she stood there in the sun with her eager little dog, Paul's name on her phone was jarring. What would she say to him? They'd been out to dinner together four days earlier but there'd been no contact between them since then. She'd thought of them as finished – one nice dinner and they were done – and felt quite relaxed (even relieved) with that outcome. Now, with a sigh, she answered her phone.

After a curt hello, Paul went straight to his news. He told her about Elizabeth's death in brief, flat statements. How it was sudden, an accident. She'd died of a brain injury from a fall when she was alone at home. She had been suffering, supposedly, from the flu.

There was no mistaking the impact this was having on him. His tone and his curtness had shocked her.

'I'm so sorry,' she said. 'How tragic for –'

'Thank you,' he cut in.

She heard an intake of breath, and waited; she guessed what was coming.

'I was hoping you and Louisa would cater for the wake.'

It made perfect sense that he should ask her, but how she wished, wholeheartedly, that he hadn't. She and Louisa were so inexperienced, floundering from one wake to the next, and there was something about Paul, an assumption of a standard. She wasn't even sure she should be doing the funerals at all.

As quickly as that, *no* had flown into her mind.

'It will be quite big,' he went on. 'It's hard to get your head around numbers without RSVPs, but I'm thinking about four hundred people.'

'Gosh,' she said reeling. 'That's a lot.'

Four hundred people. That was hundreds more than they'd done before.

Clearly, they couldn't accept. Yet to decline right in that moment, with that change in his voice, felt particularly hard. Clare thanked him for asking them, but quickly added she would need to discuss it with Louisa and would call him back. He seemed to be content with that.

But as they were ending the call, she couldn't help asking a question. 'How old was she, Paul?'

'Forty-five.'

'Oh.' Clare was forty-five. 'What did she do?'

'She was a high school English teacher. She was adored.'

They said goodbye, and seconds later she phoned Louisa. Louisa was in the Royal Botanic Garden giving one of her tours,

4

and in Clare's view there really was no question it was over. She waited, still standing on the verge under that brilliant sky.

'Good timing Clare,' Louisa said when she answered. 'I've just finished up.' She said it briskly, as if it had involved some great efficiency on her part.

'I've just had a call from Paul Swan,' Clare said, and hurriedly explained that it wasn't about their dinner. (Between them, Louisa liked to call it a date, and Clare didn't.)

She then recounted their conversation almost word for word, and couldn't help expressing it like a decision already made.

Louisa was entirely on board. 'Seriously?' she asked. 'He called four hundred people *"quite big"*?'

'Yep.'

'*Huge* would have been my choice. There's no way we can do it. Does he know it's just the two of us?'

'Yes, he does,' Clare said, and drew in a long breath. She didn't like the thought of it – of that huge wake waiting just for them – and she suggested they ring Paul together. Louisa had a certain bluntness about her that Clare realised could be helpful; her presence felt necessary.

And so, half an hour later when Louisa got home, they called Paul back and put him on speakerphone.

He answered immediately, and this time it was the Paul Swan who Clare thought she knew. The man who had the ease and confidence to ask her out at a wake, and the warmth that had her saying, unexpectedly, *yes*. Clare fumbled from the beginning, thrown off balance by the unexpected return of his warmth, and Louisa, unfortunately, followed suit. With less firmness than they'd intended, they broached concern at their lack of experience, especially with an event of that size, but he wouldn't have a bar of it. In stepped the Paul Swan who ran his own advertising agency and was skilled in persuasion, adept at praise: he flooded them with compliments, recalling the food they had served in observant, elaborate detail.

'Your food,' he concluded, 'has just the right *tone* for a wake.'

Then he emphasised how much it would mean to him and the family to have Clare and Louisa take the job on, how at a time like this it helped to deal with people you knew, and there they were, recklessly nodding at the phone, saying yes, yes, we can appreciate that, Paul.

But the true scope of his skill was evident in the wrapping-up. He pushed away any talk of refusal as if it was a generous thing to do. 'I know you'll do a great job,' he said, 'and you'll have plenty of time. The funeral's not for ten days. We've had delays with the police and the coroner, but that's pretty much over with now.'

Failure ran through them. Louisa looked at Clare, and was reduced to simply mouthing, *The police?* Clare stared dumbly back. When Paul said thank you and goodbye, she repeated his words back to him, and when he hung up, she and Louisa frowned at each other for a fairly long time.

—

The day before Elizabeth's funeral dawned warm and clear. It was the last day of spring.

Clare walked into her kitchen at four that morning to find Louisa already there, hunched over the bench, reading their work schedule for the day. Louisa had her own key and had apparently let herself in. Louisa turned slightly and Clare gave her an ironic good morning as she shuffled towards the kettle.

Nine days had passed since Paul's call. In theory, they'd had plenty of time, but the *amount* of time was never the issue; it was all in the timing: the inevitable late-in-the-day preparations, the issue of freshness. They'd kept their menu leaning high-end, not thinking it through well enough, and it was full of last-minute fiddly things they now basically detested.

Clare filled the kettle. Her eyes felt heavy-lidded and dry, and oh god was she tired. She'd had three hours sleep in the past twenty-four hours, and her first task that morning was to roast eight chickens.

She looked at the neat piles of ingredients placed on the bench around Louisa. 'How long have you been here?' she asked.

Louisa shrugged. 'About half an hour, or maybe an hour. I couldn't sleep. Can you believe that? I got home, showered, went to bed, lay completely still, and then I gradually became more alert.'

Clare had done the opposite. She'd fallen immediately into a deep, dreamless sleep; into an oblivion in which life's commitments had ceased to exist. When her alarm went off – having been set very loud to guarantee impact – she'd been shocked awake, ripped from a sweet dark unconsciousness and left sitting bolt upright in bed, startled and mindless.

Clare plugged in the kettle, put some leaves in a teapot, and leant back against a cupboard to wait. She held both her hands up in front of her. How they ached. They ached liked they belonged to somebody else.

Louisa straightened. 'Right,' she said, 'we should get started. And I know it's early, but I might have to put Elton back on.'

Elton? Clare couldn't hold back a small sigh. Elton John had been the main soundtrack to their last couple of days. She did like him, but they had listened to him *a lot.* Louisa said she found him reassuring. Sometimes, he made her think anything was possible.

—

By now, they worked in the kitchen with a sense of Elizabeth's presence. Through all the long days of cooking, amid a thousand mindless tasks, they'd fallen into imagining her. They imagined her with a baseline of exceptional – how could she be otherwise, with numbers like hers? – and used words like *clever* and *funny, kind* and *generous.* They pictured her with a warm, natural beauty. 'I'm seeing the actress Rosamund Pike,' Clare said early on, and Louisa thought that was fair. They held an image of her as a gifted teacher, standing high on a desk, urging her adoring students to *carpe diem.*

And, just once, they discussed the circumstances of her death.

Louisa had asked: 'You know how Paul mentioned the police? Have you ever considered the possibility of it being something other than an accident? Something deliberate? I mean, a fall in a house that *kills you?*'

Clare frowned. 'What are you implying? *Murder?*'

The word hung in the air, sounding too strange in the kitchen, and Louisa quickly apologised. She'd watched far too much Netflix. Back-to-back crime stories with quirky detectives who never followed the rules. It was easy to think no death was straightforward.

—

A little before seven that morning, as the last of her chickens were resting, Paul rang Clare again. They hadn't spoken to him for several days, not really feeling the need to, though they were scheduled to ring him later that morning. They mainly wanted to run through the plans for the following day, and confirm the time they would meet him and the address of the house.

The sound of Clare's ringtone tore through the kitchen and she shot an irritated look at Louisa – it was too early for a call and so inconvenient. She put down her knife, wiped her hands on her apron, and reached for her phone.

Seeing the name on the screen, she muttered 'It's Paul Swan,' to Louisa, who nodded vaguely back. Louisa was grating lemons. Everything they did, they did by the multitude. A big bowl of lemons sat before her; denuded ones lay around her. Minutes earlier Louisa had said that, as much as she loved them, she hoped to never handle another lemon for the rest of her life.

Clare answered her phone. 'Hello, Paul. How –'

An abrupt 'Clare, it's Paul' cut through her words, and when she tried again – 'How are you?' – her words were overwhelmed by the hectic flow of his. He was clearly agitated.

'First off,' he said, 'I need to say how sorry I am about calling today. I should have called you days ago, and I can't apologise enough. All I can say is my mind's been on other things.' Clare heard a shaky intake of breath, a slight suggestion of panic. 'The problem is, nobody else in the family is focusing on this. They gave me this job because I'm good with food, but I've never been good with numbers. Somehow, I was left with the numbers too.'

Clare's heart rate quickened.

'I've had a fucking awful week,' he said. 'God, sorry for swearing.'

'That's okay,' she said, but suddenly nothing felt okay.

He was flying after that, talking rapidly, as if getting it all out at once would somehow lessen the blow. He'd drastically underestimated the numbers and he was awake most of the night with it. Around two, he'd got up, sat down with a pad and worked through all his messages, went through Elizabeth's life, did some calculations, and he hadn't slept at all since then. He'd realised that he hadn't sufficiently accounted for her immense popularity, or the reality of teachers: the sheer number of ex-students they amassed. These students loved her for life. His first estimate of the mourners, he saw now, was just a bad guess. It hadn't occurred to him until late yesterday, when a friend said to him in passing, *You'd be expecting a huge number of people then?* And that question had returned to him in the middle of the night. Things felt a little *uncontainable*, but he was now thinking eight hundred people. He'd just got off the phone from Elizabeth's husband Dan and her cousin Rachel, and they both saw the sense in that number.

'Sorry, *how many?*' She'd almost hissed the words. He couldn't be serious.

'Eight hundred,' he repeated. 'It could even be more, but when do you stop?'

Clare sucked in air and pivoted to Louisa, throwing her the wildest grimace her face could make.

Louisa glared back. *What?* she mouthed. *What is it?*

Paul was now saying something about the delay with the coroner giving the news time to travel. About people being willing to travel great distances – from interstate and even from *New Zealand* – but she struggled to focus, with *eight hundred* ringing so shrilly in her head.

And then: 'Who knows?' he said. 'We might get a thousand.' As if he wanted to outbid mourning.

He'd almost lost her with that. She heard *a thousand* and was suddenly disorientated, struck by the sensation that at some point in the recent past she must have dropped concentration, opened a door, and walked into completely the wrong life.

'I realise, of course,' he went on, 'that you can't possibly cater for that many people on such short notice. I'm not necessarily asking you to do that. But you needed to know. Just do what you can. I'll call some people and ask them to bring a plate.'

Bring a plate?

'Right,' was all she said in response, and after that he gave her one final, effusive apology, said, 'See you at the funeral, Clare,' and then, abruptly, he was gone.

A strong beam of sunlight now hit the kitchen, bathing it in yellow light. Clare squinted, still clutching the phone in her hand. Her mind was almost stripped of thought.

'What was that all about?' Louisa asked.

Clare turned to her. 'Well,' she said, and stopped. Looking at Louisa she felt a sudden need to soften the news in some way. Theirs was a relatively new friendship, and there was Louisa with her expression of innocent, concerned enquiry, with her tired form bent towards a task that was now surely insignificant.

Clare described the call tentatively, skirting around its substance for a while, giving Louisa a few details about Paul and his distress. But at some point, she had to get to the number.

'HOLY FUCK!' The words exploded out of Louisa.

Clare almost shouted the same words back at her. Not once had she heard Louisa raise her voice. 'I know! I know!' she said.

'Eight hundred people?!' Still in this new voice, marginally reduced to a shriek.

'I know!' Clare said.

'Eight hundred people! You have to be kidding me!'

'I know!' She couldn't get her head around any other answer.

'He can't be serious!'

'He's serious.'

'You're telling me they're planning on fitting eight hundred people in a *house?*'

This prospect made the number even worse. Elizabeth's funeral service and wake were both being held in her cousin Rachel's home – Elizabeth's family hadn't wanted a church or a crematorium – and as a result, the funeral numbers would remain largely intact. There'd be none of the usual attrition between the service and the wake.

'I think it's more a mansion than a house,' Clare said lamely. Paul had described it to her once. It was in the Eastern Suburbs: a grand home sitting right on the harbour, all glass and light.

Louisa looked at her, seeming to not register the point. 'How can he do this?' she asked. 'He can't do this – not on the day before the funeral!'

'But that's the thing,' Clare said. 'I think he can. I remember Tim warning us about this exact situation. About large numbers at short notice being the main quirk of the business. We're probably supposed to have the resources to respond.'

Louisa's face did a thousand things with Clare's comment. A *quirk?*

'I find it very hard to believe that any part of this is normal,' Louisa said.

'It doesn't feel normal,' Clare agreed.

'What's he basing this new number on, anyway? Has he done a proper calculation this time? Used an algorithm or something? You're good with numbers – what do you think?'

'I don't know. He said he just went through her life and counted. He was very apologetic, Louisa. He did say we should just do what we can.'

'*Just do what we can?* How's that going to work? I'm already picturing it. A madding crowd of mourners hunting down a plate.'

Clare looked at Louisa and a huge wide grin she simply couldn't rein in started to spread across her face.

Louisa looked appalled. 'Why are you smiling?'

'I don't know. It must be nerves. Nothing is funny. Nothing. Well, except maybe the madding crowd thing.' And with that, the grin expanded to its full potential.

'Stop it,' Louisa said, but she, too, had a grin forming, and soon she was grinning back at Clare, trying to say she found none of it funny but grinning nonetheless. It all lasted for longer than it should have – beyond the bounds of sanity, really – but when their faces finally loosened and they had some control back, when they could look at each other with a semblance of civility, the air around them had changed a little.

Louisa pursed her lips. 'So, no question. It's a disaster.' A smile still twitched at the corners of her mouth. She picked up their work schedule from the bench. 'And this thing is now meaning-less. Do you know anyone who can help us? What about Amir?'

'Amir's busy working on the submission. Other people?' Clare paused, searching for friends, finding her available circle disconcertingly small. 'No,' she said, 'not really. None that aren't already working.' Louisa's circle, she knew, was even smaller. It would just be the two of them. A couple of univer-sity students would help them serve food at the house, and that would be the extent of it.

Louisa placed the schedule back on the bench and bent over it, breathing deeply with her hands on her hips. 'Without more people,' she said, 'we need to add time to this thing, and the only spare time we have is when we were going to sleep, so we can't go to bed tonight.'

'Nope,' Clare replied. 'And we should only increase quantities of the filling things, the bready things. And ones that aren't too fiddly or time-consuming to prepare.'

'Yep. And you know what? We have to lower our standards.' Louisa hesitated. 'We have to consider frittatas.'

'Frittatas?' The word fell out of Clare.

This would be such a terrible concession. They'd committed to never stooping to anything even resembling a frittata, as a matter of principle. Mini frittatas were everywhere now, but where was the appeal? Weren't they just a quiche with even less texture? How deflating it was to see a plate of them headed your way. They'd done a small amount of research and their main competition was a lady with scant regard for creativity and a website plastered with pictures of them. They'd believed they could stay well above that, occupying a niche of nourishment and innovation.

'We can make slabs of them and cut them into tiny, tiny squares,' Louisa said flatly.

Clare gave a dull nod.

'We can try to make them special. If that's possible.'

Clare nodded again, hearing as she did it the sound of her two teenage children stirring upstairs. It was nearing the end of the school term, and she resisted an impulse to yell up the staircase: 'Kids, don't go to school today! Stay here and cook!' Though, there was the strong chance they'd be more of a hindrance than a help.

She and Louisa sat down at the kitchen table with the schedule in front of them. To the available hours column, they added the hours they'd previously intended to sleep: five in total. Where previously they'd calculated six items of food per person, being two thousand four hundred items in total, they now reduced that to four. With eight hundred people, this equated to a target of three thousand two hundred pieces. It was well after seven, they'd already fallen behind their original plan, and now they'd increased their workload by eight hundred pieces.

'These numbers,' Louisa said, with her pen hovering over the sheet, 'they're extraordinary. I can't see how I'd get more than fifteen people at mine.'

'Fifteen? I think you'd get more than fifteen.'

'I don't think so. Where would I get them from?'

—

A little while later Louisa left the house to shop for more ingredients, in particular an unsettling number of eggs: in their unprofessional world, the egg number alone pointed to absurdity. Clare worked on in the kitchen. Her children passed through, grabbing their breakfast, and when they asked how things were going, she simply said, 'Not great.' She couldn't even begin to share it with them. After they left, she closed down Elton and put the Beatles on instead. The melancholy of 'Yesterday' filled the air and sunlight slanted into the kitchen in wide hot beams. Time was slipping away. She tried to focus on the task she was doing and what would come next, but her head was filled with Elizabeth. With Paul's word *uncontainable*. Her thoughts struggled to get past a thousand people coming to her wake. Past that level of love. That level of *life*.

And in her soul, as she worked, she placed her life next to Elizabeth's and the contrast engulfed her like a tragedy.

2

It can be uncanny, he thought later, how news travels. How it traverses the tiny meandering details of everyday life and finds you, right where it belongs.

It had just turned ten when Chris Lang sat down at the computer. For the past several minutes the department had been quiet: a long-awaited lull. In the preceding hour he'd seen a new patient every ten minutes, in the hour before that he'd been called to help out in the resuscitation area twice, and this was possibly the first time he'd sat down properly in close to eight hours. He sank deep in the chair, released his shoulders and took in a long slow breath, and with that one small indulgence the cumulative effect of three twelve-hour shifts in three days hit him like a stun gun, sending him into a debilitating depth of fatigue. He rotated his neck and tilted his head back, blinking into the harsh overhead light.

He'd walked into the hospital with Amelia, who'd parked right beside him, and she'd thought it necessary to tell him how tired he looked for the start of an afternoon shift. As if he'd have no idea unless she'd pointed it out.

'You look *so tired*,' she said. 'You look like I feel at the *end* of a shift, God help you.'

He'd given her something close to a smile, and said nothing. He couldn't tell her that almost everything in his life was in a state of flux. That he couldn't sleep during the day in a state like that.

It had been a bad week for rostering; they were a specialist and two registrars down, and this was his fourth afternoon shift in a row. Two until midnight. On top of that, he'd stayed hours after his finishing time on the shifts he'd done, feeling a reluctance to leave that became more and more irrational. He lived in Waverton, less than ten minutes from the hospital. He'd drive home around three and go to bed by four. Hear the birds start up about two hours later. Thankfully, for this shift he was rostered on the walking wounded, and so no lives were depending on him – theoretically, at least. Amelia, with her brisk walk and her switched-on air, was on acute. Their immediate world would be okay.

They negotiated the car park and Amelia stayed on the subject, telling him her nephew was a registrar in New Zealand and he was a *mess*. She'd talked to him on the weekend and he'd come off twelve sixteen-hour shifts in a row. 'Things aren't good there,' she said. 'They're considering striking.' And it occurred to Chris that just talking about tiredness can make you more tired.

'*Twelve sixteen-hour shifts in a row*,' she repeated when he didn't respond. 'There's a whole universe of tiredness in that sentence. Remember that? The brutal hours we worked in our residencies? I have a distinct memory of sleeping on the floor of the ward, curled up against the wall near my desk with people forced to step over me. Too exhausted to find somewhere soft.'

He couldn't imagine her doing that; she was meticulous. And now his own awful memories were coming forward.

'The hardest part,' he said, stupidly entering the conversation, 'was being that tired and having to continually deal with people lying on a bed.'

Amelia laughed hard enough at that she had to stop walking, forcing him to stop beside her. 'Yes,' she said, still smiling, 'the bed thing, that was the epicentre of the torture,' but her expression quickly flipped. 'It wasn't funny at the time though. It was literally torture. But you couldn't say anything like that out loud because nobody would touch you if you admitted to any kind of weakness. I got to the point of thinking I couldn't function in my life anymore, that my life wasn't even *viable,* but I was so hemmed in by the system the only way I could see out of it was to stop living. I had thoughts, a few times.'

She'd gone from sleep to suicide in a matter of seconds.

'I'm sorry,' he said.

But Amelia had already resumed walking. 'We should remember all that stuff,' she said. 'Hang on to our empathy. The hours some of those orthopaedic registrars are doing? It's shit. The system's still crazy. I really feel for them.'

'Yes,' he said as the ED doors slid open and they entered the ward. 'You'd have to be a clinical psychopath not to.'

—

Now, staring at the computer screen, Chris forced his eyes wide open with his facial muscles. His next patient was a woman with a cut index finger. He levered himself out of his chair and walked to her cubicle, and when he pushed back the curtain and looked at her, it was like a window cracked, a blast of fresh air.

She was perched on the very edge of the bed, sitting tall and solid with large dark-rimmed glasses and thick dark hair. It was her hair, possibly, that affected him the most: the short cut with its flyaway fringe, the winning combination of aerodynamics and I don't care. Or maybe it was her expression, the *You have got to be kidding me* blaring so clearly from her face? He had the distinct impression he knew her. In his mind he repeated the name he'd read on the computer – Louisa Shaw – but it triggered nothing. Maybe he'd seen her on television?

He smiled at her. She'd woken him up a bit.

He asked her what had happened and off she went, waking him up further. She told him about cutting onions with an extremely sharp knife and not really paying enough attention. About blood being everywhere and not being very good with *injuries*. As he moved closer to the bed, she apologised for her deep smell of egg – it was now part of her: its smell was in her pores, in the fabric of her clothes, the taste of it sat in the back of her throat. And then she apologised for talking so much. She didn't usually but she was feeling edgy, a little bit panicked.

He'd guessed that already. Panicky *fucks* had dotted her conversation in a fairly entertaining way. All in all, he'd had to stifle a few smiles. He made a quick mental note to get her some painkillers, something to settle her.

He gently unwrapped her finger and she turned her head the other way. Syrupy blood rose and oozed. The wound was deep but the ribbon of white tendon was intact. He asked her to hold her finger upright and try to bend it and she followed his instructions with her head still averted. Then he returned her hand to his, palm up.

'Right,' he said. 'On the positive side, you haven't cut the tendon and the blood flow is pretty slow.'

'Oh good,' she said, flicking a glance at her hand. 'Good. Does that mean I won't be here very long? There's this thing I have to do. And on that, we did try to advance my place in the queue with the triage nurse by telling her we were close friends of yours, which obviously we aren't, and I apologise. Though the nurse didn't seem to really *care*.'

He pressed her finger either side of the cut: 'Can you feel that?'
'Yep.'

Then, realising what she'd said about them being friends, he looked from her hand to her face. 'Have we met?' Surely she was a person he wouldn't forget.

'No,' she said. 'But you've met Clare, my friend who brought me in. At the funerals; we're funeral caterers. You haven't met me because I stay in the kitchen most of the time. I'm not good with the bigger groups.'

Funeral Clare? There was a time in his early thirties, a spring, when he went to a wedding a week, almost. This spring, it had been funerals.

'Is Clare here, in the hospital?' he asked. The surprise of the news shot through him. He tried to keep the emotion in it off his face.

'No, she's gone. She left straight after we'd finished with the – *oh fuck that hurts*.'

'I'm sorry,' he said. He'd pressed near her cut again. Now he pressed the other finger: 'Does that feel the same as the cut finger?'

'Yes,' she said.

'Good. The nerve doesn't appear to be damaged either,' he said, just as an intense memory of their food struck him. He hadn't eaten in so long and he almost swayed with emptiness. The only thing he'd put in his system was coffee.

'Your food is excellent,' he said. 'Very good for a funeral.'

'Thank you.'

'Have you eaten in the past six hours?'

'Have I eaten? I've been tasting food since well before dawn.' She told him about an enormous funeral they were doing the next day. 'Princess Di level,' she added. 'Why are you asking?'

'In case you need to go to theatre.'

'*Theatre?*'

He would have liked to have taken a photo of her face right then.

'Look, you'll probably avoid it,' he said. 'It's more than likely it will just need to be flushed out and stitched, but that said I still want to run it by the hand surgeon. The cut *is* deep and you have to be careful with hands – and this is your index finger. She's here, the surgeon, I've just seen her. I'll do my best to have you seen quickly.'

She wasn't at all happy with that – couldn't he just stitch it? – but he stood his ground. Well, no, he actually walked away, telling her he'd be back to check on the outcome. He walked away thinking about Clare. He contacted the hand surgeon, organised pain relief, and headed straight to the cafeteria for another coffee.

—

The department was now full. He saw nine patients in the next hour. He supervised an intern while she examined an elderly lady with a fever and signs of delirium, and then he went to a dangerously drunk teenager. Next, he consulted on a man in his mid-forties who'd ruptured his Achilles while playing volleyball. The man was quite light-hearted given his pain; this was a genuinely brave face, Chris thought. The man was the same age as Chris. Chris told him that this particular injury highlighted the hazards of middle-aged men playing explosive sports part-time, and the man thought the point valid. From there he went to a mild asthma attack, and from there he attended to a young woman who'd been dancing at a party and attempted the splits. She'd done a short run-up, and a preparatory (ill-advised) mid-air leap. It was one of those stories that made him wince even after all these years. She lay on the bed with her hand clutching a bulge high on her leg. '*Is this my hamstring?*' she shrieked at him the second he'd pulled back the curtain.

As soon as he had a spare five minutes, he went back to Louisa Shaw's cubicle, but she was gone. He checked the computer. She'd been lucky; it had been quick. Her finger had been stitched by the hand surgeon and she was discharged. He stood staring at the computer, hesitant, thinking about possibilities, about what he should do. He turned, and after a few steps he hit a slow run out of the ward, an awkward, tired-limb loping movement that got him to Louisa just before the exit doors. He called her name and she whipped around, holding her bandaged finger high in the air. It made her look like she was on the brink of saying something vital.

'I just wanted to check everything went well?' he said, quite breathless.

She nodded. 'Thank you. The hand surgeon was very efficient, and I was given some top-shelf painkillers that should see me through tomorrow, which is very quickly becoming *today.*'

'Great.'

She moved her hand and some fingers. 'I can get a pincer action with my thumb and my three good fingers, so a thousand frittatas are eminently possible.'

He looked at her and wondered about the painkillers.

'How are you getting home?' he asked.

'Uber,' she said. 'It's almost here.'

He nodded. He had nothing else. He wasn't a natural at this, and his dulled brain was incapable of invention.

She turned to go, saying thank you again and goodbye, and he watched her leave. Watched as the automatic doors opened and shut, and she walked through the dimly lit car park and finally out of view.

He went back into the ward and sat down at the computer station. It was near midnight. He'd see one or two more patients before leaving for the night.

A moment later the hand surgeon, Catherine Reddy, sat down at the computer beside him.

'That patient of yours,' she said while she typed. 'She was quite entertaining. Very droll.'

'Yes, she had me smiling.' He kept his eyes on the screen, scrolling through the results of a blood test.

'I actually know the funeral she's doing tomorrow,' Catherine said. 'The woman who died taught my niece. She was an English

24

teacher. It's very sad. She was only forty-five, really unexpected. My niece is going to the funeral. She adored her, absolutely idolised her. My sister says a day wouldn't go by without a mention of Mrs Swan. What Mrs Swan said, what Mrs Swan wore.'

'Swan?'

'Elizabeth Swan.'

And it was done. As simple as a name said without turning and he knew. *Beth's dead.* He continued to stare at his computer as his heart snatched at the news, changing rhythm; a cry came from its depths – *No! No! No!* – and he had to hold it in.

'Do you know her?'

'I did,' he said.

He asked Catherine questions with his heart pounding and his thoughts hurtling. Forced out steady, half-interested words. What happened? When? And in the shock of the news then came the picture, inevitable and clear. Of the two of them: of him, standing with his arms raised and his head turned; of Paul Swan running.

FOUR MONTHS EARLIER

3

Clare Shepard's established adult life, lovingly built and carefully maintained for over two decades, was cracked wide open on a Monday night in winter. She was in the lounge room when it happened, sitting slumped in an armchair, thinking about whether she felt like watching television or reading her book; and around her there was an almost-precious stillness: the dishes were done, her husband David was making tea, and their two children had disappeared into their bedrooms upstairs. She was staring into the near distance, deciding, when David walked in and stood directly in front of her. He delivered some rushed sentences into the short space between them. In truth, she was so fully occupied with her own thoughts she only managed to catch one word worthy of note: 'unhappy'.

Unhappy? Her response to him was basic and reactive: 'What? About the dishes?'

Their children, Alex and Grace, had become experts in evading the dishes. They would both clear some plates and cutlery from the table, stack a few more things into the dishwasher, and then leave the kitchen with an unquestionable air of *well, that's my part definitely done.* For some reason, David saw it as Clare's job to correct their behaviour – to redress what he saw as inadequate dishes training – but so often after a long day at work she lacked the energy and commitment to see it through. Their children were consummate arguers. It was so much easier to do them herself. But everything about that irritated David. Quite a few things irritated him lately. She'd told herself he was overworked. She gave him some space to be cranky.

It wasn't the dishes. When he didn't answer, she'd looked up at him properly, and the expression on his face was so unusual for him, so intense, she'd sat up straight and tried to focus all her attention on him. What was he unhappy about? He sat down opposite her, on the ochre-coloured sofa they'd recently bought which wasn't particularly comfortable and which had her wondering, every time her eyes rested on it, whether they'd made a terrible mistake. She tried to push the worry of the sofa out of her head.

When David next spoke it was in lowered tones, from which she gathered he didn't want to be heard upstairs, but still she felt nothing more than a stirred, and only marginally concerned, curiosity.

He told her again he was unhappy. Increasingly so. He tried to describe the unhappiness so she'd understand, because he knew she was largely unaware of it. He talked softly and rapidly and gave her no opportunity to comment. He talked about feelings of emptiness and numbness, and on those days teaching in the classroom was difficult. Sometimes, and this happened mainly at night in bed, he'd feel a terrible sensation – like an obscure, shifting distress. He was losing – he paused for the right word – *stability*. And with that he was also losing confidence in himself and the future. He knew he should have told her how he was feeling before now, but in the beginning he hadn't wanted to be that person, hadn't wanted her to think of him in that way. But after a little while he became hurt (irrationally maybe) that she hadn't noticed the change in him or realised the magnitude of it. He began watching and waiting for her to comment or ask, not at all sure he even wanted her to, but obsessively watching nonetheless. And that was when he saw how they were.

'You do not want to watch the two of us,' he said, whispering loudly. 'We can be amusing, but at the same time we can be really depressing.'

Her body slackened in shock. What was happening? It felt surreal, him saying these things. It had come out of nowhere, there'd been no warning. Confused, her mind went back to dinner. Had he drunk too much wine? She would admit that dinner hadn't been *fun*. Alex spent most of it filling them in on the planet's impending insect apocalypse. Biology was the school subject Alex most actively engaged with, and she was genuinely interested in it, but biodiversity was proving to be an alarming subject to be constantly brought up to date on.

'Should you see someone?' she asked.

He told her he'd started seeing a psychologist recommended by a friend. He'd been only once so far. The psychologist thought he might be suffering from depression (David didn't agree) and that he may have been for several years.

And you did all that without telling me? Her heart began hammering lightly against her chest.

He told her he'd been through something like this once before. He'd had periods of anxiety when he was a teenager. He wasn't a particularly happy teenager, a fact he'd never expressed out loud to anybody – truly, how could he have brought something like that up in his house? 'Look at my family,' he pointed out. 'A constant fucking comedy competition.' Anyway, it went away with time. He'd faked his way through it.

Her eyes widened. She loved his family and he did too. His warm generous home with its light Scottish accents and flying anecdotes. In almost twenty years he hadn't once mentioned an unhappy upbringing. She was struggling to keep up with him. Why were the two of them depressing?

And work wasn't going well; he'd lost all respect for Norton. He was actually a bully, and probably more interested in a wider stage, possibly politics. Norton had called him passive aggressive, of all things. And his passion for teaching was waning. So much administration, so many complications, they'd just about ruined English. All its inherent pleasures were disappearing. When he thought it through, what he felt was denigrated. Denigrated by the system.

Denigrated? She thought about his job, head of English at a girls' high school. She'd thought he loved it, despite its difficulties. What was he currently teaching? Was it something dire? She was so far behind him. And Norton called him passive aggressive?

'Why are we so depressing?' she asked, and just posing the question jolted her. Nothing about this was *them*. They never talked about themselves as a couple, not with this sort of serious-ness. They generally operated with humour and lightness, even when things were bleak. That's who they were.

'We just exist,' he said.

'But that's a bit –'

'We'll exist like this and then we'll die.'

'That's how you see it? Surely there's more to us and the children –'

'I love the kids, but I'm not relevant to them right now. They always go to you for anything important.'

Everything he said was so severe and extreme. So unyielding. It wasn't like him. Something had happened. There were so many positives in their lives, she knew that, he knew that, but then a thought flew into her mind: when had they last had sex? She couldn't remember the last time. A month, two? *Six?*

'Norton called you passive aggressive?' she asked.

'Yes! Can you believe that, coming from him?'

He'd seen a psychologist, Norton had called him passive aggressive, and he'd said nothing to her. In her mind, she lived in a world where her husband told her everything.

'Why haven't you told me any of this before? Has something else happened?'

He stood up without answering her or looking at her. His acute hesitation stunned her. She stared at him as he settled into an almost confronting position – legs slightly apart, shoulders back, hands on his hips. She followed his eyes as they landed on the book sitting on the little table beside her.

'You're reading *To the Lighthouse* again?' he said.

'Yes.'

'*Again?*'

Was that disgust on his face?

'You re-read so many books,' he said. 'I've seen you read that one at least three times.'

She'd read it a lot more than that. She swallowed. Why was he bringing this old argument up now? The old, stupid re-reading argument? They were not really arguers, but this one was eternal. David simply couldn't fathom her position. With all the great books to read before she died, what made her think she had the time to re-read to the extent she did? 'I understand you re-reading *Wuthering Heights*,' he once said. 'It's good. But nearly every Christmas? And nobody – *nobody* – has the time to re-read *Middlemarch*. It's nine hundred pages long!'

Invariably, the argument left her feeling deficient in a way she knew made no sense.

She looked at him sharply. That was it. He needed her to be deficient, right now. Needed evidence of it, no matter how small. Needed help with whatever he was doing.

Her eyes were still on his face when it changed. She saw him getting ready to speak, saw him trying to find the perfect words for this crucial speech.

Her heart was pounding in her chest now. She heard the words in her head before he said them.

'I've been thinking about us,' he said. 'I'm worried I don't love you anymore.' He paused. 'It's hard, isn't it? To be sure about love.'

—

Later, she would try to remember precisely all the things he said next, all his answers to her questions. As they were coming at her, she could only catch them in parts; there was too much noise in her head.

Alone in her bed that night she re-created them relentlessly.

She remembered him justifying it. How it was all about truth. He needed to start telling the truth about himself, he said. All of it. It was the only way things could get better for him.

She remembered he said 'I'm sorry' more times than she could stand.

She remembered saying to him at some point, very softly, surprising herself as the words left her mouth, 'Please tell me, you have to tell me, does this have anything to do with Hope?'

'Hope?' he'd repeated, and she could see he'd misinterpreted her. And then he paused long enough for her to think Hope wasn't a part of it at all. That he might be trying to remember who she was.

'Hope Walker,' she said.

'Hope Walker from forever ago?' he'd said.

'Yes.'

'Why would you ask me that? Of course it doesn't. This is about *me*.'

She remembered him complimenting her – how he'd loved their life together for a long time, how she was the best partner he could ever hope to find, how his family adored her. Compliments she didn't want to hear then, because they were meaningless.

And she remembered that in the middle of it all there was a scream in her soul for their children. What would happen to them? She felt like she was going to be sick.

Near the end, he became more confident and extravagant. As though he was hearing his own speech for the first time and it was giving him courage. He told her that every day at school he discussed love in some form. 'Love and death, that's really about it for literature,' he said. Love was always there in a text, *because love was important, maybe the point of existence,* and he could therefore never truly avoid thinking of it, and this was the moment she began to consider him the cruellest man she'd ever known.

And not once did he ask her how she felt.

After the part about love and literature she told him to stop talking. She couldn't bear for him to say another thing. She'd said it softly, matching her voice to his, while feeling close to angry. But only close. Anger wasn't a natural emotion for either of them; they were both mild people. The rare times when one of them had become angry, the emotion had looked so absurd on their face the other had laughed.

He told her he would stay the night at Mike's. His brother had a beautiful home with many spare rooms and a very lovely garden. This statement, that he was sorted for the night, was the one that emptied her of everything. She had nothing to say. She couldn't even move from her chair.

He went to their bedroom and emerged a few minutes later with a small bag. Her eyes followed him with the thought that his small bag was already packed, long-ago packed, and the realisation kept her rooted in her chair. He gave her a sad smile and left, throwing more soft apologies as he went, and within seconds of the door closing, Clare heard footsteps coming down the stairs. She quickly scraped together an expression for Grace, one that wouldn't raise suspicion, and she had to follow it with a white lie about David's departure – something about Grandma calling to say she'd had a fall, nothing too serious – and then, then, she had to summon the will to listen to the questions Grace was now firing at her with a twelve-year-old's insistence on immediate gratification: *But I need Dad! Have you ever read* The Rime of the Ancient Mariner? *Mum, it is SO LONG.* Grace read out a handful of lines which were making no sense to her, wanting Clare's help in David's absence, and so there she sat, engulfed by a hot confusion, discussing snakes and albatrosses and the techniques of poetry.

Apparently satisfied, Grace disappeared upstairs with her book.

Clare pulled herself out of the chair and went to her bedroom. A severe storm had been predicted and she now heard the rising wind, the first hard fall of rain. She went to the room's line of windows, checked they were shut, and closed all the shutters. Then she slowly turned back to the near-dark room, hesitant, and went no further, standing motionless with her arms hanging by her sides. She took in long, deep breaths, concentrating on self-control, on steadying herself, on drawing in and exhaling one slow lungful of air after another. But it didn't work. Each breath became shakier than the one before it. It felt like something was coming for her from a long way off. Something vast and old, and now unstoppable. Half a breath and it was there, welling in her and flooding her chest, catching in her throat and turning into great jarring sobs that rose and vented into the empty room. Tears poured down her face. And David wasn't even part of it. It was *her*, and *hers* alone, a terrible thing she'd always known was there and held mostly at bay. It was an unfathomable sense of separation. The absolute loneliness of a life.

With time the pain lessened and her crying slowed, eventually stopping. She undressed and changed into her pyjamas and cleaned her teeth, rituals of bedtime which now appeared crucial, a line of known action to cling to. She slipped into bed and turned her body away from the wide empty space beside her. The bedroom door was open and she stared through it. A streetlamp filled the hallway with pale squares of light, and just below the picture rail she could see the poor moth that had been in the same spot for days, seemingly stuck to the wall. She and David had discussed it only the night before as they lay in bed, acknowledging someone needed to collect it up and place it outside.

'I've read they can lose their bearings sometimes,' she said, 'and that if you take them back outside, they might find their way again.'

'I don't know,' David replied. 'I think it's just at the end of its life cycle. No energy left to do anything but wait to die.'

She stared at the moth for a long time. When she finally fell asleep, it was to the thought she'd lived out a predetermined idea of a marriage, of a life, while the real one carried on somewhere else entirely.

4

It was a night of wild weather. A raging storm had hit an hour or so earlier. First came a howling wind that whipped around the corner of the house, sending gust-torn branches hurtling and scraping across their deck just metres from where he sat, and then an onslaught of rain, heavy slanted sheets of it falling from the sky. It was worrying, of course, these extreme weather events. But for all that, he did feel a kind of paradoxical pleasure in it, seeing out nature's wild threatening elements from the safety and comfort of his cosy back room.

Chris Lang sat camped at a dining table with the budget reports for his department spread before him. He'd been there for hours, since just after dinner, but he was making very slow progress. It was a difficult part of his job and tonight his attention was easily taken away – by the Armageddon outside, and by the nearby television, where Q+A was on. There had been a time when he'd watched Q+A religiously, believing it kept him informed and made him a little smarter; believing it was an enjoyable pastime to watch self-interested politicians evading questions, to critique their shady replies, to witness their occasional squirming. But on one particularly frustrating night he realised the whole thing was simply draining. That if you focused on the arcane detail, if you listened hard to the political hair-splitting, to the intricate combative theorising on budgets and laws and markets, the end point of centuries of civilisation began to look ridiculous. They were an argumentative species living in an overly complicated world – who'd thought that outcome through? From that revelation onwards, he'd switched channels, usually to any sports coverage on offer.

But tonight, when Q+A came on, he'd stuck with it. One of the guests on the panel was a harebrained new senator with very big teeth and she had been horribly riveting. Her statements were either bigoted or plainly stupid, and usually so illogical they suppressed any return argument. Every time she spoke, his mind exclaimed: *This woman is the world gone mad!* (And he had a brief straying thought: *Trump will be re-elected!*) She was currently trying to sidestep a dinner invitation from a young Muslim woman in the audience who'd spoken nothing but searing reasonableness: *Please, just come into my home, sit with us, have a meal, get to know us.*

It was during their deteriorating dinner discussions – the senator appeared to have an insurmountable issue with halal – that his wife Sarah walked into the room. She sat down beside him and placed several sheets of paper on the table next to his reports. Sarah had disappeared into the study straight after dinner, printing off articles and research she'd gathered sporadically over the past few months, and she needed to talk to him. She knew he was busy, but when was he not busy? And so there he sat as Sarah talked and referred to her papers, as she quoted statistics and the opinions of strangers. There he sat, watching and listening as she unfolded the soft slow tragedy of his life.

'We're running out of time,' she said, finishing. 'Seriously running out of time. We need to register with the adoption agency by the end of the month.'

He raked his hand through his hair and began pulling all his reports into a pile in front of him. Out of the corner of his eye he could see the senator revving up. The dinner was definitely off. 'We're officially giving up?' he asked. 'We're done?'

She shrank a little as he said that. 'Done? Giving up? You make it sound like we have a choice, like there's something there to give up.' She sighed, a deep, frustrated exhale. 'And do you have to get that childish look on your face every time I bring this up? This is why we get nowhere. It drives me insane.'

Childish? Sarah believed she knew his entire repertoire of looks and tones of voice. She often announced them well before he was even conscious of employing them. How disheartening it was to be so apparently readable, so easily misunderstood. He certainly felt nothing close to childish; in fact, an ageing degree of regret and dread had washed through him moments after she'd sat down beside him with her papers. He could find nothing in himself to embrace what she wanted, no matter how much she wanted it.

'I can't believe you're still thinking we're going to conceive naturally after all this time,' she said, pointing at him now, for some reason. (Pointing really got his goat.) There was a time when they would have used the phrase 'fall pregnant' – he couldn't remember when 'conceive' had taken over, when something as natural and lively as falling was no longer theirs. It was probably around the time the art of happy conversation had begun to desert them, when banter had become a mine-riddled excursion.

'Just suddenly conceive after everything we've been through?' she demanded, her voice rising.

They'd been through long years of infertility and seven IVF treatments; a month or so ago Sarah had said she couldn't stand hanging on to hope one moment longer. He'd agreed with her that they should give up on IVF. Each failure was heartbreaking; watching her go through the whole process, the coping with loss, all became increasingly hard. But when she'd suggested they stop, what he'd thought was, *Now. Now she'll fall pregnant.* Now the stress of hoping had left her. He was still a world away from thinking about adoption.

The simple fact was they'd started too late. How badly they'd misjudged and mistimed things from the very beginning. Frequently, these past months, he'd felt the terrible lament of it: that somewhere in among all those long years of happy held-back readiness and heedless lovemaking, somewhere in all those years that followed, when the passing of time became palpable, when seasons and years came swifter and sadder, somewhere in that great accumulation of years was their baby, not missed after all with the slightest change in step.

This night he failed to properly adjust his face, failed to open his mind to her convictions, failed to completely take his eyes off the television during their discussion, and so they ended up sleeping with their backs to each other and with enough space between them that there would be no touching, even accidentally. He sensed, rather than heard, that she was crying. He thought he should probably turn over and gather her up and try to broker some sort of accord in the dark, something that would allow the morning to begin on a decent footing, but he didn't. He lay brooding and feigning sleep.

Before long, her crying stopped and her breathing became faint and eventually inaudible. He lay on his back and searched within himself. He'd always been able to find the comfort of expectation; the prospect, however small, of a future existence with his child: the child his soul assumed would always be there. But now the words *we're done* rolled around in his head and he couldn't see or feel anything else there. It was over.

—

They both woke in the early hours of the morning, and by dawn they'd come to a heart-wrenching impasse. How could there be a child? Sarah didn't have it in her to do another round of IVF, she felt too old and tired and destroyed by the rollercoaster of it, and he couldn't bring himself to say yes to adoption. There was a moment when he came close, when he wavered, but in the end he couldn't say the words, couldn't commit to it.

'Can't you imagine the day our teenage son sits us down and tells us he's off to find his *real* parents?' he demanded.

'Can't you imagine the beauty and joy before that moment?' she retorted. 'And why do you always imagine sons?'

He couldn't answer that.

He rose and headed to the shower, gripped by a sense of hollowness and defeat – of what would never be, what he would never have, what he would never witness; of a world, not far away, from which he had vanished. Completely vanished. For without a child, who would remember him?

5

Clare took David's call from the car. He was on his way to work and she'd been at her desk for hours. He was surprised to hear she was there already, but she'd woken at dawn and couldn't bear to stay in bed, then couldn't bear to stay in the house, so she'd left a note for Grace and Alex and come to work. David had her on speaker and his words sounded far away and slightly yelled. He asked her how she was and she answered quietly, 'I'm okay,' and it seemed to be enough for him. He turned to other things with no mention of the night before. She stared at the phone waiting for it, numb, but it didn't come. He rabbited on, filling her in on his sleeping arrangements and some strangeness with his sister-in-law over breakfast and a school executive meeting he had on that morning which was worrying him. He told her about a new young English teacher on staff who'd conducted parent meetings in a red velvet jacket – very red and very velvet – and everyone thought he was fabulous. 'It's a fine line,' he said, 'pulling that one off.'

She listened, frowning more deeply with each new banal detail and saying almost nothing. What was he doing? In all of this, she had to worry about him too, about the state of his mind? Tears gathered and pushed behind her eyes and she pressed her fingers to them. As she was doing this, he stopped speaking midway through a sentence and she supposed he'd finally registered her silence. When he next spoke, his voice was softer and it cracked here and there. 'I'm so sorry,' he said twice. Then came a groan. 'I have year nine first thing this morning,' he said. 'We're doing *Ethan Frome* of all things.' She said nothing. She had no idea what that was.

He was pulling into the school car park and so they quickly had the discussion they had to have – what, exactly, he would tell their children: he wanted to tell them he was leaving for a while with as little uncomfortable detail as possible. But he had to give them something substantial. They had to know he wouldn't leave on a whim. He said he would come to the house that night for dinner and try his best, the prospect of which was so awful she could hardly bear to contemplate it.

Their goodbye was as strange as the call itself. It was as if they'd both been playing a part and the scene was now finished. As if none of it was real.

She returned to her work.

Before her, a document more than a thousand pages long was open on her computer screen. She was up to page two hundred and forty-three. She'd been there for hours, reading, hardly registering any of it. She sighed. She couldn't afford not to focus. She worked in the regulatory affairs division of a large pharmaceutical company. She was a pharmacist by training but had only worked (a little half-heartedly) in pharmacies for about four years. One day, she met someone working in regulatory affairs and it sounded perfect for her. The document in front of her was a small section of a much larger document – a regulatory submission for a new migraine drug. It was a compilation of work from various departments. It was her job to do a high-level review of it so they could be confident it met Australian protocols and procedures. In its entirety, the document included data on clinical trials, manufacturing and product information, information on proper usage and possible side effects, details of labelling: everything necessary to ensure the Therapeutic Goods Administration could make a decision on the new drug's safety and efficacy. That was essentially what had drawn her to the job: the idea of bringing breakthrough medicines to people who needed them, and making sure they were all *safe*. She was an inherently patient and detail-oriented person, so in principle the role suited her. But the road to easing life's struggles for humanity was *so* inundated with detail you could get hopelessly lost in it.

She trained her eyes on the document, tried hard to hang on to the words. But David's words – *Ethan Frome Ethan Frome Ethan Frome* – now droned rhythmically and idiotically through every sentence she attempted. It felt like she was going mad.

She was staring blankly into space when Amir appeared in the doorway, smiling and walking in with one of his quick little knocks. He was a regulatory affairs specialist too, and they'd worked together for more than a decade. In many ways, he was her closest friend.

On any ordinary day, she would have already started telling him exactly what was on her mind by the time he'd settled in the chair opposite her, just as he was doing right now, but not today; she had no desire to share what had happened with David, not even the smallest part of it. She looked back at him with a dreadful exhaustion seeping through her.

His face changed. The smile was replaced by a frown. He'd probably come in to share something jovial, and now he looked thrown.

'Are you okay?' he asked.

She wondered whether she could even speak normally. She tried to restore a little of herself by sitting more upright, giving her head a quick shake, forming something almost like a smile.

'I'm fine,' she said, but from her end it didn't sound convincing.

'Are you sure?'

'I slept *very* badly,' she said, and the basic honesty in the statement helped her cause.

He looked relieved. 'I can see that,' he said, half-smiling. 'Anyway, I came in to tell you there are farewell cupcakes in the kitchen. In case you miss them, which would be a terrible shame.'

'Farewell cupcakes? Who for?'

'For the CEO. It's his last day, remember?' He was frowning again.

'I can't believe I forgot that,' she said.

Now Amir broke into a grin. He had one of those grins you couldn't help responding to. Her face tried to smile again.

'The thing is,' he said, 'the cupcakes have his face on them.'

'Whose face?'

'The CEO's. His face is printed on the icing. It's edible, apparently, but off-putting – though not enough to stop me eating one.'

'His face! How can it be that everyone in the company likes him except for the two of us?'

'I can't explain that.'

'Maybe it's irony? Maybe his face on the cupcakes is meant to be ironic?'

Amir considered this. 'Wouldn't that be great? But I don't think so. It was a flattering photo.'

And there he was, making her attempt another smile.

Amir was even more suited to regulatory affairs than she was. He was detail-oriented too, but he was more rigorous than she was, and he had an outstanding memory. He admitted to knowing all the words to pretty much every song from his favourite musicals. Particularly *Hamilton*. As outrageous as that sounded, she thought it entirely plausible, though she'd never heard him sing any. And he could recite the last line of all his favourite novels. That was probably the thing she loved most about him.

'Have you ever heard of *Ethan Frome*?' she asked.

'*Ethan Frome*.' Then he groaned just like David had.

'Is it a novel?' she asked.

He had a pained expression. 'Yes. Though it's really a novella; it's very short. Edith Wharton wrote it. It's *beyond bleak*.'

She told him David was teaching it to year nine.

'Year nine girls? They're in for a happy time.'

'I've never read it.'

'Well, it's set in a brutal winter in rural America in the late 1800s – are you getting a feel for it? Ethan marries his dead mother's nurse Zeena, because he's worried about living alone, but he realises pretty quickly that he's made a mistake, that he doesn't love her at all – she's a very silent person – and he becomes disillusioned with life. Then Zeena's younger cousin Mattie comes to stay and she's beautiful and sunny and appreciates life, and

Mattie and Ethan fall in love but their love is doomed, because the rules of society mean they can never be together, and so they agree to commit suicide together. They get on a sled and drive it down a snowy slope straight into a tree. (Not the most airtight of suicide plans.) They survive, but they're both terribly injured – Ethan is *crippled* – and they have to rely on Zeena to look after them. And she's of course not a particularly sympathetic nurse because she knows the whole story. Mattie ends up a bitter crone, and all three live on in this bitter tragic silence.'

'Right,' Clare said faintly. 'Yes, that does sound bleak.'

Amir leant forward. 'Are you *sure* you're okay?'

There was such a deep kindness in his tone, it unsteadied her. Tears pushed at her eyes again.

'Yes, thanks, I'll be fine,' she said. 'It's just that my mind's foggy and that's not good with this thing.' She gestured at her computer screen.

He stood up. 'Well, I'll let you get on with it.' But when he got to the door he turned. 'Just promise me you'll stay away from that novel,' he said.

—

She'd made a vegetable lasagne for dinner. She'd chosen it because it was an old family favourite and comfort food, but it was a mistake. It took too long – all the layers and sauces – and she was in the kitchen for ages. Layer by layer the lasagne drained her of her last drops of stamina. More than anything else in this world, she longed to sit. Longed to sit alone, and in silence.

As they'd agreed, she sent David a text ten minutes before the lasagne was due to come out of the oven. She'd been unable to bear the thought of him arriving early and standing and talking to her while she cooked. Their son Alex came downstairs a few minutes before she sent the text. He was tall for fifteen, much taller than Clare. He set the table for her and she glanced at him several times while he was doing it. Just looking at him was breaking her heart. He was such a gentle soul, not big on homework but curious about the world. Deeply concerned about the planet. When the table was done, he sat on one of the stools by the kitchen bench and told her a funny story from school – he was never without a funny story from school; an entire day with his friends was too rife with potential – and she listened and laughed as she usually would.

David arrived on cue, as if just getting home from work, and given the way he walked in, the warm words of greeting he spoke, a stranger – even the two adolescents who lived under the same roof – wouldn't have guessed anything was wrong. Wouldn't have guessed the small world of that house had changed irrevocably.

It threw her to see the act he was putting on. To witness how easily he slipped into this attitude of near-happiness. Where was the line? Where did the real person start? (He would tell her later he'd wanted to convey a feeling of optimism and she'd looked at him blankly, unable to find a place for the word.)

The four of them took their usual seats at the table and dinner began like any other weekday night. Grace was particularly animated. She'd handed in her English homework, *The Rime of the Ancient Mariner* was behind her forever, and life was good again. Clare mentioned the cupcakes; she'd had three of them.

David told them what he was planning as the last mouthfuls of food were being eaten. He did a remarkable job of normalising something Clare was finding unspeakably strange. He described what he was going through as a low and difficult period. He'd lost sight of himself (his exact words) and felt on the edge of anxiety and depression. But only on the edge; he would be okay. He was getting help, and he just needed some time to calm himself down and essentially get back to himself. He was staying at Mike's house for a while, in his brother's granny flat, to give his life smaller boundaries, to give himself some solitude and quiet.

He said nothing about Clare and the absence of love. Fair enough, Clare thought, it wasn't for this table. She had no desire to hear about it. No desire to see the reality of it written on her children's faces.

Alex and Grace were understandably shocked, though in a normal sort of way, if such a thing were possible. Alex needed some things repeated, but there was no terrible distress in their responses. Their eyes had flown to Clare, and she put everything she had, *everything*, into an expression of limitless reassurance: *we're sensible adults, we love you, you will be okay.*

The children accepted that, slowly. You could see it settle in them. Yes, they knew they were loved. And that was probably enough, for now.

6

Once they let go of their child, Chris and Sarah had to settle into a dramatically changed reality. They settled in badly, hunkering down into their work lives, and giving less to each other. Weeks passed in this way, and when Sarah proposed marriage counselling one evening, it was both unexpected and obvious.

Chris was convinced the whole thing would achieve a result fairly close to zero (he put marriage counsellors in the same quirkily designed box as naturopaths and chiropractors), but he agreed to sit on a lounge and receive vague advice because any form of overt negativity on his part had begun to feel dangerous. Their counsellor, Joanne, was everything he had expected. She was young, to his mind a little given to cliché, and from her very first soft, caring hello she planted a seed of annoyance in him that lodged so deep it was going to take a cataclysmic change in her behaviour to uproot it. He knew this was an intrinsic fault of his (though *fault* might be too harsh a term), how he made snap judgements that were never easily undone, but he did feel the need after their first session to check with Sarah: 'Was Joanne actually *recommended* to us by someone? Someone we like?'

A session with Joanne was a litany of calm, searching sentences, controlled gazes and long conversational spaces he or Sarah were supposed to fill. Sarah did the bulk of the filling. Once, during one of those long, awful spaces, he was tempted to cut to the chase; to say, 'The truth is, Joanne, Sarah and I have both had to relinquish a paramount and lifelong dream, and it's basically a matter of waiting to see if we can be enough for each other without it.'

But he didn't say it. He sat back on the lounge and listened, spoke when requested, feigned open-mindedness and patience.

One day, though, to her credit, Joanne managed to completely surprise him. They'd been discussing his and Sarah's last serious argument, held on his forty-sixth birthday a few weeks earlier. Sarah had given him a linen shirt and a new book on Vladimir Putin, and he'd been offended and unable to hide it (and these days a look was all it took; a look could ignite anything). Sarah *hated* Putin – she called him a sociopath, pure evil – and yet she'd given him a book on the man! He didn't like or admire Putin – there was no question about that – but he couldn't help being intrigued by how such a man could be made, how he could hang on to influence and power. The gift troubled him; didn't Sarah *care* anymore what he did with his time? She said it was meant in a light-hearted way – basically a joke – but she could see now that simple light-hearted exchanges were beyond them. Everything was loaded and misfiring. Their argument ran deep and personal and intense. They never resurrected his birthday.

In its retelling, the story did neither of them any favours; there was one of those long, considered silences in its aftermath. Joanne looked at them both intently, started with a point about the self-perpetuating nature of a negative mindset, and then stopped. Had there been a particular look on his face? (He did find her point fairly obvious.) After another thoughtful silence, Joanne leant forward in her chair and pressed her fingertips together in front of her chest.

'I'd like to ask you both one important question,' she said softly, though he already assumed it was for him. 'Are you willing to give your marriage one last try?'

One last try? Her words and expression threw him. Joanne believed their marriage was in its terminal stages, and she'd come to that position in barely three sessions! Had Sarah been here without him? And could a marriage really be saved by one last try? Were they supposed to perform – like actors auditioning for a remake of their marriage?

He nodded, Sarah nodded, both of them floundering with the severity of the question.

When they arrived home, Sarah suggested they get away. Friends of theirs who now lived in Brisbane, Julie and Steve Turner, were heading to Yamba for a beach holiday. What if they joined them? It had been so long since they'd seen the Turners. It coincided with the beginning of the school holidays – that was a negative – but Julie said late September wasn't usually too busy. Not like Christmas. Sarah reasoned they would have plenty of time together just the two of them, but it was always nice, she thought, to have someone else to share a meal with on a holiday, even to have extra players for a game.

He barely heard the last half of what she'd said. His mind had pulled up and veered off with the mention of Yamba. He'd never been there and wasn't even sure where it was, but the name had leapt through him. *Yamba!*

'What do you think?' she asked.

He nodded vaguely.

'Why are you frowning?'

He raised his eyebrows. 'No, no, it sounds good,' he said. 'I can probably organise some time off.' Was he just agreeing to a short holiday? He couldn't admit he hadn't been listening, not under the circumstances, not given the session they'd just had. He would double back later, ask Sarah about it again as if he was simply rechecking the plan.

—

It came to him an hour or so later, when they were both watching television. The significance of the name. Its truth flushed into his face, but he kept his eyes fixed on the screen, and his body still.

Yamba belonged to Beth.

He remembered it now. He pictured Beth curled up on the shabby brown lounge in his Ealing Common flat, telling him how she went there every Christmas holiday for the first twenty years of her life and sometimes other holidays as well. She loved it beyond words. Those family beach holidays were the highlight of her childhood, the cornerstone of her childhood contentment. They were always huge family gatherings. She'd grown up on a farm in Moree and her grandparents owned a big old house by the sea.

He took a long, quiet breath in. He hadn't thought about Beth in a long time. Over the years, he'd trained himself not to think about her. Caught in her memory were questions he hadn't faced, and images so beautiful that to evoke them was almost traumatic.

—

They met when he was living in London. He was twenty-eight and working at St Thomas' Hospital when Beth came to London to stay with her sister. She intended on staying for a month – she'd ended a long-term relationship and missed her sister – but because of Chris, she'd stretched it to six. She only left when her mother became sick, saying she simply couldn't live so far away from her family. *I'll follow you home soon*, he told her, utterly believing it. He couldn't give up his job, not right at that moment. He was learning too much.

Beth arrived in the early days of winter, when the weather was bleak and the pavements were covered in a treacherous black ice. She'd slipped over near the Tate – shooting up from the tube station, she'd rounded a corner at a pointless pace, coming from nowhere and heading towards nothing, so lonely she could barely breathe. His flatmate, Paul Swan – a saviour, now sitting so patiently in the waiting room – had picked Beth up from the pavement and brought her in to St Thomas', where Chris was working in Emergency. When Chris pulled back the curtain to the cubicle she was in, it was like a jolt to the heart. She was staggeringly beautiful; he'd registered that fact with a feeling close to alarm.

As Chris examined her, Beth told him how she'd flown halfway around the world to be with her sister, but her sister worked long hours in a law firm and was rarely home. Beth spent most days wandering about the city and wallowing in self-pity. That morning she'd sat in Westminster Abbey and heard accounts of its long history and all its *people* and she found herself envying a church! Then she'd apologised for all the detail, all the *blah*, telling him his Australian accent was undoing her.

Chris responded, working hard on the quality of his conversation. He attempted to cheer her up. He told her people were slipping over constantly on the icy pavements and there'd been such an unprecedented number of broken bones that his hospital was on the brink of running out of plaster of Paris. He'd quoted Monty Python – a cheese-shop-without-cheese quip – and she'd chuckled and then clutched at her bruised ribs. And when her discharge papers were done, he'd heedlessly blurted out an invitation to coffee, or dinner, or anything really, even though he guessed that Paul, still sitting in the waiting room, probably felt similarly compelled. (Chris would later apologise to Paul, and Paul would reply that it was fine. He didn't know Beth any more than Chris did, and it was Beth's decision after all.)

Beth had hesitated, but then she'd smiled weakly and said something like, *Why not?*

Why not? Now, he looked through his life. Why not?

Six months with Beth and she was firmly in his history. She was a feeling and a place and a time he could return to; and he often did, in the early years. And she was this, now – this hopeless wondering, this guilty regret. And she may even be that deeper thing, that indescribable sadness he sometimes felt, long removed from her but maybe her nonetheless.

There'd been three letters between them in total. The first came from Beth shortly after she'd returned home to Australia. *I miss you already* breathed through every line. Then a reply from him that took so much longer than he'd intended. He struggled to express himself romantically in written form. He'd start a letter, leave it, read it over and hate it all. He rang her instead, a phone call which he couldn't really afford, and the time delays made the conversation awkward. He swore he'd avoid phone calls in the future, use them as a last resort. After that, he'd started again on his letter and he sent it this time. But her reply took far longer than the one before it and its tone was different. Altered in a way it took him a few readings to place. It was more informational, that was the key. Her mother was undergoing chemotherapy but she was handling it well and the prognosis was good; Beth had a new teaching job and she loved it, and it felt like she'd stay there for life. She didn't say she missed him until the very last line. The next letter he wrote would remain in his possession forever. He was busy at work and taking his time with it, trying to revitalise the emotion that felt diminished in hers. When it was partially written there came another letter from Beth – a relatively short one this time. A series of lovely statements about their time together and the memories she'd keep. She'd met someone else. She was saying goodbye.

'I'm making coffee,' Sarah said, and he was hurled back into the present. He turned and smiled at Sarah and said that would be nice. He went with her to the kitchen and opened the pantry, thinking they needed a biscuit or some nice chocolate with their coffee. He couldn't make a decision so he piled a selection onto a small plate and carried it back to the lounge room where he waited for Sarah. Hanging on to his marriage, with Beth still in his head.

—

He managed to get the time off work, calling in a few rostering favours, and a week later they prepared to go. Early in the piece he'd made the suggestion they try somewhere else – after all, it was a nine-hour car trip to Yamba with stops. *Nine hours*, was that sensible? He badly wanted to change their destination. That morning he'd googled *Beth Tennant* before leaving home for his shift, and for a few minutes he went down a rabbit hole of Beth Tennants. None of them were her.

But Sarah was disappointed. She'd always wanted to see Yamba and she'd locked in the Turners for at least one lunch. And so he backed down, and instead worked on settling his memories, on keeping all his wayward thoughts at bay.

And as they packed their beach gear and light clothing, they softened towards each other. Their conversations loosened and a more positive air blew through them. They had a plan, a path, and maybe they would see each other as they had been before. Maybe it was still possible to find what they had lost?

7

David rang Clare almost every day. In every call he apologised, and in some form or another he told her he missed her. She didn't enjoy the calls and often made a face at the phone when they were done. But she always answered her phone when his name appeared. Maybe she answered because occasionally he said something that would be a reminder of the man she'd lived with so happily. It would arouse in her a sudden, intense familiarity and comfort and she'd think, *There, there it is, that's* us.

With every call she thought: *Today, I'll learn what set this all off, and I'll understand.* But with every call she understood less of what they were, or what they had been. What was a marriage anyway? A couple of clear honest sentences and it was gone.

And with every call he was doing something new and strange to her: he was beginning to make love seem irrelevant.

Almost a month had passed since he'd left. It was a work day, and he called her as she was on the way home from the office. He told her how much he was enjoying Mike's granny flat – boutique hotel to be more accurate – and about the virtues of meditation.

He'd never tried it before. Mike's wife Caro had suggested a great app and it did seem to suit him; his anxiety was lessening. There was such an unexpected benefit, he'd found, in *not thinking*. He asked her how she was, and she told him she was taking some time off work. She had long service leave accrued and she was intending on using it. A couple of months – maybe even three, to take her up to Christmas.

This surprised him. 'That's a long time,' he said. 'Are you going anywhere?'

'No.'

'Why are you taking it off?'

She told him she needed a break. She hadn't slept properly for almost two weeks, and she simply couldn't do her job without sleep. It required a level of focus she didn't have, and the responsibility was too great.

'But you must have got some sleep in two weeks!'

'I don't think so. It doesn't feel like I have. I don't remember any.' The first couple of weeks he was gone, she'd felt like she could sleep forever. Then it changed completely.

'How is it possible to not sleep for two weeks?'

'You tell me.'

It was as if she'd lost the fundamental skill of *falling asleep*. She'd tried everything and none of it worked. She'd go to bed, arrange her body into a position she imagined was conducive to sleep, and then she'd try to blacken her mind and deaden all thought. To that she'd added meditation, soothing music, sleep-inducing herbal teas and alcohol. At one point she'd given in and taken some light sleeping pills, but they left her feeling displaced and largely awake. She'd only ever flirted around the edges of sleep; deep, sound sleep now appeared to be a peculiar and ultimately unattainable state.

'You're giving up work because you can't sleep?'

He made it sound ridiculous. *But maybe my life is ridiculous now*, she was about to say, but he'd jumped in with an apology. He could see, of course, that it was probably him, after all, killing her sleep.

'I'm sorry,' he said. She could sense him giving her a hopeless shrug.

With sleeplessness she was becoming more vulnerable and emotional. She'd grown up in a family where difficult emotions were contained. She was feeling much less able to do that. She would now cry easily and for small reasons. Sometimes tears would slip down her face before she was even aware of being moved.

That morning, she'd sobbed in front of Amir, something she couldn't remember ever having done before. An unstoppable, hopeless weeping. He'd been one of the few people she'd talked to about David leaving – she'd told him four days later – and after that, he'd checked on her every day. He saw her reduce every day, he understood the incremental declines wrought by sleeplessness. Unexpectedly that day, he suggested she take a break, offering to finish her part in the submission; he could bring in another team member to help him.

His kindness was heartbreaking and she started to sob.

She finished work the next day. She'd spent the entire day doing a handover with Amir, and when she finally closed down the document it was with a sense of relief. She knew she was doing the right thing.

—

After work she rode the bus home, staring unseeing out the window. When the bus arrived at her stop she had trouble with the stairs, taking them awkwardly. An ache ran down her right side and it interfered with the movement of her leg. She limped the five-block walk to her street, and had just rounded the corner when she heard it: '*Clare!*'

She was slow to react. She was so deep within herself, so closed over, the word barely permeated her. Certainly it was unexpected: *nothing* about her would have suggested she was in the mood for interaction.

But it came again, louder this time: '*CLARE!*'

She turned her head and there, across the street, standing in Lara's front garden, was the woman who'd recently bought the house. From memory, she'd been living there about a month. Lara was in her early nineties and had moved in with her daughter. What an awful day it had been, the day Lara left. Lara and her husband Emin – a beautiful and generous Armenian couple – were living in the old house at the end of the street when Clare and David bought their house shortly after they were married. Emin died a few years later and Lara stayed on in the house. Lara liked to have tea on her porch, and as she became older, she often sat at her open front window and watched the world go by. Clare would stop and talk to her almost every day. 'You remind me of myself,' Lara would say to Clare. 'I moved into this street and raised my children, just like you.' Lara was a kind, friendly witness to Clare's life. Clare would see her when she passed by on her way to the bus stop, when she took her children to school, when she walked her little dog Stuart. Lara gave Clare cooking lessons in her kitchen and told Clare she could raid her garden for herbs and vegetables whenever she liked. That Lara's life in the street was over was heartbreaking.

And this lady who'd moved in – Clare was struggling to retrieve her name – was an entirely different ball game. Clare remembered she'd moved here to Willoughby from Five Dock, Inner West to Lower North Shore. She'd said she liked to move, and she'd been lured to Willoughby by the greenery. 'It feels very villagey here,' she'd said, 'which is nice.'

Clare also remembered, with an inner wince, that she'd offered to have the woman in for a cup of tea, but weeks had passed and she'd done nothing.

Clare walked across the street, tearing through the alphabet in her head, searching for a name.

'It's Louisa,' the woman said. 'Louisa Shaw.'

Louisa Shaw stood beneath Lara's large Robinia, under a lime-green canopy so bright it was if the air around her was alight. Clare's first impression of Louisa came rushing back: the tall, wide-hipped physique; the short, wayward hairstyle; the pretty face up close.

Clare hauled herself upright. 'I'm sorry, Louisa,' she said. She tried hard to round up some enthusiasm for a conversation, something hospitable, but inside her came the childish cry: *I need Lara back.* 'How are you? Have you settled in?'

'Almost! It's still a bit messy inside but I'll get there.'

A tall shaggy dog came around the side of the house and sat next to her, and she fondled his ear.

He was an outstanding-looking dog.

'This is Gilbert,' Louisa said. 'He's a groodle. He's living with me for six months while his owners travel the world.'

Clare nodded.

'He's funny, isn't he?' Louisa said. 'I think he looks like a person in a dog suit.'

Clare smiled. He did.

'And the haircut? His owner cuts it herself *with scissors*. When he looks at me from a certain angle, I get Ed Sheeran.'

Clare smiled again, a little wider this time. She could actually see that.

'I've been looking out for you,' Louisa said. 'I wanted to say how sorry I was. About your husband.'

Clare's eyes flew up the street to her own house. How had that news travelled? She'd told such a small, select group of people. She turned back to Louisa.

'What a dick,' Louisa said.

Who on earth had she been talking to? And what exactly did she know?

'Anyway,' Louisa said, 'I thought maybe I could mow your lawn for you?'

Now Clare's eyes swung up to her house again, up to her unkempt lawn with its spring growth and sloppy edges. What a woefully public statement on her life that was.

'I love mowing, such big results for so little effort. I mow for a living. Well, not really *a living* per se. Anyway, I've got time. How about I do it next time I've got the mower out?'

More unbearable kindness! It was becoming too much for one day.

'That's very generous,' Clare said. 'Thank you. But my son Alex is supposed to be in charge of our mowing. The thing is, he has this theory of keeping our garden as wild as possible to attract beneficial insects, but I think he's going too far with the lawn. It might be more about teenage laziness than habitat.' She ran a weary hand across her forehead.

'Good on him. That will do me out of business but we do need more insects.'

Clare nodded.

'If you don't mind me saying,' Louisa said, 'you look very tired.'

'No, that's okay. It's true. I'm not sleeping at all and I know how bad I look. I don't have eyelids anymore. They're miniature lead blankets.' This terrible tiredness hadn't only let in emotion; flamboyance had come too.

She'd caught Louisa off guard; Louisa laughed and snorted, then immediately apologised for the snort.

'Don't apologise,' Clare said. 'I love a good snort.'

'When you think about it,' Louisa mused, 'a snort is really an accelerated laugh.'

'True!' Clare was getting close to laughing herself. 'Anyway' – Clare bent to pick up her bag – 'I'd better be getting home. Thanks again for the mowing offer. It was very kind but I'll remind Alex.'

'Sure. Now try for an early night. Tie down those blankets.'

Clare put her bag back down. 'Would you believe I have a school reunion to go to tonight?'

'Stop it! You go to those things?'

'Yes. Don't you?'

'No!'

Clare gave her a look, half grimace, half desperation. 'Not one part of me wants to go, but I promised an old school friend I would. I said yes ages ago.'

'Tell your friend you can't anymore!'

'I don't think I can. She's so keen to go and I know she won't go alone.'

'Surely she understands where you're at right now?'

'No, she doesn't,' Clare said. 'I haven't told many people. Just family.' She couldn't help looking up the street again. Just how had Louisa found out? 'And to be honest,' she added, 'it feels like far too much effort to ring Helen and explain what's happened, why I haven't told her, apologise for pulling out at the last minute, et cetera, et cetera. It seems easier to go. There are some people I guess I wouldn't mind seeing. I'll just avoid the questions about myself.'

'Are you kidding me? With your body language your old classmates are going to eat you alive.'

And with that a laugh burst out of Clare. Such an alien sensation.

'Why is this Helen so desperate to go?' Louisa asked.

'It's all about this boy, Parker Wild, who she liked at school. He's never been to a reunion but he's going to this one.'

'Parker Wild? Now there's a name. Was he a Parker or was he wild?'

'He was a Parker, not at all wild. His brother was though. He had two fingers missing.' She winced. There was the flamboyance again, the oversharing. Her filter was shot.

'What's Helen's interest after all this time?'

Clare shrugged. 'I don't think she's particularly happy in her marriage at the moment. Helen and Parker were close friends at school, both shy, and Helen *supposedly* has always wondered what would have happened if she'd had the courage to speak up or make some sort of romantic move. Or he had. She says she wants to sort it out once and for all.'

'Sort it out?' Louisa gave Clare a highly quizzical look. It struck Clare, then, that Louisa had a face extremely well equipped for the expression of thoughts. Every question about Helen's hopeless position was in Louisa's look.

'I agree,' Clare said. 'Anyway, I'd better go.'

Then Louisa knelt down, picked up a pair of gardening shears and cut purple crocuses for Clare from an abundant clump near her feet.

Clare took the flowers, picked up her bag, said thanks and goodbye, and limped up the street. The flowers jiggled in front of her as she walked, each flower head a natural perfection of six identical segments. She walked through her door speaking to them in her head: *Good on you*, she told them. *Those who planted you are gone, that new, slightly odd person is there, and up you come regardless, intricate and perfect.* She found a vase for them, these almost-friends, and placed them in the kitchen. And all this she did on the verge of tears.

—

It was a significant mistake, of course. She knew that within minutes. A reunion, *obviously*, was a question-based event. If you didn't want to answer questions, you shouldn't go to a school reunion. And she also remembered within minutes that you needed a certain buoyancy for a reunion. Something she definitely didn't have.

She'd met Helen out the front. They'd walked in together with Helen kindly asking about her limp. Clare explained she hadn't actually hurt herself, or pulled anything, the limp just arrived. She said she assumed it was stress as she'd had a lot on at work. They were given their sticky name labels at the entrance table and they slapped them onto their chests as they headed into the bowling club.

Two hours later, standing on hard mustard carpet with a chardonnay in her hand, she felt weighted to the spot by torpor. Conversation was arduous. She tried to summon some interest in other people's stories but it wasn't easy. When forced to answer questions about herself she responded with vague banalities, injecting false warmth into her voice, and when friends asked after David she said he was *fine*. That part was true, at least.

And things hadn't gone at all well with Parker. They'd stumbled upon him early and found him very much improved with age. They'd both almost flinched with approval. He headed up a social enterprise group, something they didn't entirely follow but interpreted as a means by which he generously and professionally contributed to society. He was married and liked to take his young family to culture-rich places. He seemed genuinely pleased to see them and he answered their questions thoughtfully and with some very well-placed jokes. But his old group came to monopolise him and he easily put Helen aside with no hint of loss or lost opportunity. There was no flirtation, no pining. All in all, they were given, perhaps, fifteen minutes of his time.

Helen had muttered, 'Shit, shit, SHIT,' as soon as he was gone. Then she went to the bar.

Helen now arrived at her elbow.

'Would you like to sit down for a bit?' she asked in a gentle tone.

'Oh, yes,' Clare blurted.

They found a secluded table near the bathrooms. Clare sank into her chair, saying she was beyond exhausted and had drunk a little bit too much chardonnay. People kept buying her a glass.

'The chardonnay's a little thin, isn't it?' she said.

'They might be buying you wine because you look so ...' Helen paused. 'I don't know the word. Clare, what on earth has happened to you?'

So Clare told her the story. But she couldn't retrieve the finer points that gave it nuance, made it theirs – maybe it was the wine? She couldn't find the words to give her story its fundamental distinction. It came out like a cliché: her husband, in mid-life, had left her with no warning, saying there was nobody else and that he probably didn't love her and possibly never had. It appalled her how it sounded, told at that table.

Helen was shocked. She couldn't believe it! They were a great couple! She loved David! She couldn't believe it of him!

Clare nodded and nodded, collapsing a little more with each heartfelt exclamation. *This*, she thought to herself, *is why I haven't told many people. This shock.* She hated having to witness this shock.

Clare took another mouthful of wine, much larger than she'd intended, and it seemed to go straight to the back of her eyes. It was like a glare had hit them.

'What if,' she said to Helen, 'instead of love, David and I were just attracted to each other because we're the same? Bound together by mutual caution? You know how cautious I am. You know what Mum was like. And David's not so different to me.' Clare's mother had raised her on a doctrine of stay small, stay safe, stay sensible. Clare had been handed caution like it was an inheritance.

'That's ridiculous,' Helen said. 'There's a lot more to you than just *caution*. You are an amazing human being.' She looked straight at Clare, demanding her attention. 'You don't want to get me started on your mum. She undervalued you. What was that thing she used to say to you?'

'That I should know my limitations.'

'There it is. That's what I'm talking about. How about that for parenting? For negativity? Your mum's cup wasn't half-empty – it was filled to the brim with something she didn't like the taste of.'

It was hard not to smile at that.

'Where is she now? Is she still living up the coast?'

'Yes.' Clare sighed. She didn't want to talk about her mother. 'I should have called our marriage off before the wedding,' she said, instead. Though she wasn't sure why she chose to make that particular admission.

'*What?* Why are you *changing everything?* You're such a great couple. You're so suited to each other and it's not about this caution thing. I had you two on a pedestal. I had your marriage on a pedestal. I can't believe David has said these things. He's always so *sweet*. God, it feels like he's dead! Like he's dead to us! And we all had that great holiday together last year.' She drew in a long breath and let it out slowly. 'This is far, far too sad.

I need to pee and blow my nose. I'm sorry, I'll have to go to the bathroom. I'll be back.'

Clare waited alone, sipping her wine. Her gaze took in the entire room before settling on a group of women who'd begun dancing. It came to her that the sort of happy abandon required for dancing was forever lost to her now. She would never dance again. And as she watched the dancing women, she began to feel peculiar: a parched emptiness started in her throat and continued through her, an awful bodiless sensation, an unbearable fluttering lightness that made her want to flee. Remaining seated felt impossible.

She stood up and headed for the bathroom. She'd tell Helen she was leaving.

She pushed open the heavy bathroom door and the small exertion that act required left her disorientated and dizzy. The door banged behind her and she swayed. She grabbed the edge of the basin and thought, for a fraction of a moment, she should call out to Helen in the cubicle, but in the next fraction there was only the sense of impending doom, and then there was no time at all, no time for hands to be employed, there was only the floor rising far too quickly towards her and the sick, hard thud as her undefended face hit the tiles.

8

Chris lifted his sunglasses to catch the true colours of the sea. His eyes ran over the sun-dazzled water. Over white-crested waves of aquamarine and slow-rising swathes of blue, then across the stretch of ultramarine that took his eyes to the horizon. He sighed. How different would he be if he woke to this every day? He replaced his sunglasses and sat low in his beach chair. Time passed, and he was aware of nothing but beauty, nothing but the sea. And when he eventually looked away a thought went with him, about his childlessness, about his great despair: life hadn't offered him everything he'd wanted – that was it in a nutshell – and before that vast sea, from that privileged sunlit vantage point, it seemed absurdly egotistical to have presumed it would.

He heard Sarah laugh. A soft, contented sound. She was sitting beside him reading her book, and as he turned towards her, she raised her eyes from the page and smiled, and a flash of pride and love went through him. Her dark, shoulder-length hair was pulled back into a ponytail and she looked vibrant and beautiful.

They were relaxed and comfortable with their legs outstretched on the warm, soft sand. The school holidays did mean a busy beach, but it wasn't really bothering them and the weather was perfect. They hadn't had sex yet – they'd arrived two nights ago – but he thought that had a lot to do with how desperately tired they were on arrival. That nine-hour car trip! He was feeling fairly confident it would happen that night.

He opened his book and had only read a couple of lines when the big group arrived. They came from behind him in a deluge of voices and laughing, and then passed close by him like a loose, colourful parade. It was impossible to ignore them. His book lay open on his lap, abandoned, as he shifted his attention to the group. He counted at least thirty people across three generations, and easily decided they were a family. There was a refined-looking couple (late seventies, he guessed), nearly a dozen adults around his age, and countless teenagers. He watched as two large, bright cabanas were erected with admirable efficiency (they'd done this before), and he smiled as negotiations took place for the limited shade. Surfboards, towels and bags now spread across the sand; their party took up an extraordinary amount of territory. He stared at the group and without really meaning to, he eavesdropped on their lively conversations. People can be surprisingly loud on a beach, he realised, and there was very little attempt to keep things private.

But gradually, as he watched and listened on the sidelines, as the sea's presence diminished and was even forgotten, an uneasy feeling rose in him. It was envy or regret, maybe a mixture of both, and impossible to quell. There he and Sarah sat – a neat little twosome – with this riotous happy family nearly blocking out the sun.

He almost jumped when Sarah spoke. He heard, 'Aren't you?' and flung his head around to face her. She was standing, and stretching.

'Sorry?' he said.

'Aren't you hot?' She looked towards the water. 'I am. I'm going in. Are you coming?'

'Sure,' he said, feeling almost dazed as he yanked his thoughts off the group.

Sarah set off immediately for the water and he had to hurriedly find a safe place for his sunglasses before trying to catch up. She reached the shore before he did and started taking tentative hops in really small waves – 'It's a bit cold!' she called out to him over her shoulder – and he couldn't resist. He hit a run and pounded past her, thrashing through the shallows and wetting her thoroughly. He caught the edge of her scream as he dived through a breaker. After that, waves broke before him in quick succession, forcing him to dive again and again, and by the time he got to calmer water he'd become quite breathless. It struck him that he was really unfit. He turned and saw Sarah still standing in the shallows.

He'd annoyed her. It was the absolute worst way to get wet, she told him when she finally reached him. Nothing about it was funny on the receiving end. *Nothing.*

He apologised, though it was hard to put his heart into it. He hadn't meant any harm and her sense of grave injustice was funny. She was trying to get wet and he'd just made her a little wetter.

They didn't talk for a while as they trod water next to each other, waiting patiently for a decent wave. His thoughts drifted back to the shore. He turned slightly and his eyes went to the sand, to that great pack of people, and this was the first time it occurred to him: that family could be hers. Beth could actually be coming to this beach! She'd talked mainly about Christmas holidays, but she'd mentioned other seasons as well. Now his eyes scanned the beach carefully, picking through the chaos of bodies in the water and out across the crowded sand, up to the kiosk and along to the far sea baths. Searching for a Beth-like figure.

Once or twice his heart lurched, thinking he'd found her on the beach, only to discover he was wrong. He was so distracted he missed a seriously good wave. Sarah caught it, though, and hurtled to shore, riding it well. She stood up in the white wash with her hair plastered to her head and holding both thumbs up, triumphant. He watched her as she made her way back to him.

In their attic was a box he never opened. It had a scribbled label: *Chris – London*. Occasionally, when he went up there, he'd catch sight of it and recall its contents with a swift, soft heart-ache. Inside it were three books and a thick winter coat. They were Beth's. He knew the books were special – early editions she'd found in an old bookshop; there was *Ulysses*, *Middlemarch* and one other he'd forgotten. They were all extraordinarily large books and they'd both agreed it was too expensive (not to mention physically impossible) to put them in her luggage going home. The coat, too. It had been made for an English winter and was close to useless in Australia. But there was cashmere in it, and it was a lovely colour; not something you could give up easily. He'd offered to keep them for her and send them home in a crate along with his things when he returned. It was simply accepted between them they would be together again. And here he was, eighteen years later, having never given them back. How rapidly time built on itself.

He could see no more good waves forming in the distance. He turned his head left and right, taking in again all the nearby swimmers, and then his eyes flitted over the rest of the surf. The water was more crowded than before. The sun blasted down.

Sarah was now floating on her back with her face turned to the sky.

'This is glorious,' she said. 'Though way too warm for this time of year, don't you think?'

Sarah was finely attuned to climate change. She would admit to a low-level anxiety over it. Evidence, for her, was everywhere. Her worry could sometimes run so strong just being in its presence exhausted him.

At dinner the previous night she'd brought up Bangladesh (of all possible subjects). Had he read about it? 'By 2050,' she said, 'the sea may have risen high enough to make the whole country uninhabitable. The most densely populated country in the world rendered uninhabitable. At least one hundred and sixty million poor, vulnerable people needing somewhere to live.' She'd paused. 'They may even need to come here,' she added.

'Here?' he'd responded reactively, and that really exasperated her. He realised this was a subject he probably needed to catch up on.

They were well out the back now, far beyond the breaking waves. He bobbed up and down in the high swell, keeping his eyes trained on the beach for the most part, now and then glancing over at Sarah.

He couldn't adequately explain why he wanted to see Beth so badly. Why he was so deeply interested in the fact she might be here. Why the distinct possibility of seeing her again was beginning to devour him.

Except to say that the past looked beautiful.

Once he'd taken himself there again, memories rose up in him with an ethereal quality that could make him sigh out loud. His mind held a clear picture of him living in London and working at St Thomas' Hospital, and loving it all. His soul told him they were, without question, the best years of his life.

'What about the Turkish cafe for lunch?' Sarah asked.

'The Turkish cafe?' he repeated, and furtively corralled his thoughts. 'Again? But we've been there twice already.'

'That was for breakfast. And the food's *so good*. I'd love to try their lunches. Those creamy scrambled eggs I had with the side of spicy Turkish sausage?' She'd eaten the same thing twice. She'd said the perfection of her breakfast made her feel emotional.

'Why don't we –' he began, but his sentence remained unfinished. A woman walking along the shore had caught his eye. Was it Beth? Sarah was saying something but all his attention was fixed on this woman walking. His heart skipped a beat as she stopped and turned, looking seawards with one hand raised to shield her eyes, searching for someone in the surf.

It wasn't her.

And then an enormous wave whacked him from behind.

He was held under water for an alarmingly long time, and when he eventually surfaced, gasping for air, Sarah was gone. He swivelled, wheezing and heaving for breath. Had she said she was going?

He caught sight of her wading through the shallows and leaving the water, crisscrossing the sand, dodging wide camps of towels. He threw himself onto the next good wave and catapulted to shore, then strode to their towels not far behind her. He kept his eyes off the family and firmly on Sarah.

They shook the sand out of their towels, dried themselves off and gathered up their belongings, and by the time they left the beach they were already feeling hot again. Under a searing sun, they trudged up the path towards home. Chris couldn't think of one thing to say to Sarah and she wasn't talking to him. The silence felt awkward, unnatural. Sarah was good with conversation and liked it to be happening; they rarely operated in silence. And while he was in the shower she sent a text to the Turners and asked them to lunch. He was getting dressed when she told him and it sent a flutter of something through him; something like panic.

It was a ten-minute walk to the cafe. He commented on the blast-furnace heat, agreeing with her earlier comment about climate change – it was definitely too hot for September – but he got very little back from her. He quoted a few things from the latest piece he'd read about Trump, from one of those excellent *New Yorker* articles, even though he knew the subject matter was jarring. Who wanted to talk about Trump on a holiday? He felt, viscerally, the tightrope of their marriage.

The cafe was small; a hole-in-the-wall with a tiny kitchen inside and two rows of little tables outside. Its limited tables were like gold.

Julie and Steve were already there, they had a precious table, and Steve had the demeanour of a jubilant conqueror. He waved at them when they were still some distance away: *Look what we have!* Amid their hellos, he couldn't help stressing his success.

'He was so embarrassing,' Julie said as they all sat down. 'You should have seen him. He literally raced this other group for the table. They were ahead of us coming down the hill and he broke into this nonchalant power walk. With his long legs the others didn't stand a chance. I can't look at them.' She tilted her head a fraction towards four people still waiting for a table. 'Thank goodness they seem like relaxed people, happy to be on holidays.'

They went on to order an enormous amount of food. Braised broad beans with dill and garlic yoghurt and a side of warm Turkish bread. Yamba prawns. A beetroot and feta salad with dukkah and pomegranate. Lamb kofta. Sardines. Chargrilled chicken with green chillies and tomato. And when every shared plate was scraped clean, they ordered the freshly baked cake of the day – fig and hazelnut – and mint tea.

Over lunch, Chris had trouble engaging in the conversation in any meaningful way. His emotional turmoil – over Sarah, over Beth – seemed to have stripped him of a personality. After one period of silence he'd asked what sports the Turner boys were currently playing and even bored himself with the question. For a while, he watched a toddler chasing a bush turkey, and when he tuned back into the conversation Julie was telling Sarah she hadn't used Glad Wrap for a year now.

But then Steve said something that changed everything; said it just as Chris was raising his little Turkish cup to his lips.

Steve was eating a slice of the cake. 'I can't believe how much the food scene has changed since I last came here,' he said, and his cake fork in the air backed the point; a delectable morsel sat poised on its tines.

'When were you last here?' Sarah asked him.

Steve paused. 'I'm trying to remember,' he said. 'More than ten years. Maybe close to fifteen. When I was young my family came here almost every school holiday. I grew up on a farm in Grafton, so it was very close. There was no food like this, though. Fish and chips were pretty much it.'

He grew up on a farm. He came here every year.

Steve had Chris's full attention now. But he couldn't ask the question that had leapt into his head. Not while Sarah was here. Sarah would see through him. She knew Beth's name and a little of their history. She would recognise the depth of his feeling, hear the conflict in his question.

It wasn't until all the tea was drunk and they were waiting to pay the bill that Chris got his moment with Steve. Julie and Sarah had left to look through a homewares store up the street. He got straight to the point, thinking Steve wasn't a person who needed a preamble.

'Hey, Steve, did you know the Tennant family back when you used to come here as a kid? I think they holidayed in Yamba too.' He said it with an exemplary casualness.

Steve smiled broadly. 'Of course I did,' he said. 'Why? Do you know them?'

Chris hadn't bargained on such a quick confirmation. He scrambled for an answer.

'I knew Beth Tennant,' he said. 'I met her in London.' A silly amount of pride lay under his admission.

'Beth Tennant?' Steve sighed. 'What a lovely person.'

'Yes. Have you seen her recently?' he asked.

'No, not for ages. I stopped coming here for holidays in my twenties. I don't think I've actually seen her since then. It's a shame, losing contact. She was great. Lots of fun.' He paused. 'She could be here now, though,' he said, as if the thought had just occurred to him and he found it particularly pleasing. 'Her family used to come here nearly every holiday. Her grandparents had a big house near Convent Beach, though it might have been turned into apartments by now. Most of the family would stay around there.'

—

Chris jogged along the small road that ran high along the line of Convent Beach. His breathing was a little ragged and so he kept his pace slow. To his left was a small grassy verge, a line of hardy shrubs, and a steep descent to a blue bowl of water; to his right was a row of holiday houses and apartments. There was no footpath so he stayed on the road, looking up at balconies as he ran, looking through glass doors and down driveways. But there was hardly a sign to be seen of the people staying there. Almost nothing and nobody stirred. Sarah was back at the unit taking an afternoon nap, which was probably what most of the occupants of these houses were doing. His heart railed at the exercise – he'd never been a happy runner – but he kept going, conscious of the stupidity and futility of what he was doing, yet unable to stop.

He'd seen just the one person.

On his first trip along the road there was an elderly lady sitting at a small table on a balcony with a book in her hand, and she'd looked his way in the same moment he was scanning her house. She gave him a half-smile and a small nod and bent her head back to her book. *She might be Beth's mother.* That thought had spurred him on and inspired this second trip down the road. This time the elderly lady's gaze caught him early and she waved, and it occurred to him he was now confusing her; she'd be searching her memory, thinking they must know each other. He gave her a small wave back and kept running. And he couldn't quite stop himself going for a third lap. The lady's eyes were on him the moment he entered the street; she strained to see him, excessively watchful, and he imagined her heading inside to hide her jewellery, considering under what circumstances a person was warranted in dialling the police.

He stopped running and stepped onto the grass. He stood with his hands on his hips, with his unruly heart and his laboured breathing, and looked forlornly at the line of houses that were offering him nothing. How stupid. Beth could be a thousand miles from here, oceans away; she could be holidaying in fucking Thailand. It was time to give up. He swallowed, feeling slightly nauseous.

He turned and headed along the seaward track that hugged the headland, glancing back over his shoulder now and again in case, miraculously, she should appear. But still nothing stirred. The world before him was silent and deserted. Beth wasn't here.

He looked up at the sky, a faultless enormous blue. With shortening breaths, he reached the brim of the headland. Pippi Beach stretched out before him, and for a few minutes he watched the long white-fringed waves sliding towards shore. And this was when he began to feel very unwell. A heaviness pressed on his chest and he raised one hand to his jaw, aware now of an ache that was spreading along it.

He frowned heavily, and worry took flight. He pulled his eyes and his thoughts off the beach and threw up both his hands and cupped them in front of him. Were they clammy from the running and the heat?

He homed in on himself, logging it all quickly: his breathing, his hands, the nausea, the pain in his jaw, the heaviness in his chest. He sank onto his knees, down onto the hard ground. He was having a heart attack. He fought to keep calm. He'd ring Sarah. His hand went to his shorts. He had no phone! He'd thrown on a pair of old pocket-less sports shorts.

He forced himself to take steady breaths and tried to think. Think! What was at his disposal? He looked down at himself. Nothing! He could do nothing with his own hands. *He was going to die? This young? He was done?*

His eyes went to the edge of the land and out to sea. Nothing to help him! With his heart pounding too hard, he scanned Pippi Beach. He spotted two people, but they were far too distant, dark stick figures bent over the sand. *This was his death?* His eyes swung back around and at the tip of the land, through the hazy scrub, he saw a splash of colour, a young man sauntering along the narrow path and staring out to sea, with a large-lensed camera in his hand.

Chris yelled, trying to keep his voice steady: 'Hey! Hey!' He gestured to the man, trying to fuel urgency and gravity into every controlled arc of his arm.

The man's head turned abruptly from the sea, and as he caught sight of Chris he fell into an ungainly, camera-hampered run towards him.

'What's wrong? Are you okay?' he asked the moment he reached Chris.

'No, look, I'm having a heart attack and –'

The man's eyes flared with panic. 'Shit! A heart attack? How do you know that?'

'I'm a doctor.'

'You're a doctor! Oh, thank god!' the man said, before the terrible inadequacy of that comfort seemed to strike him. 'Fuck! Fuck! I don't think I'll get CPR right. It's been ages since –'

'Please don't panic,' Chris begged. 'Can you call an ambulance? I don't have a phone on me.'

'Yes! Yes! I'll do that!'

The young man – Tom, he introduced himself as he was dialling – spoke to emergency services, explained where they were and hung up, all done with an unwavering scrutiny of Chris's face. Now his eyes swooped around the headland, searching for backup.

'Now, Tom, just in case I go into cardiac arrest before they get here, can we have a quick run through –'

'Yes! Yes! Quick! *Quick!*'

Chris shifted his knees and lay down on his back; he placed his hands on his chest and spoke rapidly. 'You need to press hard and fast, and I mean really hard, don't worry about my ribs, and do it in the centre of my chest – here – and you want the rate to be about a hundred beats a minute – like this – and keep going until they get here.'

Tom was staring at Chris's chest, frowning deeply.

'I sing "Stayin' Alive" in my head while I'm doing CPR,' Chris said. 'The Bee Gees song? It's got the right beat.'

'God, I've gone blank! How does it go again?'

How does it go again? Who forgets that song?

Chris sat up carefully and sang a few hurried, mumbled bars, and Tom attempted to sing along, a word or two behind him.

'Right, got it.' Tom's shoulders and arms moved in a small nervous bounce to the beat.

They sat side by side in a tightly wound silence, looking out to sea. Chris couldn't even ring Sarah on Tom's phone because he couldn't remember her number. It was always there in his phone for him. He had no phone numbers in his head. When he heard Tom humming softly again, Chris turned to him. 'When my mother was in high school, she caught the school bus with the Bee Gees boys. Of course, they weren't the Bee Gees then. Their last name was Gibb.' His mother was wonderful.

A half-smile hit Tom's face before it fell back into its resting expression of alarm.

The Bee Gees were in Chris's head now. The Bee Gees, his mother, Sarah and his heart-pumping thoughts about dying. How desperately he wished he could calm his own heart, but he knew too much. He knew its workings intimately. He knew the amazing precision of a properly functioning heart, and he understood the awful vulnerability of precision. His thoughts now centred in on it. On the imagined small site of the blockage.

He began to think he'd be all right. The heaviness in his chest hadn't worsened; the pain in his jaw might have softened. He tried to think of anything but his own heart. He went back to the Bee Gees. He didn't really like 'Stayin' Alive'. He tried to sing 'To Love Somebody' but Tom complained – would he mind stopping? He was at risk of losing his beat.

And Chris felt a strange sort of calm settle in him. Some light-headedness. The ambulance would be on its way, he thought, and Tom was beside him. Anything that happened would be witnessed. He wasn't alone.

9

Clare's face absorbed most of the impact of her fall. Across the right side, various parts snapped and bruised under the pressure.

Her nose broke across the bridge. Her right cheekbone was badly bruised, and thousands of capillaries in the soft tissue covering it were broken. The area swelled and discoloured with the blood. Both of her eyes were swollen and black, and two of her front teeth were chipped. And there was an injury to her jaw the doctors couldn't fully explain. The X-rays showed nothing broken, but it was excruciating to open it more than the smallest amount, and so she didn't. That should heal itself, her doctor told her in a tone she didn't find reassuring, and the lack of anything scientific made her panic. She imagined never being able to open her mouth properly again, imagined her words and her thoughts – *the core of her* – forever locked.

The fall left her concussed and briefly unconscious. She had no memory of the fall or its aftermath and she felt grateful for that. Helen said there had been mayhem, which was mainly Helen's fault. She'd never been good with blood and there was so much of it – who knew a nose could produce that much blood? Helen had bounded out of her cubicle and in those first few moments she thought Clare was dead. So in her defence, she said, she was reacting to *death*. She'd screamed out the bathroom door, *Doctor! We need a doctor!* and she'd immediately got five. Five in one year for a public high school was an impressive amount, Helen thought, and three of them were specialists. But no neurosurgeons unfortunately. The gynaecologist (out of the sporty group she hadn't had much to do with) was the best of the lot, a no-nonsense sort of woman. We're underperformers, she said to Clare later, in the hospital.

At the hospital, Clare was given a local anaesthetic and her nose was manually realigned. When they were happy with her condition, she was sent home with gauze stuffed up her nose and some heavy-duty painkillers.

The following morning she woke at dawn, gripped by terror. Her heart thrashed and she struggled to breathe – she couldn't get air through her nose and couldn't get enough through her mouth – and the terror escalated as she fought for breath, convinced she could suffocate. She opened her mouth as far as she could and dragged in air, each breath making a sucking, hissing sound as tears slid down her face. She felt so broken, and so deeply alone. Her children were in the house and were capable of caring for her in an emergency, but that did little to reduce her fear.

There were many mornings of terror. Terror would be waiting for her in the moment she woke up. The first waking thing she did was try to tamp it down, to reason with it. For several days she couldn't open her mouth wide enough to eat and the prospect of chewing raised her anxiety. She pureed her food and sucked it in through a straw she placed in an opening near one of her chipped teeth. She spoke minimally, and painfully.

Her interactions were limited to her children and David and her dog. David called in every day on his way home from work. He brought pureed meals with him – dishes he'd invented or ones that Caro had cooked the night before – and it felt to her, then, that her humiliation was complete. David would recount the details of his day, what he'd read in the news or heard on the radio. He'd relay interesting conversations with his colleagues.

Flowers arrived in the beginning.

Friends would text her and she would text back, telling them she was out of action for a while, waiting for her face and whatever was wrong with her jaw to heal. *So, please don't call in*, she would write. *I can't actually talk*.

Eventually the messages tapered off.

It came to her she didn't have nearly as many friends as she'd assumed. She'd always accepted the background presence in her life of a standard number of friends – on the lower side, yet surely around standard – but nothing like that sort of number appeared, and you could count them pretty easily when something like this happened. Not that she wanted people around her, but still, the smallness of the group concerned her. After a long, full-time commitment to her job, her casual friend circle had shrunk. Most of her friends were work friends, and with that context removed they didn't feel quite as close. Well, apart from Amir.

And on this front, she certainly hadn't helped herself. She chose not to broadcast her accident or initiate contact. There was something about passing out on the brown-tiled bathroom floor of a suburban bowling club that lent itself to silence. Helen and her closest friend Jen had each dropped by in person, once – visits full of kindness and sympathy – but they stayed for only a short while. Clare didn't make it easy for them. She told them she was too worn out and not ready for company, and they fell back into texting. Amir sent her regular texts too. The injured face emoji was in almost every text she got.

It was almost too easy to do, physically separating herself from people.

But once separated, she was left predominantly with time; time to *think*. She sat in vast, quiet spaces of time and relentlessly replayed the night David told her he was leaving. She'd lost all defence to it now. Over and over, she pulled apart his speech and scrutinised it, feeling a persistent uncertainty about his true motivations. And what about her? After all these years, why did *she* ask about Hope? Clare and David had been together for over twenty years and Hope was the tiniest fragment of that time, and long gone. What had made her ask? The possible meaning in the question came close to unravelling her.

A few times she picked up her novel and tried to read, but there was no pleasure in it anymore; she could hear herself thinking above the words. And so, in the end, she took to watching a degrading amount of television.

She became addicted to *Breaking Bad* first. She watched an entire season in a day and came close to losing any workable concept of daily life. But two full days of Walt was all she could take; he began to stress her unbearably. Then she switched to *Grace and Frankie* and found it surprisingly funny. She went overboard again, taking herself to the point where she was getting annoyed by Brianna (which she knew wasn't supposed to happen) and wanting to rename Coyote. And with that, she returned to *Friends* and watched a truly uncountable number of episodes; they were so short, and one episode flowed into the next if you didn't touch the remote. How she longed to live with them all. *Longed.* And if not all of them, then at least Ross. It occurred to her she'd only ever lived with her parents (mainly her mother) and David, and that seemed to her now to be a truly depressing outcome.

She lived, largely, in a world of fiction and silence. Some days she couldn't shape herself into existence. Couldn't remember her part in it all.

—

Five days after her accident, on a warm spring day that she'd spent entirely indoors, there was a knock on the door.

Her attention lifted from the television, briefly. She felt extremely put out. Who would knock on her door in the middle of the day? She decided to ignore it. It had to be marketing. But it came again, a little louder this time, and she sighed heavily and her eyes swept the room. There was an extraordinary mess before her: her own things – medicines, teacups, washing to be sorted – and the detritus of two teenage children who obviously hadn't been trained well enough. She wasn't as prone to tidying up as she used to be. Housework now appeared to her as a particularly futile enterprise. She heaved herself off the lounge and went to the door and her little dog went with her. Stuart, these days, was always by her side.

Bright sunlight hit her in the eyes the second she opened the door. She frowned, trying to adjust to the light and the fresh, flowing air. It was Louisa Shaw. She stood on the doorstep, and in one hand she held up a small branch from a frangipani tree laden with flowers. Her shock on seeing Clare was palpable. She didn't even manage hello. There was a soft, 'Whoa,' a short silence, then a solid, 'Fuck that's nasty.'

Clare nodded a few times, tight-lipped inclines of her head designed to keep her front teeth from view. She agreed wholeheartedly with Louisa. It was nasty.

Louisa stared at her in silence, looking thrown by the grimness, and Clare stood rigid, feeling ever more hesitant and unwilling to speak. A voice in her head said, *Please, Louisa* – please – *just give me the flowers and let me go back inside.*

'I did warn you,' Louisa said suddenly, her voice loud in the silence, 'about school reunions.' Then she held up the frangipanis telling Clare they were the first ones from her tree, and so beautiful and summery, *but, fuck – it's only spring!* Louisa suggested Clare pick off the flowers and float them in a bowl full of water.

And Clare stood there, with the strange sensation of warm sunlight on her skin, with Louisa and her flowers and her odd declarations, and something shifted in her very slightly. In the smallest unit of measurement known to man, she felt better.

'Thank you,' she said, and surprisingly she added, 'Would you like to come in?'

There was a chance Louisa hadn't understood a word Clare had said. Although her jaw was softening and opening up a little, Clare continued to protect it and so her speech remained odd. She'd fallen into the habit of moving her lips more than her mouth.

Louisa hesitated before appearing to grasp Clare's invitation. 'That would be lovely,' she replied, but she said it in a way that made Clare wonder if Louisa had now seen her teeth – was there a repressed smile in her reply? It was incredible what two chipped teeth could do to your appearance.

They walked down the hallway together with Stuart taking the lead.

'I love the energy in your dog,' Louisa remarked. Then: 'I've just finished work and I'd kill for a cup of tea. Can you drink tea?'

'As of yesterday, yes,' Clare said, but she'd caught that look on Louisa's face again; the pushed-down smile.

'It's okay,' Clare said. 'About my teeth.'

'What?'

'My teeth. I've come to terms with them.' She hadn't really.

'Your teeth are fine,' Louisa said.

'They going to be fixed with crowns,' Clare said. 'When I can open my mouth wide enough.'

'Oh thank god for that.'

Clare brewed tea, moved the washing, and they sat on the couches amid all the mess. Louisa did almost all the talking. Clare would look back on her visit and realise she'd never felt talked *at*, though; she felt entertained. She could have listened to Louisa's voice all day. She had a voice you could make a living with – a honey timbre, a droll delivery, and her words were paced in a way that made you think you shouldn't be rushing your day. And her facial expressions. They were another joy entirely.

Louisa told her four bush turkeys had crossed the pedestrian crossing in front of her that morning. In single file. An Abbey Road of turkeys. They were smart birds; they'd worked out the road system. The word was the turkeys were heading south-east, only held back for the moment while they sorted out how to cross the harbour.

She talked about books. She was reading *The Overstory,* and thought Clare should read it. It was a very thick novel and very dense writing, Louisa warned, but it was worth it. It was about the beauty and importance of trees and forests, about the destruction mankind had wrought on the planet and mankind's likely extinction as a result. She paused on the word *extinction.* She decided Clare shouldn't read it right now. Wait until you're feeling more resilient, she suggested.

That morning Louisa had done her first stint as a volunteer tour guide in the Royal Botanic Garden. She might not go back. She knew quite a bit about trees, but she wasn't a leader. All morning she'd struggled to keep her group in anything even resembling a group-like structure. 'The thing is,' she said, 'garden lovers are natural wanderers.'

On leaving, Louisa admitted to knowing nothing about reunions. She'd never been to one in her life. They just sounded dreadful to her in principle.

—

Louisa's second visit came two days after the first.

Clare had had a particularly bad night. Her instinct was to ignore the knock, but Stuart had scurried down the hallway and stood barking at the door with an unusual enthusiasm. Clare turned off the television, hauled herself off the lounge, and opened the door with Stuart by her side. She stood facing Louisa with her aching teeth and her painful face and a brow she couldn't fully unknit.

Louisa couldn't hide a small start. 'So, how is your face today?' she asked. Her expression made the question rhetorical.

Clare shrugged a little hopelessly and invited her in.

What an excellent question, Clare thought as she walked down her hall. How was her face? No, how was her *life*? And what the fuck was this crap called *existence*?

She felt extraordinarily pissed off. Mental and physical had collided. She'd reached her soft-food limit of tolerance. She'd heaved her way through her breakfast.

'I am so fucking tired of continually redefining rock bottom,' she said, and it was ridiculous, of course, the unwieldy words she'd chosen for that sentence.

Louisa frowned and looked at her. 'Pardon?'

'I'm so fucking tired,' she started again, but gave up. And besides, it wasn't like her to swear. She wasn't a natural.

They sat on the couches and had tea. Louisa told her Gilbert the groodle had started coming into her bedroom as she was waking up. He'd stand beside the bed and stare at her without a sound. No, he must be coming in just before she woke up, because he was already there. But how did he know she was about to wake up? Or did he make a small noise to wake her? She couldn't be sure. He stood face-height with the bed and so she opened her eyes directly into his wide loving gaze, only centimetres from her own. It was a little freaky at first, but it had quickly turned into a really nice way to start the day.

'I'm beginning to think,' she said, 'that I can't give him back. His owners are just going to have to get another dog.'

She told Clare about specific vegetables she'd been planting to supplement the ones already in her garden, the ones Lara must have planted. Her goal was to eventually become vegetable self-sufficient. She said *eventually become vegetable self-sufficient* a few times before she was happy with it, and on the third time Clare felt her jaw relax and her eyebrows soften.

Louisa said she'd read that morning that the comprehension of music – the ability to remember a song – was one of the last cognitive faculties a dementia patient retains.

Louisa even talked about sex with absolutely no segue. About not having had it for years, a fact she honestly didn't find concerning. Her only relationship of substance lasted five years, and within a month of breaking up it was like she'd never known him at all. Five years obliterated in a month. It did make her think they probably weren't ever that close.

—

That night, quite late, David dropped by. He texted Clare first to check she was still up, saying his visit would be short. She was watching television and he sat on the lounge beside her, speaking gently with his face full of warmth.

He said, 'I hate seeing you so physically hurt. I hate that I made you so depressed.'

He told her he regretted all the big statements he'd made. He'd been wanting to tell her for a while, and suddenly felt the need to say it as soon as possible. The night he left, he'd worked himself into a strange dark place where nothing looked right, he'd lost all perspective. His reaction was dramatic and extreme.

He didn't use the word *love*. She should have asked about that, of course, but the question felt too big, there was too much attached to it for that time of night. She was holding the threads of her life clutched in her hand and couldn't let go for a moment.

She nodded, sometimes she shrugged; she was barely responding to him. He said he appreciated her hearing him out, and right as he was leaving, he said, 'I think I realised what I had almost the minute I gave it up,' and despite the enormity of his confession she gave him one of her noncommittal nods. Then she watched him walk down their front path and across the street to his car, a bent silhouette against a late, bruised sky.

—

Louisa continued to call in. She was like a benign force of nature coursing up the street and diverting through Clare's door. She'd sweep in with her wit and her energy and change the air in the room. Clare would hear a knock and a small smile would form. Stuart's little ears would prick.

On the third visit, Louisa insisted she was antisocial. 'That day in the street when we talked, that was a very strange thing I did. I *never* call out to people,' she said. But she'd stood up from her weeding to see Clare limping up the street with an apology to the world written all over her.

'I wanted to tell you there was no need to apologise, that we were all fine about it,' Louisa said.

On her next visit she walked in with a: 'For fuck's sake have you heard Ed Sheeran singing "Perfect" with Andrea Bocelli? Talk about nailing perfection.' She'd played it loudly *numerous* times. Clare worried about her neighbours. And that day Louisa asked, 'Have you ever listened to Archie Roach while the sun's setting?'

The visit after that, she arrived carrying a one-thousand-piece jigsaw puzzle – a beautiful Tuscan landscape with a disconcerting amount of uninterrupted blue sky and mottled green poplar.

'I'm thinking a mindless activity is a good way for you to go,' she said. 'But watch out for puzzler's neck. The last thing you need is another ailment.'

Clare started it after Louisa left and was addicted to it within five minutes. She had what was surely puzzler's neck by nightfall. But it was worth the pain. Working on the puzzle she had felt a long, muted peace. All she'd thought about for hours was where to place the annoying blues and greens and golds of Tuscany. Alex and Grace chose to help her with it instead of doing their homework (though it wasn't actually a choice on their part, she conceded, as this thing was *compelling*).

Not once, in all her visits, did Louisa ask about David. And if Louisa's visits were a charitable project (which of course they could be), Clare was never made to feel it.

Weeks passed and she now relied on them both: David and Louisa. Her life was distilled through these two very different people. And their paths never crossed.

10

It was a mild heart attack. Chris inserted the adjective *mild* whenever it was spoken about. The mild part was important.

He had a blockage in a minor artery. There was mild damage to a small part of his heart and the damage was unlikely to be permanent. There'd been no cardiac arrest and no need for Tom to put his newly acquired skills into use. Chris had been taken to Gold Coast University Hospital, and the cardiologist there had been prompt and skilful. He had an angiogram, and a stent was put in the artery to allow the blood to flow freely. Chris expressed his eternal thanks to Tom as he was loaded into the ambulance, and then Tom went to their unit to let Sarah know what had happened.

The event didn't bring Chris and Sarah any closer together. It didn't evoke any epiphanies: *Hey, look, our time together is finite and precious!* In fact, rather than bringing them together it did the opposite. Once it was clear he would be fine, he saw the change in Sarah. He saw, with a terrible clarity, the particular quality of her relief. He was going to be okay: it was therefore okay for her to leave if she wanted to. He'd taken a little time off work to recover from his heart event, but his unusual presence in the house made no difference. A decision was being made; a curtain was being pulled. Their last try was failing in its infancy.

'Let's admit it,' Sarah said to him on their last day. 'Love can die away for no other reason than its time is done.'

—

They were in bed. Pale morning light was slipping through the shutters when he woke and unusually for him he hadn't got up straight away.

Sarah was just waking too. She rolled over to face him, and the very first thing she said to him was, 'I've been thinking about London. Those two years we had in London. They were so good.'

And for long, lovely minutes they threw all the good things at each other. The theatre, the cosy pubs, all the different nights out; the beautiful parks, Hampstead Heath, and the tube in a good way, the ones with the crazily long escalators; gorgeous weekends in the gentle rolling countryside and extra-cute pubs and wandering through castles. The food. The chickens that didn't taste like the chickens at home. ('It's the chicken ancestry,' he said.) A weekend in France. A summer break in Italy. A second summer break in Italy, gorging on pasta that sent them home chubby. The dramatic change in colour with each season. They went on and on, and nearing the end of it he held on to the smallest, smallest hope they might be okay – how could they not be with a history like theirs?

He and Sarah had met in a London pub on a crisp autumn night. Sarah was working as an intern at Guy's Hospital and they discovered their lives were littered with mutual acquaintances.

Sarah had short dark hair tucked behind her ears and one of those draw-you-in smiles. He remembered his immediate sense of ease with her. He even remembered the jumper she had on that night: a pale grey turtleneck that was cosy and soft. Beth had been gone for five months when they met.

'And Paul Swan?' Sarah said, smiling widely at the ceiling. 'He was funny.'

Paul shared the flat in Ealing Common with Chris. They were high school friends and arrived in London around the same time as each other. Together, they found the flat and they'd been living there for a year and a half when Chris met Sarah.

'He was so much fun,' Sarah said.

Chris frowned slightly. It was hard not to read his own failings into that sentence. Was *he* fun? Had he been enough fun in their marriage?

'Do you think it was hard for Paul,' Sarah asked, 'having a brother like Dan? I think it was.'

'Probably,' Chris said.

Paul's brother Dan had stayed with them in London before he headed to Europe. Dan had been a year ahead of them at school. He was a charismatic and respected school captain, a true leader, and he was funny and smart and a gifted guitarist. If Chris was honest, he might have preferred Dan to Paul. Paul was great, but Dan shone.

'Don't take this the wrong way,' Sarah was now saying, 'but I was never convinced Paul really liked you.'

'What?' His head jerked off the pillow. 'How do I take that the right way?'

'No, no, what I meant to say is he liked you, but I think he also envied you, which meant he couldn't *really* like you. Sorry, I'm not explaining myself well. It was just a feeling.' She paused. 'And in my defence, you haven't seen him once since we got home from London. He didn't even come to our wedding. How good a friend can he have been?'

That was easily explained. When they arrived home from London, Chris worked ridiculous hours. It was an effort to look after his own life, let alone extend it to others. In that period, many school friendships had been left behind and were never recovered. It had nothing to do with whether he was liked or not, surely? And he was, obviously, a hopeless communicator. He wasn't good at picking up the phone, maintaining friendships that weren't directly in his view.

He thought about friendship. He actually had only one friend from school left: Max. Over the years, Max had filled him in on a little of Paul's news. He knew Paul was doing well in advertising. That he'd had a few long relationships but hadn't had children. And that was about it.

Sarah was lying back on her pillow and out of nowhere she laughed. She turned her head towards him. 'I just had this vision of Paul on cocaine. That's when he was fun. It's terrible to say that, isn't it? But he'd talk so fast, and he was so entertaining. Remember that flip thing he did on the tube? With all the passengers cheering?' She laughed again and he laughed along with her.

'We really should have taken him to hospital,' he said. 'That cut should have been stitched.'

'He wouldn't let us!'

The cocaine had come into their flat via a cousin of Paul's who'd stayed with them for a few months. The cousin was a newly qualified anaesthetist, three years their senior and with easy access (never fully explained) to medical-grade cocaine. He brought one hundred per cent pure cocaine into their flat – a thoughtful gift in lieu of rent. This gift was no congenial aid to bring you out of yourself at a drab dinner party. This didn't give you something as benign as a bit of joy and some more focus and energy. For Chris, it unleashed in him an intense optimism about life and a consuming awareness of his capabilities – on it, he'd see how naturally gifted he was; how with enough hard work, anything could be his. *Anything.* A medical award of some sort maybe; even something international, like the Nobel Prize. He'd only used it a couple of times. It was far too good; it screamed addiction, and of course it was a bad idea with his job. Paul stuck with it for a bit longer. It didn't seem to interfere with his work and in fact, it probably helped him, probably shot his creativity through the roof. *But this won't end well,* Chris thought as he watched Paul tell funny story after funny story, outpacing Robin Williams. Thankfully, Paul had to stop. The biggest favour the anaesthetist cousin did for them was to continue on his way to America.

—

They'd been lying there talking for over an hour when Sarah brought up his heart attack.

She propped herself on one elbow. 'I've never properly asked you,' she said. 'How did you *feel* on the headland when you thought you were going to die? You've never talked about how you felt.'

Her question stunned him. It was jarring after the conversation they'd just been having.

'Well . . .' He reluctantly cast his mind back.

'I'm only asking,' she went on, 'because I've always had this sense you see death very differently from me. And that might be fair, given your job, given what you see. You're trained to preserve life, which means death is a form of failure. But I think that's made death almost abstract for you.'

Abstract? He was floundering in the conversation now. With her huge questions and propositions. Sarah worked in general practice but she knew, intimately, how it was for him. He wasn't inundated by death. It hadn't been turned abstract for him! He didn't see as much death as people assumed. He'd only witness about four or five deaths a month. If a patient died, it was more likely to happen in the ward he sent them on to.

She didn't seem to need an answer.

'I've been thinking about death quite a bit since it happened,' she said. 'Not only your death, but death in general. Mine too.' She let out a small sigh. 'The thing about death is, it makes life important. It gives our choices meaning.'

She lowered herself back down onto the bed and said something about choices in a voice that wavered, a voice too soft for him to hear. Then, a little louder now, speaking to the ceiling, she said: 'Chris, at some point we just stopped paying attention to each other. We stopped being generous towards each other.'

And she rolled over to face him for that last time. For those last few sentences. She told him, gently, about some loves being finite, about her love dying. She told him she'd made her choice and she was going.

And after that he faced her, open-hearted, already beginning to mourn.

11

Louisa bowled into Clare's house with an air of change about her. She strode down the hallway while Clare was still shutting the door. Stuart scuttled after her. Words were bursting out of Louisa and she threw them over her shoulder as she walked through the house. Things about a brand-new plan, a new living, a big question. But Clare already had a visitor. There was Amir, sitting on one of the couches in the living room, turning curiously now towards the source of all the noise, and the surprising sight of him stopped Louisa in her tracks. She turned to Clare, with the expression on her face demanding: *And who the hell is this?*

It was a fair reaction, Clare thought. She never had visitors.

Clare introduced them. Her instinct was to give Louisa some time, let her rearrange her bearings, and with that intent her introductions turned a little longwinded, a touch formal.

'Louisa,' she said, 'this is Amir. He's a work colleague of mine and a very good friend. He has an amazing memory, particularly for musical theatre, and he often goes birdwatching on his holidays.' Amir had so many positive attributes to choose from, she'd gone for the more unusual ones; had she made him sound too quirky? She turned to Amir with an apologetic grin. 'Amir, this is Louisa, a new friend of mine. Louisa lives at the end of my street. She volunteers in the Royal Botanic Garden, taking small informational tour groups about, and she's an excellent landscape gardener.'

Louisa and Amir nodded at each other graciously through the introductions. Then Louisa looked from Clare to Amir. Amir had a full cup of tea sitting on the coffee table before him. He wasn't going anywhere. You could see it on Louisa's face, the moment that fact became clear to her, standing there with her held-in excitement. The announcement of her information – still obviously crucial to her – would have to be shared.

Clare made tea for Louisa and the three of them sat on the couches. Amir sat opposite Louisa and there was a new expression on his face, a mixture of happiness and anticipation. Right from the beginning, he'd looked astonished by Louisa. Clare smiled broadly at the two of them. Her teeth had been capped the day before.

'Oh, look at you with your big perfect grin,' Louisa said to her, and then she shot a glance at Amir. 'You missed the teeth, Amir. You should have come earlier.'

Amir rushed in with an apology. He hadn't come earlier because he'd thought Clare needed some quiet time and privacy. Clare reassured him she'd got plenty of that.

Louisa now looked settled, even content with Amir's presence. She raised a teacup to her lips. 'So, Amir,' she said. 'Birds?'

He told Louisa he used the sound of the birdsong to identify a bird and he also used an app to help him. He did most of his birdwatching on his hiking holidays. One of the first things he'd do when he arrived in a town was to visit the local birdwatching group. They'd tell him the particular birds he'd be most likely to see.

Louisa said she had a special love for birds too. Her favourite had to be the puffin, though it was hard to go past the kookaburra. 'They call puffins the clowns of the sea,' she said, 'and for good reason. You just have to look at them! And their babies are called pufflings.'

'I've got a pair of pufflings at home,' Amir replied, and Clare and Louisa both hesitated, briefly bemused.

'Oh, it's a joke, you mean *cufflinks*,' Clare said, and Louisa huffed with laughter. Clare smiled wildly again. How lovely it was to have these two special friends together. How grateful she felt right at that moment.

But Louisa was done with small talk. She sat forward in her seat and began to deliver her news, directing most of her statements to Clare, with the occasional inclusive glance at Amir.

She gave them a preamble packed with honesty. She explained she was currently a little low on income. The North Shore mowing market was proving a hard nut to crack. She'd used the money from the sale of her house in Five Dock and a small inheritance she'd kept aside to pay for Lara's place, but she needed to do something to improve her income stream. It was a pittance.

'If I were a Jane Austen character,' she said, 'I'd be sorely tempted to accept Mr Collins right now.'

Another big smile rose out of Clare. Truly, few things were as heartwarming as a Jane Austen joke.

Louisa had had breakfast that morning with a man called Tim, the son of her mother's best friend. Louisa said *Tim* in rather a funny way, Clare thought – quickly and with emphasis, as if it wasn't actually a name – and Louisa would say it that way every time she spoke about him. (Later, Louisa told Clare she'd spent most of her life calling Tim a nickname that no longer felt appropriate, certainly not in a business sense. But how hard it was to change someone's name; to call them something else with ease.) Tim had been living in Melbourne for the last fifteen years, but a few months ago he moved to Sydney, and they'd caught up.

'Tim's bought his own funeral home and he's offered me some work,' Louisa said.

Clare instantly frowned. 'Work?'

'Your face did something very funny just then, Clare,' Louisa said.

'What sort of work would you do in a funeral home?' she asked.

'Catering,' Louisa said. 'Funeral catering. In the industry it's actually called *bereavement catering*. Tim said he could pass work on to me. The lady the funeral home has been using has moved to New Zealand and there's an opening.'

'Can you cook?' Amir asked.

Louisa nodded. 'I worked as a chef in my early thirties. Nothing too serious, but I'm good.'

'You've never mentioned that,' Clare said. Though it did strike her there was potentially a lot Louisa hadn't mentioned.

'And apparently,' Louisa went on, 'the New Zealand lady was making *a killing*.'

Amir openly appreciated her remark.

'Are you being serious?' Clare asked. She really couldn't tell.

'Yes, I'm being serious. If you think about it, it's an excellent business idea. It involves catering for the wakes and Tim says it's a solid money earner and there's plenty of work. The baby boomers aren't young anymore. And Tim pointed out all the practical advantages of it. The working hours are particularly reasonable for a cooking job – no nights, no weekends. Funerals are almost always on a weekday and during the day. So that's great. *And* the client expectations are supposedly very low. There's no pressure to produce anything too fancy. He said that all people need at a wake is a bit of nourishment, and they'd be over the moon just to be eating anything other than Aunty Edna's egg sandwiches.'

'I'm loving the sound of this,' Amir said.

Clare sat silent. This was such unexpected news. Already, she felt a little bereft at the thought of Louisa's absence.

'It's obvious when you think about it,' Louisa said, with her enthusiasm clearly rising. At least half of her sentences were now directed at Amir; her head swivelled between the two of them. 'We're living in an era where everything is outsourced.'

That was true.

'I'm not sure of the logical market, though,' Louisa added, as though the subject had suddenly occurred to her. 'The more food-centric cultures might not be interested. They'd probably all pitch in with the food.' She paused. 'The stoic Anglo-Saxons? They're not generally so handy with food.'

'Hindus don't have any food at their funerals,' Amir said. 'So rule us out.'

Clare sagged in her seat. Louisa was plainly serious. And it was so unsettling how easily she talked about funerals, about markets. Clare ran a hand across the back of her neck. Any talk of funerals – even simply the word – made her uncomfortable. The discomfort came from the depths of her, something dark and instinctual.

—

Clare's father had left for work one morning in his usual fashion – there'd been a funny commotion about a shoelace, a *my goodness, June, this lunch looks great*, a jaunty head poked around Clare's bedroom door to say goodbye to a daughter running late enough (or perhaps distressed enough about her hair) to only half-acknowledge him – and then he drove off in his car to have a cardiac arrest only ten minutes later and never return. That evening he wasn't going to pull into the driveway or stride up the path. There'd be no flinging open of the flimsy screen door, no asking what was for dinner. The news of his death had just been delivered when Helen's perky tap sounded on the door – *I'm here!* – ready to walk to school. Helen read the news on Clare's face as she was absorbing it herself. Helen got to see exactly what never-returning meant.

All Clare remembered of the actual funeral service was sitting on a pew next to her mother with her head bent and tears streaming down her face. No, she also remembered the slow singing of Psalm 23. '*The Lord is my shepherd . . .*'

But she remembered clearly what happened afterwards. She was standing outside the church on the verge with her mother. The hearse was parked in front of them. She watched, transfixed, as her father's coffin was loaded into the back of it, the boot was shut, and the driver slid behind the wheel. He closed his car door and she frowned. Somebody distracted her, it may have been her mother, and when she turned back around the hearse was driving away. Her heart exploded. *Where is it going?!* she asked her mother. Her eyes were glued to the hearse as it made its achingly slow way down the street. She watched it taking her father away, nobody but the driver with him, nobody following. He was alone with the driver – a stranger! It was as if she'd stopped breathing. The hearse reached the corner, the indicator blinked, and it turned to the left. And slowly, so slowly, it disappeared from view.

She'd rounded on her mother. Flung questions at her with a rising hysteria. *Why was he alone? Why weren't we with him? Why didn't we follow him to the very last place?*

Her mother shrugged and said, *This is how it's done, Clare – and please lower your voice.*

—

Clare straightened in her seat, realising Louisa was now addressing her.

'The thing is, Clare,' Louisa was saying calmly, 'I was wondering if I could ask you for a little help – just with the first wake, and maybe even the second? Just while I get established and follow up a couple of leads with some people I know in the hospitality industry. I'm worried that if I hold off too long Tim will find someone else.'

Clare almost started. 'Help from *me?*'

'All I really need is another pair of hands. You don't need to be a good cook. Although,' Louisa said, with her head now turned towards the kitchen, and a finger flicked towards the block of heavy-weight knives on the bench, the shelves of cookbooks, the row of steel utensils hanging above the cooktop, 'it's pretty obvious somebody in this house can cook.'

Clare acknowledged that with a half-smile. She and David both adored cooking.

'I just thought,' Louisa said, 'that it might be a good way for you to fill in some of your free time while you're on your long service leave. We could have some fun *and* make some money.'

Have some fun? She couldn't do that. She couldn't work at a funeral.

'I've eaten Clare's cooking,' Amir said. 'I'd turn up at one of your funerals.'

Louisa leant forward. 'What if you come with me when I meet Tim again tomorrow morning, Clare? You could hear it all from the horse's mouth and then decide.'

—

They swung into Tim's driveway in a gravel-crunching arc. He was waiting for them, standing in the doorway at the front of his building, and he smiled and waved the moment he saw them. He directed them to park beside a hearse being washed and Clare's stomach lurched as Louisa's small ute followed the path of his arm. Her eyes went from the large funeral home sign to Tim and then to the hearse, big and black and glinting in the sunlight. She felt queasy by the time they pulled up.

Tim met them at the car. He looked about Clare's age, and he smiled at them warmly; he was a generous-looking person, she decided. He was average height with light brown hair, and he was wearing tailored beige pants, a white open-necked business shirt and stylish pointy-toed brown shoes. Where was the dark suit and the tall thin figure she'd had in her mind for some reason? She looked again at Tim. There was not one obvious concession to oddity.

He turned out to be thoroughly likeable. He led them into an office decorated in Scandinavian tones, with polished blond wood and fine minimalist furniture. Sunlight streamed into the room, and it all created an aura of warmth Clare would have very much liked to have pulled off in her own home. They sat in three comfortable armchairs placed in a circle around a small coffee table and held cups of tea on their laps.

Early in the conversation, Clare sensed Tim zoning in on her. Had he sensed her discomfort or had Louisa forewarned him? He went out of his way to explain to her why he did what he did; what it was about his job that he found so satisfying. He'd now been a funeral director for ten years. Before that, he'd worked as a builder.

'I was having trouble with my back,' he explained, 'and I was tired of being exposed to the elements. I started looking for a different type of job, and when I saw an ad to work in a funeral home, I answered it mainly as a personal dare, not really expecting to get the job and not really understanding what was involved. And here I am, ten years later.'

He didn't think what he did was so extraordinary. Dying was the one thing they were all going to do. He simply provided a much-needed service, and his role was varied: a first responder, a guardian, a carer; sometimes a provider of comfort, a friend in grief. Acknowledgement of a mourner's grief, of its existence and importance, often its magnitude, was the first step in helping them to heal, he'd found. He loved his job, and not only for the acts of giving it involved. 'We can learn a lot about something from its opposite,' he said. 'Like learning about peace from war. This job gives me daily reminders about life.'

He paused for a moment, allowing a silence to settle, then got down to business. 'Okay,' he said, clasping his hands together. 'This catering idea. If you can get the ball rolling quickly enough, I'm more than happy to start referring work to you. I really want to help you do this.' He turned to Clare. 'Isn't Louisa's cooking amazing?'

'I haven't actually tasted any of her cooking,' Clare said.

'None? Not even the lemon tart?'

'*Tarte au citron*,' Louisa corrected. She turned to Clare. 'It's my speciality.'

'Piquant,' Tim said, 'doesn't even begin to describe it.'

Clare smiled.

'The quality of the cooking isn't under question,' Tim went on. 'What you need to consider with this business is its quirks. The short notice and the numbers. The numbers can vary a lot, and occasionally they're very big. It requires good organisation.'

Clare looked at Louisa.

Good organisation hung in the air between them.

Tim was looking at Clare again and his point was obvious. He thought she was on board. And he was telling her that she would be the carrier of the organisational banner.

'I've improved, Tim,' Louisa said, and Tim gave her what looked to Clare like a completely unconvinced nod.

—

As they left the funeral home, stepping through the door into the hard light of midday, Clare felt unmoored. This wasn't her life; this was nothing she knew. Funeral homes and mourners and Louisa, who wasn't straightforward.

'I'm sorry,' Louisa said in the car. 'It was a bit much for you, I know.'

'It's fine.'

'I'm not good at reading a room. You said you didn't like funerals and –'

'No, it's –'

'I can get caught up in things and I can be a bit naive. I probably won't go ahead with it, so –'

'But you can't not do it because of me.'

Louisa turned to Clare with one of her self-deprecating grins. It was an expression Clare had come to enjoy quite a lot. 'I'd not do it because of *me*,' Louisa said. 'I have trouble opening and dealing with mail. I'm incapable of keeping up with texts and emails because I find their constancy off-putting and intrusive. And I'm not on social media because it all looks too administrative to me.' She grimaced. 'In other words, I'm not particularly *businessy*.'

Louisa stopped the ute in front of Clare's house.

Clare unbuckled her seatbelt and opened her door, unsure of how to finish the discussion. As she got out, she turned around impulsively. 'Don't say no to Tim just yet,' she said. 'Let me think about it overnight.'

She walked into the house. Gratitude lay under her impulsive words. A deep gratitude for this rare, funny friend; impossible to ignore.

—

Early that evening, Louisa arrived with a lemon tart. 'Save it for dessert, Clare,' she said as she handed it over at the front door. But as she turned to walk back down the garden path, David was coming up it. They both stopped.

'Hello, David,' Louisa said with a crisp nod. There was enough judgement in her tone that Clare saw him wince.

'Hello,' David replied, a little quietly, but Louisa was already heading down the path. She walked through the gate without turning, and disappeared down the street.

'That was Louisa,' Clare said, as they stood together for a few moments on the path. To this point, she hadn't said a word to David about Louisa. 'She lives in Lara's old house,' she added.

David didn't stay long. He spent an hour helping Grace with some Ted Hughes – 'She's doing well,' he said to Clare – and then left.

After dinner, Clare snuggled into a corner of her lounge; *Middlemarch* sat on her lap, and a large slice of tart sat on a white porcelain plate beside her. She picked up her book. She was about a third of the way in. Dorothea was firmly installed in her disastrous marriage. She turned the page to Mary Garth. Mary sat alone in the early hours of the morning before an open fire: 'perfectly still, enjoying the outer stillness and the subdued light'. Mary, who'd decided life was a comedy in which she wouldn't take a mean part. There was a hint of Mary Garth in Louisa. Clare turned slightly, picked up her dessert fork and lifted a small piece of lemon tart to her mouth.

Before she went to bed, she sent a text message to Louisa: *The tart. I'm happy to help you with the first wake.* She put a drooling emoji in between the two sentences.

Louisa's reply was immediate. She sent back two lines of emojis with multiple thankful hands and two girls dancing. In among them was one coffin emoji. Possibly a step too far, Clare thought.

—

Three days later, Clare and Louisa were back in Tim's office. He'd had a call from a lovely man. His wife – a mother, a grandmother, an impressive woman – had died. There would be an autopsy so there was plenty of time. Her name was Greta Henry.

12

Death was everywhere. As if it had never been, and suddenly was. That was how it felt to him. Chris sat on his lounge with his phone in his hand, battling a strong urge to ring Sarah. He wanted to share the feeling, as absurd as it was, wanted to know that someone else understood. She was the only one he could begin to describe it to. Sarah had been gone over a week now. She was staying at her sister's place in what she called a transitional move, and most of her belongings remained in the house. He wanted to tell her about his day, then tell her what had happened as he'd walked in his door.

—

It had been late morning when the bat phone went off. The ambulance was six minutes away: twenty-year-old female, bee sting, anaphylactic shock, cardiac arrest, two doses of adrenaline already administered. His team assembled in three. The trolley came in with her friend stumbling behind it, stunned and crying. She would later demand of Chris: *How can this be happening?!*

She was fetching a frisbee in the bushes! They tried everything they knew and they tried for so long, but nothing worked. When her mother arrived, Chris walked to the family room and gave her the news, the part of his job he would never get used to. Never become good at. He gently explained the process of her death, and then offered his sympathy, offered the best comfort he could. Comfort? It was like standing on the doorstep of a flooded world, cradling a raindrop.

From there, he'd consulted on a man who'd shoved a sizeable screw-top jar into his anus and had it move entirely out of his reach. Chris stood in the bay and rotated his head on its neck, still reeling from failure, while the man complained of abdominal pain and expressed complete disbelief that a jar of that size could just disappear like that. Chris explained (possibly too abruptly) the particular power of internal suction, then listened (possibly unprofessionally vaguely) to the man's account of an implausible accident, then sent him off for an X-ray.

He'd been back at the computer all of two minutes when the bat phone went off again. An older lady this time, airlifted. Seventy-three-year-old female, bike accident, cardiac and respiratory arrest, resuscitated on the scene, suspected spinal cord injury, sedated and intubated at the scene. Her husband arrived after her; he'd been driven to the hospital in the ambulance.

A great deal of vital information was circulated quickly in that small room, and every piece of it ended up with him. Stand-out facts about the woman's past, her precise medical and personal position in the present, her potential future. Her name was Greta Henry. A high cervical cord lesion was suspected.

From her husband would come frantically relayed information and insistent panicked questions. There was information he needed others to understand, and so much he needed to understand himself. First, what could have happened? It was a charity bike race and they'd barely started and already he was a kilometre behind her – *She's very fast*, he said. Supposedly she'd been flying down a hill and left the road and crashed, nothing and nobody else involved, just her, so could it have been a stone on the road, a slip of a foot, a lapse in concentration? But that wasn't like her; she was always so focused! Could it have been a medical episode of some sort? Could that be relevant?

Her husband knew, though, what was relevant.

'You need to know *her*,' he said. 'She – *we* have four daughters and she understands medicine. She was a doctor before she switched to law.' He paused. 'She has an advance care directive in place,' he said, and everything in Chris went quiet.

A copy of the directive was sent in by one of her daughters and it was the best-written advance care directive Chris had ever seen. When his registrar read it he asked for a copy for himself. Greta Henry understood law and medicine. She knew what she was doing and there was no ambiguity.

If I have any injury, she'd written, *and on balance it is more likely than not* . . . She was making the decision clean and obvious. The balance of probabilities: the scales only needed the slightest tip.

If it is more likely than not that I will be unable to attend to my own personal needs – that is, to dress myself, feed myself, look after myself – I do not want to be kept alive artificially.

Medical investigations were done. A CAT scan confirmed a high cervical cord lesion and no damage to the brain. With her injury, she would more likely than not be a C3 to C4 quadriplegic, on a ventilator for the rest of her life and unable to move her arms or her legs.

The scales of probability were absolutely tipped.

Three daughters arrived quickly and the fourth followed an hour or so later, flying in from Melbourne on the first plane available. All four daughters knew about the directive. Their mother had emailed it to them a few years ago and yes, they'd all agreed to follow it. But had the notion of actually having to do so ever taken root in their minds? No! A life force like her? She would live to one hundred and die in her sleep!

But Greta's husband softly defended his wife's actions; this was what she wanted, and they had to stay true to her wishes. She'd told him she was too independent at heart, and couldn't imagine herself living any other way. *And let's not be greedy*, she'd told him when she decided on the directive. *What a privilege to have what I've had already. I'm satisfied, I'm grateful.*

Chris took the family into the relatives' room and he felt the emotions within it swirl around him. Something deep inside him railed against the directive; his long-held, deeply precious instinct to preserve a life. He wanted her sent to theatre, wheeled out of emergency and into the hands of specialists, his job done and her life preserved and her future open to chance. He certainly couldn't have done what his patient had done; he was firmly in the land of even the smallest probability.

Two of Greta's daughters argued vehemently with each other while the other two and their father stayed silent. The oldest, Nina, wanted the document questioned. Their mother was still too young, too vibrant, it was too soon. *And what does* likely *mean? Have we defined likely? Isn't likely subjective?*

No, Suzie argued, *it's not subjective; it's a legal phrase,* the balance of probabilities. *All it requires is for it to be greater than fifty per cent – it can be as low as fifty-point-one per cent, Nina,* and she looked at Chris for confirmation.

But Nina was exploding. *Maths!* she almost screamed. *This has to be wrong if we're talking about* maths!

In the end, none of Nina's arguments could beat her mother's thoughtful, well-written document, her *more likely than not.* Chris's medical decision was agonisingly straightforward: none of the treatment options – surgery and drugs and therapy – would reverse the damage that had been done. Should she survive this injury, it was more likely than not that for the remainder of her life she would require a ventilator to breathe and assistance to complete the most basic of daily functions, the ones she'd listed. Her rudiments of living. Her bottom line.

Greta Henry was transferred to intensive care and two spinal doctors were brought in for their opinions. They agreed that, on balance, she sat well beyond her *more likely than not.* She probably sat around ninety-five per cent, they advised.

A social worker was brought in.

Chris stayed on hours after his shift to follow Greta's outcome. The family made calls and more people arrived. One was her mother, who was over ninety. Greta Henry was given morphine, and around eight that night her ventilator was unhooked. She died a few minutes later.

—

He'd finally gone home, and as he stood on his doorstep fumbling with his house keys, his phone had rung. It was late for a call, almost nine, and he'd frowned as he pulled his phone from his pocket. Then he saw the caller ID: *Max Duncan.*

In the course of their long friendship, Chris and Max had learnt to keep administration to a minimum. Or maybe it was simply that Max understood Chris and made the necessary adjustments? Whatever the case, it was the only school friend-ship Chris could still genuinely lay claim to. A decade ago, he and Max had agreed to meet twice a year for dinner in the months of January and June, and those dinners were enough to keep their friendship alive – even thriving, from Chris's point of view. Some years, their wives had taken charge and they'd seen each other more than twice. Chris had rarely missed a dinner; if work forced him to cancel, he would immediately reschedule.

It was late October. The realisation of the month, along with the time of night, had Chris still frowning as he said hello, opened his door, and walked down the hallway into his stark empty house.

He'd sat on his lounge listening as Max told him he wanted to bring next year's dinner forward because he had pancreatic cancer and it was going to be quick. Max explained the situation in the same tone he might have used if he'd been heading off for an extended holiday overseas and wanted to catch Chris before he left. There were other things written in that tone. *No hero intervention needed, Chris, this is all sorted,* was in there. And it was true, Chris had plans forming in his mind as soon as the word *cancer* was uttered: the names of specialists, a rapid course of action. He didn't get to mention any of them. The cancer had made it to Max's liver and his spine before Max had sought any sort of help. Up to that point, he'd found some benign reason for every symptom he had. 'And you know what I'm like,' Max said. 'I'm not good with anything medical.' By the time Max saw a doctor, things were relatively far gone. Max said he had now seen a couple of specialists. It was clear to everyone what was going to happen.

They organised to meet for dinner the following night. 'Okay, see you then,' Chris said, and hung up his phone.

Now he stared at it, consumed by the vastness of Max's news, by the feeling this day had created in him. Was it too late to ring Sarah? Did he need to wait until morning? Sarah called Max the most warm-hearted man they knew; said she admired him *wholeheartedly*. Max had been highly successful from very early on – he'd skipped university and gone straight into IT – but for a few years now he'd donated all his time and skills to a green-energy start-up. *Could I love him any more?* Sarah had declared when he did that. She would be as devastated by Max's news as Chris was. He decided he couldn't break it to her at this time of night.

—

He saw it as early as Max's entrance in the restaurant.

Chris arrived first and from their table he could see the door. He saw the physical change, the depletion in Max, as an arm extended to push the door open, as a long leg stepped in with it. Chris saw the shape of him with a sickening roll in his stomach and an aching pull in his chest, but there was Max fully through the doorway with a jovial, almost-triumphant wave of the hand.

So good to see you! Ridiculously, that hand gesture alone gave Chris hope.

It was their favourite restaurant. A waiter arrived at their table and greeted them warmly, asking them how they'd been, and they both nodded – *good*. What else could you say? He gave them their menus and the wine list and said he'd be back with some water. And as soon as he'd left Max apologised to Chris. The truth was, his appetite was gone, and he had the unhappy suspicion it might be gone for good. But he'd wanted one last dinner regardless. Chris felt the strangest sensation as Max said that; a tingling pressure that began at the base of his skull and extended around his head.

Max said he would pick at something small, maybe a side dish, but he insisted Chris had to eat. '*Someone* at this table has to eat or it just won't make any sense,' he said.

Chris skimmed his menu, its cryptic descriptions blurring illegibly, and when their waiter came by their table he asked for fish, any kind of fish the waiter wanted to bring, really. He couldn't face choosing, or describing a dish. Max gave a small shake of his head when the waiter looked his way. Max was drinking, though (he'd have a taste – well, maybe more than a taste), and they spent an inordinate amount of time choosing their wine.

And for a while they talked about everything but the cancer. On sitting down, Max said immediately, 'Let's talk about the serious stuff later,' and Chris raked his mind for any good stories he had.

But in the end, Max turned to the subject with a kind of ease. 'It was interesting,' he said, 'when I was given the news. It's a pretty harsh thing to take on board, and then to have to cope with the thought of leaving Jill and the boys. But the strange thing was, it didn't take me long to accept it. To see that, right, okay, it's *that time*. That's what I've got to do now.'

Chris shook his head. 'I'm not sure I could do that. I think I'd be the opposite.'

'Maybe you wouldn't be.'

Chris couldn't tell Max about his heart attack, his mild heart attack. He couldn't bring that news into the dinner. But he remembered how it had felt for him. The urge to scream *help me!* to the world.

Max leant in. 'I'm finding that swearing really flamboyantly – mainly in my head or when I'm alone, occasionally to other people – really does help. Somehow it cuts through the weirdness of dying. The thought of leaving and never coming back.' It was funny, he'd never been much of a swearer to this point, but recently he'd run into a friend who hadn't heard the news, took one good look at him and asked pointedly how he was, and Max had simply said: *Well, Pete, my life plans have gone right up the fuck.* This method of delivering the news had definitely helped an awkward conversation along. *Holy shit, Jesus* and a simple *fuck* were handy in the early days, when the bad news was flooding in.

Chris looked at him with so many emotions rising. It was like Max was a thousand miles ahead of him, a conqueror of worlds he couldn't even imagine.

'But Dad's struggling,' Max said. 'And Jill. Particularly with the short timeframe. Right now, Jill's planning a family trip to Africa. Ever since we were married, we've talked about going there, but she's always baulked at it for the fear of getting eaten alive – which, strangely, doesn't seem to worry her as much now. I can't bring myself to convince her it's not going to happen. She's spent days and days on the internet researching African safaris and the proximity of hospitals, and last night she did this mini presentation to me. I sat there listening, but in my mind, I'm going, *No, no, no, Jill. I'm going to be dying, sweetheart, not going to bloody Burkina Faso.*'

'Tourism has reached Burkina Faso?'

'Apparently.'

'I wouldn't be too confident about the hospitals there.'

'I'm going to tell her you said that. It will mean more coming from you. Though she'll probably just reroute us.'

Chris's food arrived, and between small mouthfuls he told Max about one of his recent cases. A man, a South Pacific–style performer who was entertaining people at a backyard wedding when his grass skirt caught on fire as he'd sashayed about with his flame sticks. The man panicked and ran straight for a pool and jumped into it, but the pool had no water in it.

'What?' Max was horrified. 'Did he *survive?*'

'He did. He's going to be okay,' Chris said. 'Amazingly no broken bones. A deep gash on his head, second-degree burns on his legs and he'll need a skin graft, but otherwise . . .'

'How could he not see there wasn't any water in the pool?'

'Who expects no water in a pool? Anyway, I think he was too busy dancing with his sticks. Then busy panicking. Remember, he was *on fire.*'

Something in Chris's look, or his last sentence, had Max dissolving into laughter. He laughed well beyond the merits of the story. The sound of it filled the small restaurant. And when he was done, he looked straight at Chris and started talking about their friendship. He told Chris how much he valued their friendship and how much he admired him. 'You say you went into emergency medicine for the excitement and challenge,' Max said, 'but I think you do what you do because you're kind.'

Kind. Max thought he was kind. The ache behind his eyes hardened then stung.

—

In the days after their dinner Chris experienced a form of trauma as he recalled the perfection of the evening. He was now acutely aware of the rarity of Max, the rarity of a friend he connected with so deeply, a peer who knew, intimately, so much of his history. A loss was coming that seemed too great.

13

They began work on Greta's wake immediately. In Louisa's case, it was as soon as she'd stepped out of Tim's door. Possible menu items were already forming in her mind. In the car trip going home, she threw them at Clare one after the other, swivelling to face her as she did so. They hurtled across the city with talk of the wake filling the small ute, and with Louisa's attention, to Clare's mind, insufficiently trained on the road.

Most of Louisa's suggestions had an Italian theme. In among the relevant details Tim gave them – a description of Greta and her family, the expected number of guests (one hundred), the time and location of the wake (they had a week) – he mentioned Greta Henry came from an Italian background, and a few close relatives were flying in from Italy. Louisa had almost barked the word back at Tim: '*Italian?*'

He had no idea what she was so concerned about.

'But Italians know about food,' Louisa insisted. 'That knowledge is just in them from birth. What happened to the low expectations you talked about? What happened to Aunty Edna's sandwiches? An *Italian barrister*?'

Louisa had an image of her first wake in her mind. Something small and non-confronting to kick off her business. She'd pictured a quiet, average elderly person with a small group of bingo friends and a peaceful uneventful death.

—

From the following day onwards, Clare and Louisa spent the greater part of each day together. At first, Clare watched Louisa with some apprehension, worried about how her lack of organisational ability would manifest itself. There was no question she struggled to engage with anything administrative. Planning, list-making, scheduling, pricing all brought a vagueness to her expression, a light glaze over her eyes, a fidgeting. But that did seem to be compensated for. When she was interested, she became fast and focused. Give her a cooking utensil and a specific task and she was impressive. She could chop with a speed that seemed to demand a competition.

On their first day of work, they'd sat down and discussed the menu again. Louisa had a thousand small food ideas stored in her head and she easily pulled out the more Italianesque ones. She suggested an Italian hand pie, like a mini calzone, filled with Italian sausage and basil and ricotta. Or maybe a slow-roasted shredded beef version with olives and rosemary and a hint of orange?

'Could we make them in advance and freeze them?' Clare asked.

'Yep.'

'Done.'

But what Louisa really wanted to do was a morning bun: a sweet version and a savoury one. She explained it was made from croissant dough that was rolled into a cylinder and cut and baked, giving you little pillows with spiralling hills in the middle. 'What sends your senses soaring is the textural thing,' she said. 'The contrast between the outside and the inside. Rich and crisp and crackly on the outside, delicate buttery folds on the inside.' They were often baked with orange-cinnamon sugar – it was a classic and they'd have to do that one – but she had an Italian version in mind too. A swirl of pesto made with zesty greens and a sharp, aged provolone.

'Croissant dough?' Clare asked.

'Laminated croissant dough, actually.'

'That sounds like a lot of work. Aren't croissants hard?'

'Not if you've made them a lot. Which I have. You just need to perfect your technique and then it's relatively easy.'

'Right.'

'They'd be outrageously good. And very comforting to sad people, I'd imagine.'

Clare nodded.

'And the croissant dough can be made ahead of time and frozen. We could even freeze the cooked buns and heat them up on the day.'

And arancini balls. Louisa had a great recipe: wild mushroom and taleggio with a green goddess sauce.

'Ooh, they sound nice. Not too much work?'

'Nah. And you can make them a day or two in advance, and then heat and crisp them up in the oven when you're ready to serve.' (It would be the arancini, strangely, out of all the intricate things Louisa put forward, that would almost be their undoing.)

On the sweeter side she suggested her lemon tart, a Persian love cake, and tartlets with goat's curd and strawberries. And again, the practicalities: the tartlet cases could be made ahead of time and frozen and the Persian love cake could be made in advance too – the oil in the ground almond base would ensure it stayed moist and lovely for a couple of days after making.

'But of course,' Louisa said that first day, 'we also need scones and little sandwiches. Funeral stalwarts and for good reason. We'd be shooting ourselves in the foot to leave those two out. And there really are endless marvellous things you can put between two slices of bread.'

'I make a pretty good chicken sandwich,' Clare said. Alex had won sandwich competitions among his school friends with it. Grace took phone calls from her school friends requesting she bring some for her lunch, and in exchange they'd bring chocolate. When Clare took a plate of them to a function she would feel, for a brief period, that she might have nailed life.

'That's enough for me,' Louisa said, and Clare's chicken sandwich made it onto the menu without an audition.

—

They worked in Louisa's kitchen with music in the background. Louisa made a playlist especially for the cooking and it leant, quite interestingly, towards Elvis. Every time he popped up Clare would be surprised; she hadn't heard so much Elvis in such a long time. 'There are times,' Louisa insisted, 'when Elvis is just *right.*' She was buoyant with purpose. She sang along loudly with 'Suspicious Minds'.

A mild nervousness arrived on day three, flitting through their conversations, and a full solid nervousness set in on day four. Elton John replaced Elvis. That day they moved their operations from Louisa's house to Clare's – Clare had a much bigger kitchen and they hoped they'd work more efficiently with the space.

Amir arrived on day five, when they were knee-deep in arancini balls and had less than two days until the wake. Minutes before his knock on the door Louisa had muttered to Clare: 'These fuckers are so time-consuming. Having to make the risotto then do all the rolling and flouring and egging and crumbing and then the cooking – what the fuck was I thinking? A hundred risotto balls?'

Clare was almost beyond thought or speech about them; they were slowly unravelling her. There were far too many of them, and the process just wouldn't finish.

Clare answered her door, covered in flour. It was a little surprising to see Amir, standing on her doorstep and smiling hello, but in the next breath she felt nothing but pleasure. She ushered him in with a near-urgent wave of her hand, and took him briskly down the hallway as if bringing in a treasure. Another person! A friendly voice to help soften the atmosphere. And, maybe, a roller of balls? Amir made numerous comments on how *good* the house smelt. 'It's rosemary and garlic, isn't it?' he said as they walked. 'And there's thyme and onion?' It was early on a Sunday afternoon. He had been sitting at home and thought he might check on how they were going.

He pulled up when he saw the kitchen. He may have sworn, softly, but Clare couldn't be sure.

The kitchen, and its surrounds, were strewn with the chaos of production. From where Clare stood, it told a pitiful story that held a tinge of hysteria. And there was Louisa in the middle of it, with her hands dipped in a large bowl of beaten egg, swivelling her torso to see who it was.

What a difference another pair of hands made! They could separate the tasks and make the whole thing cleaner and quicker; in short, keep their own hands in one product. Once the balls were all rolled, they could have one person on the flouring, one on the egging and one on the crumbing. Triumph burst into the air around Louisa.

They stood in a line at the bench. Conversation returned and the air felt lighter. Clare told Louisa that Amir knew all the lyrics to most of the songs from his favourite musicals and Louisa was impressed. He told her he liked the lyrical storytelling, particularly in *Hamilton*. 'That's lyrical genius,' he said. Louisa then asked him if he could sing one of her favourites: 'Any Dream Will Do' from *Joseph and the Amazing Technicolor Dreamcoat*.

Her request stopped Clare mid-egging. 'How do you do that?' she asked Louisa.

'Do what?'

'Have a favourite song or a favourite bird ready like that? I'd have to think for ages about which one I'd choose.'

'It's a surprising choice,' Amir said, 'but I like it. I know it.'

'What's surprising is Jason Donovan,' Louisa said. 'Do you know all of it?'

'Yes.'

Amir was on the brink of the song, within a breath of giving them that first sung word, when David appeared, quick-stepping up the deck stairs and walking through the French doors. Clare immediately deflated – was it the lack of the song, or simply David? Lately, he'd fallen into the habit of coming around the back instead of knocking on the front door, of seemingly appearing on a whim. He stopped just inside the family room when he saw them, and Clare imagined how they must appear to him: aproned and floured and so festively industrious.

In a silly sort of a way, nobody spoke. As if the three of them in the kitchen were guilty of some wrongdoing. There was the sense of David being left out of something important, as if word should have got to him, as if they'd been rude to exclude him.

Then he moved into the room, and the silence broke.

There was no need for introductions. David knew Amir and he'd met Louisa. Though to Clare it felt like she needed to intro-duce them again – or, at the very least, *explain* them.

But David spoke first. 'Nice to see you, Amir.'

'Nice to see you too,' Amir said, in a way that almost turned it into a question.

David and Amir worked out they'd last seen each other at the work Christmas party two years earlier. 'That was an awful night, wasn't it?' Amir said, but David couldn't remember it.

'I'm giving them a bit of a hand,' Amir added into the loaded silence that followed.

'That's what's confusing me,' David said. 'What are you all doing?'

Clare spoke for the first time. 'We're preparing some food for a funeral.'

'A funeral? Whose funeral? Who died?' he asked.

'A woman named Greta Henry,' Clare said. 'You don't know her.'

'Is she a friend of yours?' David asked, looking from Clare to Louisa.

'No.' Clare shook her head and Louisa did the same.

'We don't know her,' Clare added quickly, wanting to help David out now. He was appearing awkward and a little cold, and that wasn't him at all. 'Louisa is having a go at some funeral catering and I'm helping her with the first one, and Amir called in to see how I was and he's been helping us out a bit too.'

David took some time to digest it all, his eyes taking in the scene again with this new knowledge.

He looked at Louisa. 'So, this is your business?'

Business? The word raised a little smile in Clare. She simply couldn't help it. She saw its effect on Louisa.

'Yes, hopefully it is,' Louisa replied with a tight expression, and then she asked if they would all please excuse her, she needed to pop into the bathroom.

David looked so lost in his old home. His eyes went to their dining table, where slabs of Persian love cake were cooling. Fragrances of cardamom and rosewater wafted from the table. Once decorated, they would be beautiful, perhaps like a Persian garden in spring: hints of rosewater and citrus, a sprinkling of bright green pistachios and rose petals.

'What's that?' he asked.

'Persian love cake,' Clare said.

And then Amir cut in softly, saying he had finished all the balls he had and it was getting close to five and he should go.

He took off his apron, said a gracious goodbye, and disappeared out the back doors.

David looked at her intently once Amir had left. 'You've always said you hate funerals. You avoid them at all costs. I can't really believe you're doing this as work.'

'I never say *hate*, and I'm not doing this as my work.' He was making her jaw ache. 'I told you that. Louisa is doing it and I'm just helping her out while she gets started. Just this one.' She spoke softly not wanting Louisa to hear. Was it fair, saying *just this one*?

'Okay,' he said. 'But I thought you were taking a holiday.'

'It was never a holiday.'

'I thought you were taking it easy. You've completely thrown me,' he said. 'I worry about you. Well, so long as it's just –'

Clare glared at him as she heard Louisa returning.

'So, Dave,' Louisa said as she walked back into the kitchen. 'A question for you. Which business name do you like the best: Food to Die For or Waking the Bread?'

14

Greta's dying, her leaving them, felt as 'violent and unforeseen as an engine stopping in the middle of the sky'.

The words of Simone de Beauvoir, Bruce Henry said. Later, he quoted a lengthier passage from John Keats (something with much gentler imagery) and apologised for using other people's words. There was a correctness and beauty in them he simply couldn't match.

Chris didn't have any great knowledge of poetry; all he had were some leftovers from his school days, a handful of sporadic sentences which had inexplicably stayed in his brain all this time. For one, he had *I wandered lonely as a cloud* and virtually nothing after that. He had a fairly good idea there was a later mention of daffodils but he couldn't be sure. He had some sentences from the other English poets – the usual stuff: Auden, Gerard Manley Hopkins, Ted Hughes – and smatterings of Les Murray. But his favourite lines, his most intact lines, were from Emily Dickinson (she wrote wonderfully short poems): *'Hope' is the thing with feathers/That perches in the soul/And sings the tune without the words/And never stops – at all.* Chris sighed, almost content, sitting forward in his seat and listening to Bruce.

They were in the hands of a master. Grief-drenched Bruce could certainly deliver a eulogy. Chris understood Bruce had been an engineer, but he had the affecting, resonant voice of an actor. There'd been a cracked, mass-sobbing sound as early as the second sentence of his eulogy, when he'd said something like: *I've lost my favourite person in the world, the best thing about living.* It struck Chris as the sincerest sentiment he had ever heard spoken. Bruce Henry had lost the best thing about living, and not one person in that room would doubt it. And how hard it was not to project that sentiment into your own life. Was Sarah his best thing? He wasn't sure. He had a sneaking suspicion work had always been his best thing, and in Bruce Henry's company that felt like a tragedy of monumental proportions.

From memory, he'd only been to two funerals apart from his parents', and both had dismal eulogies. In one, the reference point for almost every anecdote and character point about the deceased was the eulogiser himself. The relationship between him and the deceased, what the deceased thought of him and vice versa, how *he* would struggle without him. Chris remembered thinking, *Pull it in, this isn't about you!* It had been pulled in, eventually, but maybe too late; he didn't feel as sad as he thought he should be. And then there'd been an awful religious one. The priest had declared that man is not saved by good deeds done, he is saved by mercy, and under his direction the eulogiser had mentioned not one of his cousin's admirable acts or attributes. You'd have to call it a disaster, how he gave them nothing; no stories or memories on which to hang their grief. Left them all sitting there, holding it in.

His eyes remained locked on Bruce Henry. Chris could have listened to Bruce Henry all day. And he'd even been funny, along with that terrible grief. He had a cache of wonderful anecdotes – stories of individuality and daring (Greta Henry had swum the English Channel!) – and the further he went into his eulogy the more of a well-structured masterpiece it became. There was a chance he was edging a little close to destroying his audience. Once or twice, Chris had to resist a morbid urge to turn to his neighbour – a young woman often inundated by tears – and tell her it had been in his hands to keep Greta alive. He could have saved this tremendous woman they were all hearing about.

And who would talk about *him* like this when he was gone? Sarah certainly couldn't be counted on any longer, and he was an only child, so there were no siblings to call upon. Most of his friends were work colleagues, and in any imagining of their speeches they fell well short of what he'd just heard. He understood it wasn't a competition, but all his accomplishments, going unheard!

He'd recognised Nina Henry. She saw him arrive and said she was touched that he'd come. He felt embarrassed by that. Like an imposter. He couldn't settle on why he was there. Countless patients had died in his care in the span of his career and not once had he been tempted to do this, to attend their funeral, to be so immersed in a life lost. Given his job, that would have been unsustainable.

He turned his attention back to Bruce who was now quoting John Keats, saying,

'A *thing of beauty is a joy for ever:*

Its loveliness increases; it will never
Pass into nothingness; but still will keep
A bower quiet for us, and a sleep
Full of sweet dreams, and health, and quiet breathing.'

For all his early composure, Bruce broke down in the few sentences that came next, the final ones of his eulogy. It was hard to watch, and he took most of the room down with him.

Margie Vaile, Greta Henry's best friend, stood at the lectern after Bruce. She admitted she wouldn't say much – that was rather beyond her – but she wanted to play a recording. In two weeks time it would be Greta and Bruce's fortieth wedding anniversary. Greta had been planning a surprise for which she'd enlisted Margie's help. (Margie had been her maid of honour.) Greta wanted to perform Bruce's favourite song – 'The Luckiest' by Ben Folds – at the party they were holding to mark the occasion. Margie and Greta, both musically compromised – Margie on the piano with only a few years of childhood tuition behind her and Greta, tone-deaf in a family of good singers – gave it their best. At their last practice, only a few days before Greta died, they'd taped themselves to see how they sounded. 'Well,' Margie said, standing now in that church, 'I'm not sure of the best words to describe it. But we were both highly amused by it and decided there was an entertainment value in it that was well worth going ahead with.' Margie looked at Bruce. 'I think she would want you to hear this,' she said.

And so, they got to hear Greta's voice – Chris for the first time. Her singing was earnest and a little wobbly and almost on key, and the piano playing was generally okay though prone to haphazard changes in volume and speed. All in all, it was mediocre and sometimes truly awful, and somehow that made it both ridiculously uplifting and emotionally devastating. All through the church, suppressed giggles turned into laughter that turned into sobs.

And last of all came the video. Set against beautiful music, it told the story of an undoubtedly rich and full life. And the final thing they were all shown was footage of Greta skiing down a mountain. A middle-aged Greta making quick sharp turns in the dry, powdery snow with high white peaks and a deep blue sky behind her. As she passed whomever was filming, she let out a whoop of joy, one arm and a pole thrown high in the air, then continued on, past the camera, skiing off into the distance and finally out of view. The video faded to a cloudless blue sky, then nothing.

Nothing.

What a visual onslaught of nothing. There was a kind of snuffled explosion in the room, and some commotion in the front pew Chris couldn't quite see. But he could imagine.

He wanted to blame the video for what happened next. There was another small speech and then the coffin was lifted, ready to leave. He sat still, feeling the well of some unbearable emotion, like a cry rising in him; he had no idea what it was and he worked to keep it down. It horrified him: this couldn't be for Greta, that would be absurd. Who was this for? His mother? His father? Everyone around him stood and 'The Carnival Is Over' played, and he stayed seated with his head bent, breathing deeply. Once, he lifted his head briefly and saw the bent-over body and collapsed face of Greta's mother, walking right behind the coffin, and he was back where he'd started, tamping down those surprising tears.

Afterwards, he stood in bright sunlight on the steps of the church. He was breathing normally again, and the sun felt good. But he couldn't quite leave Greta's life behind him; what an extraordinary, beautiful shape it took all around him. He stood there, above the crowd, and it hit him he might actually be feeling jealous. *Jealous.* Thank goodness thoughts couldn't be seen. And there he was having to pull himself in again, quickly and silently berating himself for the envy, reminding himself she was dead.

He wasn't a funeral person. Why had he come? He'd left the house without giving it much thought, stepping around Sarah's boxes. Sarah was now leaving permanently. Her boxes were in almost every room, slowly filling with belongings she considered to be indisputably hers. Every room was now stamped with her leaving. She was going about it in a prolonged fashion, a drawn-out removal that came either from reluctance or a lack of time, he wasn't sure which. It was hard to watch; a failure years in the making and now days and days in the execution.

And so, maybe he'd gone to the funeral to escape Sarah's boxes.

He had no real intention of attending the wake. That seemed inappropriate, if not plain weird. But a few things came into play. They were informed near the end of the funeral service that refreshments were being served in a room just a short walk away, and the word *refreshment* landed in him with considerable force. He was starving. And he was heading straight to work from the funeral; a ten-hour shift lay ahead of him. Into his mind came the image of a golden-crusted hot scone, little side dishes of jam and cream.

Most of the mourners were still loitering around the front of the church. As he weaved his way through them, there was no sign that anyone was heading yet for the refreshment room. It occurred to him he could slip in and out, largely unseen.

And he was, it appeared, *first*. He walked into the room and was greeted by a woman who burst from a side door; she must have heard him enter. It surprised her, he could see that – the fact of him being so blatantly alone – and then, of all things, she picked up a plate and offered him a scone. He thanked her, picking up the scone, and she turned and took one step away from him as if to give him some privacy. How he wished he'd gone straight to his car. He felt stupidly awkward. But then he had a good look at the scone and it was just as he imagined it. He took a small bite, and it was *excellent*. He was finishing it off when a noise made him look across the room. There was another woman in the kitchen in the corner – he caught a fleeting glimpse of her leaning back at an unusual angle, stealing a look at him before disappearing – and the quick picture of her made it hard not to smile.

But he knew the last thing he should do was smile to himself, standing there on his own.

'Excellent scone,' he said to the woman in the room. 'The crowd is on its way,' he added.

'Oh, good,' she said, with a nervous kind of smile.

A large screen on one wall caught his attention. He inclined his head towards it. 'Watch out for the video presentation,' he said. 'A fairly harrowing end.'

'Oh no,' she said, looking around, as if trying to look anywhere but at him.

He looked around too. There was food everywhere, so many plates of the most delicious-looking food. It would be a well-attended wake, but there was an extraordinary amount of food on display.

'The thing is,' he said, searching for words that might provide him with some dignity, 'I've just called in quickly because I'm due back at work. Do you think I could grab something for the road?' They could definitely spare it.

'Yes, of course you can,' she said and sprang into action, grabbing a small plate. They decided that sandwiches would be the easiest thing for him to eat in the car, and she chose a selection for him on his suggestion. And when she stood before him, holding her offerings, he appreciated for the first time how lovely she was. There was a kind of pressing on his heart as he looked at her. He took the plate and thanked her a great deal, telling himself he was opened up by the funeral, unusually susceptible to loveliness, and after that, he said quite a formal goodbye with a strange sort of half-bow. The bow arrived out of nowhere; he really couldn't account for it. On leaving, he wished her good luck over his shoulder.

He walked through the car park with his eight small sandwiches. There was no one about. How separate he suddenly felt from life itself. When he got to his car, he sat still without turning on the engine, feeling so incredibly lonely.

He chose what he assumed to be a chicken sandwich and took a bite, and for a moment all thought stopped. The sandwich was *outstanding*. Possibly the best he'd ever eaten. What on earth was in it? He picked up another one and looked at it closely, but its ingredients were too finely chopped, too amalgamated to be clear. He rarely cooked, so it wasn't really his forte, working it out. There was chicken, obviously, and mayonnaise, and in his next bite he detected herbs of some sort and a hint of citrus. But he could be wrong. He felt a fierce regret that he had only two of them; that he'd opted for a selection. The rest of the sandwiches were gone within minutes and they were all very good, though the smallest fraction short of chicken-excellence. It was a few minutes of thoughtless satisfaction, a relief, and he was tempted to go back and get more. The place would be crowded by now and he could pilfer a feast to see him through his shift. But what would he say to the caterer? More to the point, how could he return after that bow?

He stared out the window and the beautiful eulogies returned to his mind. The sound of Bruce's voice, and his words; the sound of Greta and Margie singing.

He held them close as he started the car and drove out of the church grounds.

15

In a certain light, Clare thought, a wake could look like a party.

There was plenty of wine going around. And the Henry family loved to sing. They were all very good. Bruce Henry had sung an acoustic version of 'You're Beautiful', and if you closed your eyes you could come close to thinking James Blunt was in the room. Clare had walked up to a small group who were talking about how much Greta loved music. How she would say that to be able to sing – to just stand up anywhere and sing – was to her the most beautiful gift of all. It was no coincidence, someone said, that she married a man with a lovely voice.

In the first hour, Clare was coping quite well. She moved through the gathering, keeping the word *funeral* locked well away in a little box in her mind.

In the beginning, one man arrived on his own. There was some awkwardness, she was nervous, but in the end his compliments and his kind manners helped to ease some of her tension. He made her think: *This will be okay; I can do this.* She felt a quick sense of pleasure as she compiled a small plate for him. But he didn't stay long. He left with a formal sort of exit and she went straight to the kitchen to tell Louisa all about him. She'd walked through the door saying, 'Well, he liked the scones,' and felt compelled to add, 'And he was *particularly* good-looking.' Louisa said she had noticed that.

But a wake wasn't a party. Greta's mother arrived later than everyone else, and she changed the picture of the room for Clare. One of her sons brought her in. She was ninety-three. She sat in the corner, draped in black, with a small, tight group of relatives sitting around her. She hadn't eaten a thing – she refused anything she was offered – and soon, for Clare, she made the food seem trivial and close to heartless. On her hairline were bare patches of skin where Clare assumed she'd pulled her own hair out. The only time she looked out into the room, the only time her grief seemed to give her a reprieve, was when someone was singing.

Clare worked at a very fast pace. It wasn't until people began streaming through the doors that Louisa admitted how uncomfortable she felt around crowds. Somehow, stupidly, she'd thought mourners would be different. Quieter, less of a strain on her sensibilities. But not so. The opposite, really – all those families. She disappeared into the kitchen as the room filled up. *I'll hold the fort in there*, she said with a look of concern and apology. And so Clare moved around the room in something approaching a run: she hovered by groups, raced off to the kitchen, came back, checked on what people had, offered plates and darted off again.

The chicken sandwiches disappeared quickly among floods of praise. She was asked for them on numerous occasions when arriving at a group holding a plate of something else. 'All gone,' she would answer with a small shake of her head and a regretful smile, and with an unexpected delight rising in her. The balls were popular too, but she was still too annoyed by them to care – no matter how round and crisp they looked, no matter how much pleasure people expressed when the warm taleggio arrived in their first bite. And the lemon tarts and the morning buns: in her mind, and in the opinion of others, they were spectacular.

As the wake was ending, Clare acknowledged its pervading air of celebration. It was there; it existed, alongside Greta's mother. When things calmed down a little, when people mostly gave her a little wave when she approached them, saying, 'No, thank you, we're full,' she began hearing more and more stories about Greta. Greta had a big family and there was a lot of laughter. Sometimes there were great joyous bursts of it.

And in the wake's dwindling minutes, Greta Henry's best friend walked into the kitchen when she and Louisa were cleaning up.

'Thank you so much,' she said. 'Greta would have loved that food. Is there anything I can do to help?'

'No, no,' Clare and Louisa both said.

Margie Vaile introduced herself and sat down in the only chair in the commercial kitchen.

'I heard some people talking about your song,' Clare said. 'I loved the sound of that.'

'Can I tell you something?' Margie said. And she told them about the day she said goodbye to Greta at the hospital. How she'd sat by her friend's bedside feeling such an urgency to talk. To tell her the things she remembered most, to relive one last time the funniest things, the things she was most grateful for. It felt like her only chance to do that while believing Greta might be listening.

'I went on and on and they literally had to call time on me,' she said. 'That last moment, when I knew it was the last thing that I would ever say to her, I leant in and told her I loved her and I said, *I got to live my one life with you. I'm the luckiest.* And that made me think I had to play that song.'

Clare was silent for a while after Margie Vaile left. They were busy cleaning and packing up, and she kept her back to Louisa. The things Margie had said made Clare think of Hope. One of her tightest-held memories prickled down her spine. Clare understood that level of friendship. She knew about the space left behind when a friendship like that no longer existed; she knew about the grief, about the millions of things – the funny observations, the small stories, the concerns about life – that would forever go unsaid when that friendship was gone. She knew that you'd never forget it.

—

They stacked their things into Clare's car as a pink dusk fell. The car was an ageing, roomy people mover, much bigger than Louisa's ute, and they climbed in and sat high in its front seats like a pair of tired bus drivers.

'How nice it is to finally sit,' Louisa said, and Clare nodded.

On the drive home they were so exhausted that a few minutes passed before either of them said a word; they simply stared blankly through the windscreen.

Louisa spoke first. 'Clare, is driving this slowly legal?'

'What do you mean?'

'I mean, this is very slow.'

Clare kept her eyes on the road, but she was fairly sure Louisa was grinning. She shrugged. 'This is how I always drive.'

'This isn't driving! A committed jogger would move faster than this. You must send other drivers around you *mad*.'

'I don't know about that,' Clare said, unable to resist a smile, and drove on with little change in speed. Soon, Louisa admitted she was actually finding the pace relaxing. There was a certain mindfulness to it.

'Just wondering, though,' Clare said, 'how will you do this job in the future if you don't like big groups of people?'

'That's a very good point. I'm going to have to think that one through.'

The sky was beautiful, streaked with paling pinks and blues. Clare's mind was full of Greta and her family.

'Do you have any family, Louisa?' Clare asked. It struck her that in all their hours together, in all that talking, in all those topics covered, Louisa hadn't once mentioned family. Tim, who wasn't even a relative, was the closest she'd come.

'No, I don't have any,' Louisa said. 'Not alive, anyway.'

It wasn't at all the answer Clare was expecting. She expected someone. And it was such a bad time to have asked the question. She was entering the motorway – it always worried her, merging with such fast-flowing traffic – and the concentration required left her with no opportunity to look sideways. To catch Louisa's expression, to give her a look of sympathy. *No family.*

After a silence, Louisa said, 'I never knew my father. My mother had me when she was nineteen. My father came to Australia from Ireland for a working holiday and he went back home without knowing I existed.'

'Where is he now?'

'To tell you the truth, I don't know. Ireland?'

'No one has ever contacted him?'

'No.'

'And your mother?'

'She died when I was twelve.'

'Twelve?'

Clare twisted quickly to check on Louisa, and Louisa was nodding at her almost matter-of-factly.

'How did she die?'

'In a car accident. Her car left the bend of a country road when it was raining.'

'Who did you live with then? Did you have grandparents to go to?'

'No. I lived with my mother's younger sister Janie.'

'Your mother's sister? How old was she?'

'Fifteen months younger than my mother.'

'But she's no longer alive?' Clare felt tears push at her eyes with the question.

'She died when I was seventeen. Of breast cancer.' There was something different about Louisa's voice now, and Clare knew that if she turned to look at her, the matter-of-fact expression would no longer be there. Clare couldn't look away; cars were flying by on either side of her – how narrow the lanes now felt! She wanted to stop the car, pull over and talk.

'I'm so sorry, Louisa,' Clare said. 'My father died when I was thirteen.' And there it was. Clare hadn't talked about family either.

Clare's voice had trembled, something it always did when she spoke about her father. Which was rarely. She stared straight ahead and sensed Louisa doing the same. They sat in silence for a few moments, with those deep difficult topics lying between them.

'I'm sorry . . .' Clare said again, and then her voice trailed off. She turned her head briefly towards Louisa. An inadequate flick of a glance. 'Would you like to talk about it?'

Louisa shook her head. 'No, not really,' she said. 'And I'm sorry about your dad.'

There was another silence. Clare hadn't known Louisa long enough for this territory. She didn't know how to read these silences, how to feel when Louisa's wit and wryness wasn't coming straight back at her. Clare lurched to an alternative subject.

'David keeps dropping in meals,' she said, 'even though I'm perfectly capable of cooking now. He says it makes him feel like he's contributing to the household, helping to care for the kids. The meals are lovely, he's an excellent cook, but just once it would be great if instead of cooking – which he loves, says it calms him – he suggested he would stay for a few hours and clean the house. Do the bathrooms and wash the floors, maybe?'

Louisa was still quiet.

'Sometimes,' Clare said, intent on saving the car from silence, 'I look at him when he walks in after I haven't seen him for a while, and I can't believe I once found him attractive. I think it through, and I can't see it. But then there are other times when I can, and he's nice and . . .' Off she went, listing a few of his nice attributes, trying to place evidence in the car, a reason for the existence of a twenty-year marriage.

And that little speech took her to the corner at the bottom of their street. She pulled in to the kerb in front of Louisa's house.

'I'm sorry about your mum and Janie,' she said again, turning to look at Louisa properly, but Louisa was already stretching into the back seat for her belongings. The words felt fumbled and would never be enough, and all Clare caught from Louisa was an expression cast while turning, a fleeting streak of something.

They both got out of the car and grabbed boxes from the boot and took them inside.

'Thanks so much for your help,' Louisa said. 'You were fantastic.'

'It was a pleasure,' Clare said. And it was true; it was.

Then she left, and drove the short remaining distance to her own house. Floundered into it with Louisa's loss.

16

Only hours after she said their names out loud in the car – Mum and Janie – they both appeared in Louisa's dream. They came in together, so vibrant and happy, and they were both *there* with Louisa, talking as if they'd talked to her only five minutes ago, and again only yesterday. Their faces held a stunning clarity, a *realness* that Louisa registered in the dream, and how she longed to hang on to them and take them into daylight! When had she last seen them that way? When had she last heard them? But they were there for just minutes, or that's how it seemed, and she was left grappling with their memories in her first waking thoughts.

Their memories moved in her chest and tightened in her throat the way they used to do. She felt the hard, aching sensation of a long-ago loneliness. In them, in the two of them, was a loss too great and too extraordinary. All those years ago, she'd learnt to place it aside and cover it over. They couldn't function together, that huge loss and her.

She stayed in bed for longer than usual. She shut down the memories as the day's light filtered in, diligently dragged each thought from her dream to her day. She had three lawns to mow. Three newish regulars.

She'd rung Tim before going to bed the night before. She'd told him she'd like to put a hold on the funeral work for now. She needed to think it all through, all the aspects of the business, and she planned to tell Clare all about it when she finished with her mowing.

—

Her first lawn was Frank's.

It was a clear spring morning, a perfect day for mowing. Frank was kind and elderly and so gently endearing she was reluctant to charge him. She mowed his lawn, trimmed the hedges and did some weeding, and knocked on his door when she was done. She and Frank had fallen into a quick-cup-of-tea habit. She didn't like to dwell on her rate of productivity.

'When the heck are you going to charge me?' Frank asked the second she walked in.

She stopped to think. When had she last done her accounts? Even the word *accounts* could fill her with dismay. She kept a book in her ute's glove box and in it she wrote down the details of every job she did. She'd used the tatty book process for years now; a spreadsheet seemed like overkill.

Frank had told her on numerous occasions that he had plenty of money. 'Just give me a bill and I'll pay it straight away,' he'd said.

It was as basic as that. She needed to work out how many visits Frank owed her for and times that by her rate. What was so difficult about that?

Frank already had their tea brewing. She caught up on his news: which grandchild was having a baby, the various places in which his family were holidaying. She knew the names of all his children and grandchildren, and they numbered over twenty; she'd seen photos of each of them; she knew Jaydan spelt his name with two a's. But today she was only half-listening as she sipped her tea, too aware of the tightness still lingering in her chest; it felt a little hot around her heart, and her breathing was shallow. She took in three deep breaths as she sat there.

From Frank's she went to the cranky lady's place. Here, there'd be no cups of tea. Louisa mowed the lawns and cut the edges as quickly and efficiently as possible, hoping cranky Elaine would remain in her house until the very last minute. She had the leaf blower roaring around the pool when she realised Elaine had come out and was yelling at her over the noise. Louisa cut the motor and removed her earmuffs.

Elaine wanted to say she still thought Louisa cut the lawn's edges far too hard (and Louisa really thought she didn't; any less hard and there would be no edge to speak of).

'Sure,' Louisa said nodding, and took a few more deep breaths. Her policy was to keep engagement with Elaine to a minimum – Elaine set off the bluntness in her and occasionally it ran a little out of her control – but today was different. She would have to engage.

'Have you noticed, Elaine, how many mosquitoes you've got around your pool?' Louisa swatted the air. Now the leaf blower had stopped, the mosquitoes were moving back smartly and en masse.

Elaine frowned, swatting now too, and nodding, saying she didn't come out to the pool much – or the yard, for that matter.

She adopted a highly concerned expression as her eyes ran over her clear blue pool and the significant number of mosquitoes hovering above it.

'They're coming from somewhere else,' Louisa said, frowning. She was being bitten. She almost shivered with irritation.

'But from where?'

'I'll get my ladder.'

Louisa walked to her ute, scratching both her arms and the back of her neck, and hauled out her ladder. She carried it down to the backyard with the hot sun beating down on her and positioned it against the fence. She climbed to the top, still scratching, and peered across the near neighbours' back gardens. 'The pool two houses down,' she yelled back to Elaine. 'It's green. Full of algae.' One green swimming pool could produce millions of mosquitoes. The mosquitoes were also in next door's pool. And maybe on the other side of the algae-filled pool too. She climbed back down.

'They're in your neighbour's pool as well.' Louisa tilted her head at the fence.

'Well, that's not right! What should I do?' Elaine gave her own leg a hard slap.

'Ask the perpetrators to clean their pool.'

'Ask them to clean their own pool? I hardly know them. How can I do that?'

'I don't know. They're your neighbours. Just two houses down. You have to say something – they're infecting the neighbourhood.'

'It would be too embarrassing. Couldn't you ask them?'

'No.'

'I might ask next door to do it then. What would happen if I didn't say anything?'

'Your pool will be bloody awful, Elaine.'

Louisa picked up her ladder. She tried to smile at Elaine when she said goodbye; she really did try.

—

The last garden was her favourite. Grant and Lucy lived a few suburbs from Louisa's place, and they'd only lived in the house for a couple of months. Grant was a consultant of some kind and mainly worked from home, sitting in a second-floor room at the back of the house, working and looking out at the world. In the four times she'd been there, he'd always wandered out to talk to Louisa. He was so *casual*; she loved that about him.

Today she had to trim their back hedge, a tall monster of a thing which had been left untouched for too long. Louisa hauled out her ladder again, sagging a little in the heat. Saying, *Sorry, girlfriend* in her mind to her middle-aged body. Then she went back for her hedge trimmer and the extension pole. She positioned her ladder carefully and climbed to the top, taking the trimmer with her. She started it up, stretched and leant, and just got the tip of it to the top of the hedge. Small cut branches and foliage fell all around her. Some fell on her head. She kept going; moving her ladder, climbing up, stretching and leaning, thinking about her balance and the hope of a straight line. She was tall, but this was hard. There was no sign of Grant in his little top room. The house appeared empty. The thought *I could actually die doing this* did briefly, and quite truthfully, come into her mind.

She was done, climbing down her ladder for the last time, when Grant walked into the yard. He said hello, and together they stood back, hands on their hips, surveying the hedge. It would have been generous, a serious overstatement, to call the hedge's top line a *line*.

'I caught a glimpse of you at work,' Grant said. 'You're not going back up there.'

'But look at it,' she said. 'It's terrible.'

It was so terrible she was grinning now. Tips of tall branches appeared sporadically along the back, too far away for her to reach them. The front of the hedge was very uneven, a result of the balancing act she'd been trying to pull off. The whole thing looked like the worst of haircuts – the ones that take a lifetime to grow out.

Grant was grinning too. 'What a crazy thing to plant. This hedge belongs in Versailles.'

'I think it needs someone in a crane to trim it,' she said.

'Let's leave it,' Grant said. 'The shape will even out eventually. And it's got character for the time being.'

'Are you sure? I'm a bit embarrassed by it. Let me quickly go back up and –'

'No! God, Louisa, I could see you falling. When I turned the corner of the house you were at a right angle with the ladder. I would have yelled, but I realised if I yelled out you would definitely fall. So, yes: I'm sure. I'm happy with my hedge and with my gardener who is alive and speaking to me.'

And he meant it. She could see that. He was happy. He'd walk upstairs to his office, and it was utterly conceivable he would be whistling while he did. He'd look out at his back garden as he worked. And he would be perfectly fine with the sight of his tall, ragged hedge set against a clear blue sky.

On that note, Louisa headed home. But the tightness was still there in her chest, still restricting her breathing, taking so much of her attention and energy. The fatigue was almost overwhelming.

—

Louisa showered and walked up to Clare's place. She hoped they'd do what they always did – sit and chat and have a nice cup of tea – but when she got to Clare's gate she saw David's car on the street. Her heart sank. She stopped, thinking she'd turn around and head back home, have her tea sitting outside with Gilbert instead. She didn't like David. She'd tried to (a little bit), but she couldn't. She knew she was biased, having made a decision about him well before meeting him, and maybe she could have liked him if they'd started unencumbered by what he'd done. (Which was an inane concept anyway.) Could she have liked him? He had a nice-enough face with plenty of laughter lines crinkling out from his eyes, a feature which usually drew her to a person. He was a teacher, that was a positive, and Clare supposedly loved him once, and maybe she still did.

And here he was, opening the front door with Clare, coming down the garden path towards her.

'Hello, David,' she said, and as she looked at him, her handful of stories – the ones meant for Clare – disappeared. God, she thought, he just takes the wind out of me. And in that moment, she worked out the problem: she didn't *believe in him*.

'Hi, Louisa,' he replied and smiled at her in what seemed to her an annoyingly friendly way. As if he'd read her thoughts and was ready to debunk them. *Believe me, I'm me, and I'm truly likeable.* Then he said something to her about having dropped off a chickpea curry with nigella seeds for Clare (why mention the nigella seeds?), that he had a hundred essays to mark, and that he'd heard the wake went well.

'Have you got time for a cup of tea?' Clare asked Louisa as they watched his retreating back, the happy sort of bounce in his step.

'Pretty much always,' Louisa said. She was attempting a reassessment of David. There'd been a hearty, quite genuine-looking wave in her direction as he'd ducked his head into the car. He'd seen her staring.

—

'Did I tell you the story about the teacher with the red velvet jacket?' Clare asked as they drank tea.

'Is this a fairy tale?' Louisa asked.

Clare laughed. 'No!' She raised her cup to her lips. 'Well, maybe there's a chance it could be. That hadn't crossed my mind.'

'You haven't told me about the teacher. I'd remember a line like that.'

'He started at David's school halfway through the year. He teaches English and drama. He wore a red velvet jacket to the parent–teacher night and everyone loved it. Except for David, apparently. He described it as very red and very velvet.'

'I like the sound of that jacket.'

'Everyone at the school loves him.'

'I do a bit already.'

'David brought him up in our conversation today. I know it sounds ridiculous, but he's become this sort of symbol for David.

Like the guy is saying: *Look at me living my life full-pelt, wearing a red velvet jacket because I love the feel of it and the look of it and I'm completely free of bullshit.'*

'David can read a jacket.'

Clare smiled. 'I imagine there's more to it. David said this teacher made him feel like he himself was full of bullshit. He reckons he had this sort of mid-life honesty breakdown and that led to the night he left me. When he needed to disgorge the truth.'

'Right.' Louisa downed the last bit of her tea, then cocked her head. 'What's an honesty breakdown, exactly?'

Clare frowned a little. 'His words.' She sighed. 'He asked me to think about whether he could come home, sometime in the future.'

Louisa sat back and crossed her arms. She tried to look surprised and interested, even though shock and dismay were surging through her.

'It's hard to think about, though,' Clare said. 'I don't know how to even start thinking about it. Let's change the subject.'

As she'd walked up the street, Louisa had thought she might tell Clare about the sensation in her chest. Talk about the dream with her mother and Janie. But any desire to do that had gone. Something in David had silenced her – and maybe something in what Clare had just said. Some days, Clare would tell Louisa how lonely she was; that she felt it mainly at night. 'It's such an adjustment after all these years,' she said. 'The emptiness of the bed; the quietness when the kids are upstairs; watching television alone.' Louisa also knew work calls had started coming in: questions for Clare, the expert. And Clare was almost fully recovered, apart from some ongoing tenderness around her jaw that a physio was helping her with.

Louisa looked at Clare and imagined her slipping back into her old life, how easily that could be done, how easily it could be rebuilt. All the pieces were there.

17

Chris pulled his chair close to Max's bed.

For the past few weeks, Chris had visited Max every couple of days. Chris's full-time work schedule consisted of four ten-hour days: a mixture of morning shifts, afternoon shifts and an office day. Beyond that, he was on call. A morning shift went from eight until six, and on those days he'd drive over to Max's straight from work, heading towards the harbour with the dusk gathering around him. An afternoon shift went from two until midnight, and on those days, he'd pop over in the morning, once the peak-hour traffic had died down.

In the beginning, he'd felt the need to check with Jill, ask whether he was coming too often. It crossed his mind it might be selfish.

'I'd be happy for you to come every day,' Jill had replied. 'Your presence in this house is exactly what we need. Max told me he can talk to you about anything, about how he's really feeling. Stuff he couldn't say to anyone else. Maybe not even to me.' She paused. 'For a very popular man, Max doesn't get as many visitors as you'd expect. I think people worry they'll take up somebody else's time, somebody who might be closer to him, or that Max will be too tired, or they worry they'll say the wrong thing.'

Chris nodded, thinking: *And maybe they don't realise how quick this is going to be.*

—

The cancer hadn't spread to his brain. *Max* was there, most of the time.

On Chris's first visit, Max looked thinner than at the restaurant, but he was still able to move around quite freely and the painkillers were doing their job. Chris talked about anything that came into his head. (Nearer to the end, it would seem to Chris that in these visits with Max he talked more than he'd talked in his entire life until then, if you added all the talking up. Physically impossible, of course, but that's how it seemed. And he rarely talked about work.)

That day, he told Max he'd just met Greg, the sausage dog next door, for the first time. Greg had lived next door for almost two years, supposedly, and Chris had never previously met him. How had he missed seeing Greg all that time? Greg's owners insisted Greg was fiercely intelligent.

He told Max about the time he and Sarah swam beside a whale shark off the coast of Western Australia. The gentle puppies of the ocean, they called them. It was the size of a *bus*.

And then he told Max about Sarah leaving, with sharp tears stinging his eyes, and Max said softly, 'Oh, man, I'm sorry.'

Chris left Max's house after that first visit knowing, without question, he would return as often as he could. And he did.

Sometimes, Chris would arrive and Max would smile and say: 'You again?'

One evening he sat in Max's bedroom with Max's two sons, Will and James. They were fourteen and sixteen; they were young men, aching and kind. Chris often heard them tell Max they loved him. Max's youngest son Will had read the Uluru Statement from the Heart at school that day, and Chris admitted he'd never read it. He felt ashamed he hadn't: it was so important, and only two pages long; and now over a year old. Max said, 'It's very moving, Chris, and very generous – you should read it.' The four of them sat in that big-windowed room, talking about land and connection and the structure for a voice, while outside the sun dipped and the sky streaked with pink. For the duration of the visit, Chris never stopped feeling grateful to be there.

Occasionally, Chris would cross paths with the palliative care nurse and they'd talk. Several times Max's father, Keith, would be in the house too, and Chris would stay much longer than he'd intended. Any day, it was hard to leave Keith. He was a big man with an elegant sweep of white hair, a presence in a room. Chris would talk to Keith and look into gentle eyes clouded with grief; he'd watch Keith's expressive hands giving form to tragedy in the air.

—

One morning, early in Chris's visits, he and Max sat in the garden and Max kept his gaze on the sky. 'I knew I would feel like this, exactly like this,' Max said. He knew he would feel guilt and dread about the planet he was leaving behind for his children, and for others. He wished he had done more, wished he had started earlier. 'The next generation are cleverer than us, and more engaged,' he said, 'but god, what's ahead of them.' He shook his head.

Chris had his eyes on the sky too; it was a brilliant blue.

'Time's the issue,' Max said. 'There's still hope, the solutions exist, but the world has to get going. It needs to bloody get cracking.'

In that first week they often sat outside. Max was well enough for that, and he managed a reasonable amount of laughing and talking, even though his nausea was constant and the pain was increasing. Soon it would become intractable pain, and the strongest painkillers available wouldn't quite be enough. They arranged a morphine pump and tablets for the nausea, and these managed to take the edge off for a while.

Then Max moved inside to his bed, and mostly stayed there. He was too tired and weak and nauseous – basically, he felt *too crap*, he said – to be up and about. The first time he stayed in bed for the duration of Chris's visit, Max told Chris as he was leaving: 'I can't tell you how much I'd love to get out of this bed and walk out the door like you're going to do. Just walk out of my house and into the sunshine.'

That morning, Chris stepped out of Max's door into the natural light of day with Max's words in his head. He wondered whether he would ever step outside again without them.

—

Now, Chris sat close to Max's bed. He asked Max how his night had gone, how he was feeling, was there anything he needed? And then he sat in his chair and looked at his dearest friend in the world. The soft morning light fell across the bed. I love him, he thought.

He began telling Max about his family. About his father: a humane and intelligent man who cried listening to opera, who cried watching *Lassie Come Home* ('He cried in *Lassie*?' Max interrupted, and Chris replied, 'That show could be really sad, Max; the dog was *permanently lost.*') but struggled to express any emotion to his family. 'We weren't huggers,' Chris said. He told Max about his mother, who was almost the opposite to his father – bright and funny and outwardly happy – but she followed the lead in the matter of hugging. Chris couldn't remember *I love you* ever being said in his home. The first time he told his mother he loved her was in the days leading up to her death.

Then, Chris told Max about his heart attack on the headland at Yamba. He managed to make it amusing, after emphasising *mild* a few times. He told him about training his assistant in CPR on that grassy headland. About the Bee Gees.

'I can't believe you kept that to yourself,' Max said. He paused. 'Given that you're okay and the heart attack was mild, that is a *good story*. Having to train someone? And that your mum caught the school bus with all the budding Bee Gees!' Max was smiling. 'And seriously, this guy on the headland couldn't remember "Stayin' Alive"? Surely that's impossible!'

'Apparently not.'

'Maybe it's that we're so middle-aged.' Max lay back on his pillow and started humming the song softly, and when a small ironic smile played on his lips his eyes went to Chris's. A long look passed between them with everything in it – all of it; all those years as boys, and men, all the fun and adventure and friendship. The living. Now, the bare love. 'God, life is worth it,' Max said.

—

But these days were ending. Max often lay still now, with his arms under the bedcovers, drowsy and saying very little. The life left in him was there in his eyes, sometimes shining. Chris sat leaning forward in his chair, speaking through an ache in his throat. And as he spoke, a decision was being made somewhere else in him: *This will be the day I'll start saying goodbye, saying I love you. From now on, I'll never leave this house without saying those words.*

Max told him he was tired, so tired; tired enough to leave the world without any sort of argument. That part about wanting to walk out the front door – that feeling had passed.

That day, when Chris left Max's room, he said goodbye, and after it he added his first, 'I love you.' It came out a little awkwardly – the words were spoken quietly, and he added 'mate', a word he never used – but he saw Max's face, saw the importance of what he'd said. He hoped to improve on his volume and delivery next time.

Then he found Jill in the kitchen. She was sitting bent forward with her head resting on the kitchen table. She sat upright when she heard him enter and he saw that her cheeks were wet. A small notebook lay open on her lap.

'He won't be home much longer,' she said.

He sighed. 'No.'

His eyes fell on the book she was holding.

'It's Max's funeral book,' she said. 'He made notes of things he'd like in it.'

'Is Bob Dylan one of them?' Chris asked.

She nodded with a faint smile.

A week earlier, when Max was weak and sleepy but still talking freely, they'd discussed Bob Dylan. Max and Jill were having a small disagreement about funeral songs. Max had in his mind an image of his coffin leaving with Bob Dylan singing 'Mr Tambourine Man'. He'd always loved that song; the last two verses were lyrical masterpieces, and the line about the diamond sky and the waving hand, well, that particularly touched him now.

'And really,' Max said, 'who doesn't want a good bout of harmonica playing at the end of their funeral?'

'True,' Chris said. 'True.'

'And another bonus,' Max said, 'the song is nice and long, plenty of time for slow coffin bearers – no pressure.'

But Jill found Bob Dylan a little whiny, and she had her heart set on Elvis Presley singing 'The Wonder of You'. Jill had a close friend with a strong mellow-toned voice who sang in a choir. Jill wanted this friend to belt out the song. Stand up and really belt it out.

'You do love Elvis,' Chris had said to Max.

And Max had propped himself up in the bed and half-smiled at Chris. 'But "The Wonder of You"? You don't think in that context the song is a bit *look at me, aren't I great?*'

Chris could hardly bear to look at Max in that moment. And then Max smiled, lying back on the pillows. 'Leaving with "Mr Tambourine Man" is a dream scenario for me. I told Jill I don't have much wiggle room on it.'

Now, Jill turned a few pages of the book. 'There's also a very lovely poem by Clive James in here. About dying. He's looking at a Japanese maple his daughter gave him. He's very surprising, Clive James.'

'Yes, very surprising. I haven't read his poetry. I need to read more poetry, I think.'

'You read poetry?'

'No. I think it would be a good thing to do, though.'

Jill nodded and glanced down again at her book.

'I went to a funeral a few weeks ago,' Chris said.

'Oh, I'm sorry.'

'No, don't be sorry – it was for a patient I didn't really know, so it was a bit unusual for me to go along. I'm just mentioning it because they had caterers for the wake and the food was very good. Excellent, in fact. Let me know, when the time comes, if you need help with organising anything like that.'

'Oh, Chris, thank you. I won't be able to think about food.'

'The funeral was over near me. But I imagine they'd come east. It doesn't take that long.'

'Do you have their details?'

Their details? He had nothing.

'I haven't,' he said. 'But I can make some calls.' Make some calls? It was so unlike him.

'Thank you.'

'I'll see you tomorrow,' he said.

And he turned and left, taking with him a glimpse of Jill, tears glistening in her eyes as she bent her head again and slowly turned another page of that book.

18

Clare was in the process of a complete and cleansing reorganisation of every cupboard in her house. She wanted to create a sense of order before returning to work. She attacked them sporadically in the course of a day; a cupboard, small or big, was always there in the background when there was a lull in activity. Most mornings, she took Stuart on a walk with Louisa and Gilbert and they stopped for coffee; and after that there'd be housework and shopping and cooking, the occasional work call, the kids. And the cupboards. A day was easily filled. 'Every cupboard? For how long?' Louisa had said. She couldn't get her head around the cupboards and the timeframe. When Clare embarked on the cupboard plan, she had six weeks of leave left.

Today, she'd started work on her large linen cupboard. She'd emptied it, and now its contents lay scattered in messy clumps across her lounge room, a mass so voluminous it appeared logistically impossible for it to have all come from one cupboard. It was disheartening, actually, standing back and taking it all in: the size of the task, all the decisions to be made. It almost depressed her, which was silly. And heavy rain continued to fall outside. The house was leaking in two places. At breakfast, Grace said they were all going to have to get used to weather like this. She spoke like an adult. 'This is climate change, Mum,' she said. 'The warmer air means the atmosphere holds more moisture and the extra moisture creates these huge falls of rain.' They talked for a while on the subject, and afterwards Clare felt her lack of climate action to date was ignorant and almost cruel. Her children had such a clear concept of what they were inheriting. She vowed to get her head around the details of the science as soon as possible, to finalise the papers on their solar panels, to embrace whatever else she could do. She had the time and, frankly, there was a climate change committee now living upstairs in her house. She heard in them an increasing distress at the failures of the government, and probably her failures too – and all of it was fair.

But for the moment, she had to finish what she'd started. Linen was all over the lounge room and impossible to ignore.

She was assessing her first bedsheet when Louisa arrived. It was one of Grace's, from when she was a child – quite thin, now, but full of memories and little pink flowers. Should one keep something like that? She put down the sheet, still undecided, and went to answer the door with Stuart skidding ahead of her. She opened the door to bedlam. The rain, still so heavy, was being whipped about by an extremely wild wind. Louisa's umbrella was bent out of shape and her raincoat was a piece of shiny black plastic that clung to every inch of her body. The raincoat's hood had been blown off and Louisa's thick fringe, usually so outward, sat plastered slickly to her head.

'Well, fuck,' Louisa said. 'That's *rain*.'

Louisa stayed on the doorstep for a few moments, peeling off her raincoat and her shoes and wet socks, and then padded into the house in her bare feet, saying something about the importance of her visit. She couldn't wait; she had to brave the elements. They walked through the lounge room en route to the kitchen, and Clare apologised for its state, gesturing to the mountains of linen. It looked like she could make beds for an army, and give them all towels as well, and with that she picked up a towel and handed it to Louisa. Louisa buffed her wet hair vigorously and it sprang into life, attacking the air in various directions.

'Tim's just rung me,' Louisa said without sitting down.

'Tim?' Greta Henry's funeral felt like an age ago.

'*Tim*,' Louisa said. 'He called because someone called him. We have been requested. Someone has *referred us*. Someone went to Greta's funeral and told someone else about us. They thought we were excellent. Tim's given me the woman's number to ring her directly. He's not doing this funeral.'

'Right. Wow. Referred? And what do you think about that?'

Louisa's expression was unreadable, which was not at all like her. 'I'm thinking,' she said, 'that I might have one more go. I'm thinking I might regret it if I don't. I feel like I want to do it a little bit more than I don't want to do it.'

'Right.' That surprised Clare. She'd thought Louisa had made a solid decision on this, that it wasn't for her. Clare pursed her lips. Out of the corner of one eye she could see some linen. 'And do you know anything about the person who died?' she asked.

Louisa nodded. 'A man in his forties. A couple of years older than us. I've been told he was very well-loved, with a wife and two sons. He was a popular man.'

'Well-loved and popular? What numbers are you talking?'

'A bit bigger than Greta's. One hundred and twenty.'

'Popular and only in his forties with a family? One hundred and twenty sounds like an underestimation to me.'

'Do you think? I can't get my head around numbers like that. People knowing that many people. Anyway, that's what they're asking us to do.'

Us.

They looked at each other.

'Oops,' Louisa said. 'I meant to ask first.' She placed a decent amount of begging in her expression.

It was unexpectedly tempting. 'Okay,' Clare said. 'I'll help you with one more.'

When Louisa had gone, Clare would look back on her response and wonder if it made any sense. Wonder what she had agreed to without a discussion, and so quickly. Wonder what Louisa would do when Clare could no longer help her. Wonder further when she took a work call from Amir later that day. She told him about the funeral and he sounded disproportionately excited. Any question of the sense of it seemed not to enter his mind; he simply accepted it as something she was doing for a friend. He said he had plenty of free time on the coming Saturday and offered to give them a hand. (Amir's wife had died of cancer in her mid-thirties and he hadn't had a partner since then. *I have far too much free time,* he'd often tell Clare.)

—

They were cleverer this time. By a small degree. They fiddled with the menu and lowered their ambitions by the tiniest notch (it was hard to do, though). They made the menu less Italian and drew a hard line through the balls. They went through what could be done in advance, considering each item more thoroughly this time. The final days would still be the longest, they knew that – it was a given with the style of food they were serving – but hopefully, with more planning and now having some experience, that element of last-minute, wild-minded panic would be lessened.

'Anyway, strap yourself in,' Louisa said to Clare.

—

David arrived soon after the lemon tarts came out of the oven. It was his habit, recently, to pop in every few days on his way home from work. He would come around the back and bound up the stairs, exciting the pants off poor Stuart. *Top dog is back again! Everyone! Top dog!*

David stopped in the doorway, surveying the scene, taking in their particular brand of funeral-eve madness. Stages of food preparation scattered the kitchen benchtop, boxes lined the walls, and trays of lemon tarts covered the kitchen table. In fact, the lemon tarts' existence dominated the room. And today, Gilbert was here too; he'd been hanging with them all day. Now he stood in the corner, erect and questioning, brought to attention by Stuart's sudden activity. David looked at the tarts, then quite pointedly at Gilbert, then back at Clare, frowning.

'Ed Sheeran,' she said.

But David just continued to frown.

They had discussed it on his previous visit, a few days earlier: his problem with her doing this. There was the *funeral thing*, of course – his unsubstantiated concern with the concept in general.

And there was the feeling he had that she was heading in a worrying direction. She held a prominent position at a major pharmaceutical; she was respected and earned a high, stable salary. Was that all protected, all still firmly in place? And the thing he didn't say – *this isn't our old life* – was there too, unspoken, but laced through everything. She assured him over and over that she was just helping Louisa out. That it all had a limited time span, and she was definitely returning to work.

Thankfully, his frown was short-lived. He walked in with a spreading smile. He went to the table and stood by the tarts.

'Where's Louisa?' he asked.

'She's gone to the shops for some final supplies.'

They would be working until midnight, maybe later. They'd begun doing a little extra of everything as they talked about Max Duncan. Louisa had spoken to his wife Jill several times. What a lovely woman, she'd say every time she hung up the phone. Jill had given Louisa a general picture of Max, an idea of the man, and one hundred and twenty seemed low.

'Would you mind,' David said, 'if I tried one?'

Clare hesitated. Their numbers felt precious.

'Oh, all right,' she said, giving into his smile. It was a reminder of a man she'd treasured. A man who could quote Monty Python in one breath, and Sylvia Plath in the next.

He picked up one small lemon tart and bit into it, chewed slowly, swallowed, and turned to Clare.

'Oh my god,' he said.

'I know.'

'It's so *lemony*.'

'I know.'

'But not *too* lemony.'

'I know.'

'And so creamy and crisp. Such a perfect contrast of textures.'

'It's homemade pastry.'

'That goes without saying,' he said, with a wholly contented look that made Clare's breath catch in her chest. Another reminder.

'Any chance I could have another one?' he asked.

'Absolutely not.'

He now stood by the bench, quite near her. 'I was wondering something the other day. Did you have to get a special licence to be doing this here? In our home?'

She shook her head and gave him a shrug. 'Louisa said she was getting some sort of permit for her place, but I'm not one hundred per cent sure she did.'

'But what about for here?'

Now she couldn't repress a comic grimace. 'I'm not sure about that either. But she's absolutely across occupational health and safety, I can tell you that for sure.'

'That's not like you,' he said. 'You're the biggest rule follower I know.'

'Don't say *rule follower* like it's a really bad thing.'

'What are you talking about? I'm not. Your job is essentially one big exercise in rule-following. And that's a good thing. It keeps everyone safe.'

'Right. Yep.' She nodded, feigning agreement.

In truth, he was beginning to annoy her. Her feelings towards David were so changeable lately, so highly reactive. She suddenly longed for Louisa to come bursting through the door.

Then David seemed to take himself into a field of complaint. Was Alex doing *any* mowing? And he wasn't happy about the kids spending so much time upstairs in their bedrooms. Did they ever come down?

Trying not to sound indignant, she said they always came down for dinner, and not just the times he stayed to eat. They had good, entertaining conversations around the table. And Alex had joined an interschool climate change committee that was working on a presentation to parliament. How impressive was that? They should be proud of him.

And as if on cue, Alex came thumping down the stairs and entered the kitchen. Tall and lively, so engaged with the world. An intense love for him rose in Clare.

'Hi, Dad,' he said.

David went to hug him and saw he was holding a book. 'What are you reading?' David tilted his head to see the title. '*The Uninhabitable Earth.*' Unwisely, he gave Alex an exaggerated grimace.

'You should read it, Dad,' Alex said, sounding remarkably calm in Clare's opinion. 'It's scary.' He opened the book to a page he had marked. 'It says in here that every return flight between London and New York costs the Arctic three square metres of ice.'

'Seriously?' David said. 'Gee. That's a lot.'

Alex read out a few more statistics, and Clare and David tried to absorb them. They were horrendous.

Then Alex snapped his book shut. 'We shouldn't have to read these things out to you guys,' he said. He looked at David. 'Are you staying for dinner, Dad?'

David shook his head. 'Not tonight.'

Alex turned and left with his book.

A few minutes later there was a knock, the sound of the front door opening and shutting, followed by the sound of Louisa and Alex laughing in the lounge room. *Listen to her*, Clare thought fondly, *how she just walks in the door and says something funny.* And besides that, Louisa knew the statistics. Alex didn't need to read her a thing.

She'd sensed David flinch, and tighten, as they heard Louisa's entry, and for a few seconds afterwards she wondered why he was still standing there, and wished, suddenly, that he'd leave.

He moved slightly as if reading her thoughts. 'I'll go,' he said. 'Okay,' she replied.

And as he turned to leave, saying, 'See you later,' she felt, immediately, the weight of their short, loaded exchange; the burden of everything *she'd* left unsaid. She watched him go.

19

Chris sprinted from his car into Max's funeral, only slowing his pace when he reached the crematorium doors. He stood there for a few seconds with his hands on his hips, dragging in air. His intention – formed well over a week ago – had been to arrive here early enough to ensure he got one of those coveted seats in the third or fourth rows. It felt incredibly important to him that he do that. But minutes before he was due to leave work a multi-trauma came in, and there he was helping out in the resus area with the clock ticking down. He scanned the tightly packed room: Where was a seat? Where? One seat! He turned to take a booklet from the usher and asked about seats and the usher told him it looked pretty full to him. Full! This wasn't how it was supposed to be! He felt rattled to be standing there without a seat, felt a sense of a failure that could never be reeled back.

He could imagine himself trapped at the back of the room, standing with the rest of the latecomers, given only a partial view of what was going on down the front. He searched the room one last time, and caught sight of a space of sorts in the third row from the back, three-quarters of the way along. It was almost human-sized. Big enough, surely. He walked down the aisle and began his apologies the second he reached the pew's end. He gingerly launched himself in, shuffling his sizeable form towards the space, whispering apologies, trying hard not to touch anyone's legs too much. The neighbours of the space looked understandably surprised that he was heading their way – you can't be intending to sit *here*? – but he forged ahead, avoiding their stares. When he finally sat down he decided he did almost fit – his shoulders pressed against the others but nothing too limiting – and, even better, in the next moment a thoughtful reorganisation began either side of him; everyone moved the slightest bit one way or the other, and when it was done he was able to sit there quite comfortably. They all could. He nodded a silent thank you to both flanks of the pew.

Once he was settled, he took long slow breaths. His thoughts went to Max. He was tall enough that if he stretched his torso and craned his neck, he could see over the heads of most people. He could see Max's coffin, and he registered that fact with a heart-dropping relief. He strained his neck further to have a view of the coffin in its entirety, and he gave it a tiny nod, said, *Hello, Max, I'm here* in his mind. Then he relaxed his neck and closed his eyes. But with that, he felt the threat of tears, and so he opened them again and took refuge in the funeral booklet. He focused on people's names, the songs and the readings, until he got to the last page. There was a small selection of photos of Max; Max busy living. Chris's eyes went straight to a photo of him and Max in the garden, the only one that would reflect some of the truth of Max's decline – but how good he still looked, how dear! Chris raised a hand and placed it over his mouth, and then he looked at the other photos. At one in particular. He frowned and brought the booklet closer to his face. It was a group of men at a golf course. He recognised Dan Swan immediately, and his eyes ran along the line of men until they landed on Paul. *Paul Swan*. Of course – Paul would be here!

He looked up from the booklet and scanned the room for Paul, searching pew by pew. How comforting it would be to connect with an old friend lost. And then he thought of Dan. Dan could easily be here too. Over the years, Dan had become closer to Max than Paul was. And with the thought of Dan, more warmth bled through Chris; some of the glow of his school days came with the name. But the service was starting, the celebrant was standing before them. He relinquished his search.

—

Max's three brothers and his sister delivered the first eulogies. They spoke in turns but they told one story in unison. A story of a brother, heartbreaking in its beauty and its intimacy. They had so many funny or moving anecdotes at their fingertips because they were *there* in all the days and nights of Max's childhood and adolescence, and they'd stayed in his vicinity for the span of his adulthood. They all *knew him* and loved him in a way nobody else could; and they would miss him in their own way too. His absence still came to them as implausible.

Then came the boys, Will and James, standing like men, suited and honouring. They described what their father had given them, and how they would remember him. They talked about unconditional love and fierce support, about holidays and in-jokes, about getting to hang around with a man they admired and adored. They asked the impossible question: How do we imagine our futures without him? And they finished with something so touching it almost, *almost*, reached the edge of joy. Two weeks before their father died, he'd spoken to each of them. *Make sure and take the time to picture the man you want to be*, Max had said, and he said it with a rare seriousness. There'd been no time in those two weeks to think about that, James said, but in the past few days he and Will had talked about it and realised they didn't need to think about it at all. The picture was in front of them. Their father was the man they both wanted to be.

There was so much of Max in his boys. The way they spoke, their turns of phrase, the way they stood; the enthusiasm that remained in them even in the depth of sorrow. Tears slipped from Chris's eyes and an unnameable emotion welled in him, something molten. Something quite different to grief. He bent his head and pressed his fingers to his eyes.

It was while Jill was speaking that he found Paul and Dan. And would he ever forgive himself for that – for allowing his eyes to wander in the middle of Jill's tribute? She'd actually made them all laugh in the beginning, describing how she'd met Max in a nightclub in Surfers Paradise. 'Who marries someone you meet in a place like that?' she asked. That first night, once she'd adapted to Max's individual style of dancing ('think energetic irony,' she said), she fell for him. 'He was the love of my life,' she said, and began to tell them why. Chris found Paul and Dan about halfway through. One minute he was listening to Jill (intently, he would have said) describing Max's generosity, his impeccable sense of style, his alarming sudoku speed, and the next minute his eyes were on the back of Paul's head. They seemed to simply land there, and once found, Paul was astonishingly easy to recognise. It was his distinctive hair. The light brown, well-cut hair, a little wavy and always worn slightly longer than his contemporaries, long enough to make a statement: *this is very good hair*. And with the hair confirmed, there was the familiar line of his head and shoulders. How nice it was to see him! Paul sat in almost a direct line from Chris, in the sought-after fourth row, and as he watched Paul's head, part of Chris was already imagining their reunion. And then his attention shifted slightly to the right and he recognised Dan, too. Dan sat taller than Paul, more solid, still so casually commanding even from behind. So *familiar* too.

When did he realise it was her?

At first it was nothing more than the faintest awareness of the possibility of her, something at the furthest edge of his mind, more sensation than thought. Then she was vaguely crossing into the middle of his thoughts. And then, with a head-jerking clarity, he was struck by her full presence. His eyes moved to Dan's right, and to her, and he knew immediately, with a startling certainty, that it was Beth.

His whole body clenched as he tried to draw in the shock, contain it in that incredibly small space, keep this huge thing inside himself. *The love of my life*, Jill had said in her eulogy, and the words now rang in his head. He stared at Beth, trying to relate to her presence. *I've googled you*, he thought, *and here you are. Here you are.* He tried to rationalise her sitting so close to Dan Swan.

And as he watched, Beth turned her head slightly to the right and he followed her gaze with his heart pounding, followed the line of her arm raised to touch the person beside her. He was young. A teenager. A son? Beth had a son?

His head began to swim.

But then he saw all four of them – Paul, Dan, Beth and her son – straighten in their seats and turn to fully face the front (as he should be!). It was as if they were readying themselves for an onslaught. He looked up to see Keith at the lectern. What had he missed? He fixed his attention on Keith and no one else, taking in this big, kind man who looked so demolished. Keith began slowly and hesitantly reading from his notes, and he was both mesmerising and destroying. Chris fought an impulse to get up and walk to the front and stand beside Keith, to help Keith make it through his speech, to help him in any way he could. But one sheet in, Keith stopped talking abruptly, halfway through a sentence. It was as if something had suddenly collapsed in him, rendering him desperate and silent.

They all waited, starkly silent too, while Keith looked out to the room with his shoulders slumped, and with sunlight streaming through high windows and hitting the floor around him.

Finally, Keith drew in a long slow breath, released it and said, 'We *just adored him.*'

How deeply human are the things a sentence can do. It came into the room with every word aching, and bathed them all in Keith's grief. And in doing so, for Chris, it gave his own grief a presence, a form, a sense of reason. He stayed tightly with Keith, watched the quavering heave of Keith's chest as he turned back to the speech he had written.

'There's this void,' Keith read, 'where Max once was. This absence. This gigantic unfathomable *space*. The Ancient Greeks had a name for the space that was there before time began, before anything existed. They called it Chaos. I feel that,' Keith said softly, almost apologetically, 'that sense of Chaos.'

Keith spoke for several minutes, and a sublime love replaced the chaos. Above all, Chris thought, his eulogy projected a sense of love and heartbreak that was magical, something with an unworldly dimension. Something worthy of Max.

Then the video began to play, and the sounds of 'Yellow' by Coldplay came with it. The perfection in the pairing was apparent in the video's opening moments – those lines about yellow stars shining, colouring Max's singular life – but Chris couldn't stay completely with it, even though, within seconds, he'd sensed its lasting, comforting potential. Part of his mind strayed, constructing a story of Beth and Paul and Dan. He imagined Paul returning to Sydney after Beth, looking her up and remaining her friend (something the Paul he knew would have done so well and so effortlessly). He imagined Paul recklessly introducing her to Dan. His head filled with images of Beth and her son, imagined their bond and then, almost inevitably, came the thought: *Could I have been a father in that other life with her?*

When the video finished, the funeral celebrant closed the service. 'The wake is being held in Max's home,' he said. 'The address is in your booklet. Everyone is most welcome.'

Six pallbearers – Max's brothers and his cousins – emerged from the front pews, and Chris realised what was coming. The knowledge of it clutched at his stomach.

In the end Max got both songs, and why not? The choir gathered and a pianist took his seat; the pallbearers took their positions though they didn't yet lift the coffin, they simply stood by its side. And when the time was right the pianist's hands went to the keys and the opening bars were played, as if making the lightest of suggestions. Then his fingers flittered down the scale and the man with the Elvis voice started singing.

The whole room stood without direction. It was a rapid mass-standing – a quick collective acknowledgement that no part of this moment should be wasted – and they all began singing with the same passionate intent, right along with the Elvis man. Chris sang with everything he had in him and what an immediate ecstasy there was in it, and, as quickly, what a heart-stricken cry. *The wonder of you, Max, the wonder of you!* And Keith's voice was suddenly there booming above it all, exalting in a son, in feeling like a king. Hearing him, Chris's voice faltered but he sang on through it, for what a *privilege* it was, standing there, being part of that song!

The song built, and as its final lines approached, the pallbearers bent and lifted the coffin and held it aloft on their shoulders during that stunning crescendo, as an eternity of longing, and love, was placed into that last rapturous word.

In the charged quiet when the song was all done, Chris turned to his neighbours just as they turned to him, and caught on their faces was the same insistent regret: *Oh, that it should end! That it should end!* But within moments came a lively guitar strumming, and Bob Dylan's clear voice, cutting through the air.

Chris heard Max saying, *Leaving with 'Mr Tambourine Man' is a dream scenario for me,* as the pallbearers began walking, as Max, right there in his dream, began leaving. And how dream-like the song was; how vivid, how brilliant the pictures were that now breezed through the room.

Chris followed the coffin's journey with tears filling his eyes, but as it passed him by, he registered the line of people now walking slowly behind it and the thought suddenly occurred to him (and how obvious it was): Beth would be passing by too, she would walk right by him! He pulled his eyes off the coffin. Twenty years, London, and now she was surely only a few metres away. He imagined her face, the look she would give him when she found him. Anticipation surged through him and he lost track of the song. He turned his head to see Max's coffin nearing the door, to see it leaving the room, and when he turned back around, they were there – all four of them in that long line behind the coffin – but their heads were bent! All four had their eyes on the floor, oblivious to him! Fuck. So oblivious to him.

He sat down again, and the courteous leaving procedure went on around him, row by row. He swivelled, once, saw the moment the four of them were folded into the throng outside the church, and then he returned to 'Mr Tambourine Man'. The room emptied, and he stayed on until the song ended. He sang softly to himself with the last verse and the final chorus.

Eventually, he stood up and went out into the day, readying himself for their presence. From the top step he looked through the crowd, his eyes moving from group to group, head after head. Where were they? He doubled back, checking more carefully, but they simply weren't there. He craned his neck to see the car park – nobody. *Not one of them.* As if they'd been apparitions all along.

He stood on the steps for a while, watching Max's family gathered at the rear of the hearse. He thought about Max in his coffin and that unnameable feeling rose in him again. It was even stronger now and he found he *could* name it. It was gratitude. A deep, uncomplicated gratitude that his one life had crossed with Max's.

He approached Jill and she turned and they hugged. He pledged his continued support to her – support in any way she needed, any time of day or night – and she told him she couldn't put into words what he'd done for the family. 'You made the process as gentle as it could be for him,' she said. 'We could all see that and it brought us so much comfort, so much relief.' He went to Keith next, and tried to say how sorry he was, but what an inadequate sentiment that was. And by the time he got to his car to drive to the wake, a small amount of hope had resurfaced. The wake. The apparitions. He might find them all there.

20

The food was extraordinary. *Utterly* unexpected for a wake. Where were the soggy egg sandwiches? The soul-destroying scones?

Paul Swan held a warm morning bun in his hand and his eyes swept the room for its possible creator. A short while ago he'd seen a woman with a plate racing about – she'd had an air of frantic earnestness about her that he'd found quite appealing – but there was no sign of her now. And how he'd applauded her activity once he'd tasted the bun! He looked down at it again, appreciating the skill in its tight, swirling shape. He'd eaten them before at Tartine, a bakery in San Francisco where arguably the best morning buns in the world were made, and he *adored them*. A few people were standing near him now at the table, making careless selections of food, and he was tempted to hold up the bun and demand of them: *Do you realise what these things are? Do you have any idea of the* work *that's gone into them?*

He took another bite. He was so thoroughly impressed. And for a moment, just a moment, he felt a tiny shot of joy.

He scanned the room for his next destination, for where he might find the best conversation. Beth and Dan had left (thank god), and it struck him, looking about, that he knew quite a lot of people. There were the Duncans, of course – he'd known them since he was ten – but he didn't feel ready to face Jill just yet. There was the old group from school taking up a good section of the back-yard, and in the room where he stood, he could see the men Max and Dan played golf with every Saturday; he'd occasionally join them when one of them couldn't make it. And Chris Lang would be here too. He hadn't spotted Chris yet, but he had to be here.

He was heading for the school group when he collided with Chris. It was a literal collision, and in any reasonable assessment it was largely his fault. He'd set off with a new sense of purpose and another morning bun in his hand (he was starving), and he'd hurried down the deck stairs at a mindless pace. Mid-journey, he'd even given the school group a brotherly wave, and any focus he had left was fixed on the bun. He couldn't escape the collision even as he registered Chris's presence. And Chris must have been travelling at a decent pace too.

They were the same height and there was a violent clash of shoulders, a rush of arms and hands, and did one of them yell? Right in the middle of it, he dropped the morning bun and Chris stepped on it, and it was this last fact, the only fact, that resurrected him from the jolt. A quick smile formed in him. He brushed himself down, extended an apology to Chris, then pantomimed an exaggerated *we're okay!* to the school group.

It was all quite a bit of work, and the aftermath was even harder. (But maybe their reunion was never going to be easy, not even with a civil and separated: *Hello, how are you?*)

They stood trapped in an unheard-of silence for them. Paul grappled with a world of things he might say, and not one of them was to his liking. Eventually the silence passed, as it had to, and they said proper hellos, threw some like-minded sentiments at each other. *How long has it been? You look good! What the fuck was that crash?* Sentiments that might just be capable of spanning a long, troubled history.

But they faltered again; Paul was stuck. Where should he start? He was never lost for conversation, he hated these lapses, and with something like panic he went for bare honesty.

'Good to see you, Chris' – and there *was* something good about it – 'but how hard is this? I can't believe he's gone. And that *Elvis song*.'

Chris agreed, nodding yes, it was hard, and then with barely a break he began talking about Max. It was as if he'd been holding it all in, and Paul was the sole person he could tell it to. He spoke about school days, Max dying, about biannual dinners and friendship – all of it intertwined. Once, he used the word love. *Love*. Paul took the tiniest step backwards as he listened, overwhelmed by the warmth, by the deluge of it, quite thrown by the emotion on display: that surprising flash of tears, the anguish that rose and receded and rose again on Chris's face.

And how could you not question *yourself* in the midst of all that, in the midst of that flood? Standing there, that one step back, Paul looked in on himself critically and wondered about resetting his own sadness. It appeared to him, now, to be so paltry and thin.

And there it was, returning; that old, difficult thing about Chris.

The thought went through Paul's mind of what Chris had apparently done for Max near the end – he'd heard it repeated and repeated – and a small grimace pulled tight in him. It lent Chris a kind of grandeur, the things he was capable of doing, capable of giving.

He sighed. God, he needed a drink. Near them was a small table covered in glasses of wine and now he shifted to his left, half-turning and saying, 'Would you like one, Chris? White or red?' But in that moment, Chris was elsewhere. He saw Chris's eyes flit across the room as if searching, and it came to him, then, all the other things Chris might be feeling.

He handed Chris a glass of white wine and commented, briefly, on the beauty of the service (was it *guilt* holding back the flow of his thoughts?) and for the time being that comment was all that he had. Chris did appear to be on the verge of saying something, but all he ended up offering was a nod and a small smile, and so there they were again, caught in one of those sudden periods of quiet that are a long way from comfortable.

It was the busy catering lady, in the end, who saved them. She appeared by their side, right at the edge of that silence, announcing little tartlets of finely chopped cucumber with pistachio and crème fraîche. He wasn't sure about the cucumber – what a strange ingredient to choose from the world of ingredients available – but on the back of the morning bun he'd take anything she had. He smiled openly at her; he was a little in awe of her cooking and her activity, and up close, she was exceptionally lovely.

He was reaching for a tartlet, opening his mind to the cucumber, when he saw the look passing from the caterer to

Chris. And suddenly she was introducing herself, directing herself solely to Chris.

'I'm Clare,' she said. 'Clare Shepard. We met at Greta's wake? You were first?'

Oh, they know each other, Paul thought, but Chris was so slow to acknowledge it. There was such a painful pause. It was his attention, Paul realised; it was barely with them.

Chris eventually said something like, *Right, yes, I'm Chris Lang and this is Paul Swan*, and as introductions went it was appalling. Paul simply had to go to Chris's aid, he couldn't bear it any longer. He turned to Clare Shepard and gave her his review of the morning buns. He told her about the bakery in San Francisco he'd visited, and the competitive and wholly surprising standard of their version. 'I loved it,' he said. 'I just loved it.' And as he spoke, he felt his conversation lifting, felt it hitting a near-normal altitude. He felt more like himself. And Clare smiled a beautiful smile back at him before she turned to go.

'Where did the two of you meet?' he asked Chris. 'And who is Greta?'

'We met at a patient's funeral. It's a long story.' Now Chris's eyes were on him; his focus had returned. And Paul could guess what was coming.

'I actually saw you at the crematorium,' Chris said. A casual wave of the hand failed to lighten his tone. 'With Dan. And was that Beth with Dan?'

It occurred to Paul he could save Chris a lot of trouble. He could give him a short and considerate summary. But he didn't, and he didn't dwell on why.

Paul nodded. 'But she calls herself Elizabeth now,' he said.

'Elizabeth? Since when?'

Paul shrugged. 'It's been so long I can't really remember. She was calling herself Elizabeth before she married Dan. Her mother preferred Elizabeth.'

He saw the impact his familiarity had on Chris, but he didn't admit that after all this time he, too, still thought of her as Beth.

'Is she here?' Chris asked, barking the question. 'At the wake?'

'No. She had to leave. Their son was getting some big award at school. They ran off straight from the service. And I mean literally ran. Hundred-metre-sprint style. No decorum.'

Again, he saw the emotional impact this news wrought on Chris. A husband, a son. Paul guessed what it might mean to him. They weren't so different.

'She married Dan?'

'Yes, ages ago.'

'And he still plays the guitar?'

'Yep. He's a professional musician. Dan gets to do what he loves for a living. He says his life is bliss.'

'Bliss? Right.'

They stood with the word bliss for a while, until Clare again came to their aid. She held out a plate, declaring 'little chicken sandwiches.'

'Oh, these are *very good*,' Chris said, almost too quickly. 'I highly recommend them.' He'd noticeably brightened. Paul couldn't decide whether it was on account of Clare, or her offerings; couldn't decide whether it was actually adoration on Chris's face.

Clare turned to him.

'Can I ask, Chris, was it you who recommended us to the Duncans?'

And there Chris was, smiling so easily. So unexpectedly. 'Yes, I told Jill about you,' he said. 'I thought your food was excellent. In fact, the chicken sandwiches were the best I've ever eaten.'

Clare received the compliment with an extravagant show of happiness. She was lingering longer than she had before.

Paul took a small sandwich. Their exchange slightly exasperated him. It was loaded with an odd connection he had no hope of reading, or being part of.

He took a bite.

'Whoa that's good,' he said, almost involuntarily, too.

'I told you,' Chris said.

Paul took another bite, luxuriating in its deliciousness, and then held the last precious morsel in the air. 'Is there *any chance*,' he said to Clare, 'you'll tell me exactly what's in them?'

'Well,' Clare said smiling, and with no hesitation she said, 'there's chicken, obviously, but with the chicken we marinate it overnight in –'

'No, don't tell me!' he exclaimed with a quick raise of his hand. Her warmth had disarmed him. And there was the chance a woman to their near-left was listening too. 'It's an outstanding sandwich,' he explained. 'It could well end up being your signature sandwich. Maybe you should keep its secret close to your chest?'

The smile he got back made him pleased he had said it. And then Clare showed signs of leaving, and he and Chris quickly reached for another sandwich before she walked off. He watched her for a while; admired, again, her brisk industrious journey.

—

Paul lasted with Chris until he asked about Jack. It was too much, talking with Chris about Beth and her life. He answered two questions, and that was the extent of it:

'Yes, he's Beth and Dan's son.'

'Yes, he's their only child.'

He sensed similar questions coming and he cut Chris off, jumping in with a quick apology. He told Chris he needed to go to the bathroom, and then he'd have to catch up with other people. He wasn't staying long and there were so many people he hadn't seen for years. He hadn't even talked to the Duncans. He handed Chris one of his business cards, saying, 'It's been great to see you. We should meet up for a drink in the city sometime,' and Chris smiled rather graciously, and admitted he'd love that.

And off Paul went, as he said, to the bathroom.

After the bathroom he made it to his school friends and merged into the old group seamlessly. One of his friends said: 'Look at you, Paul, with all your hair,' and he laughed contentedly. So many of his friends were *bald*. Something happened in their forties – no, it started when they had kids. Here was another plus for a solid night's sleep, for the stress reliever of a long Sunday lie-in: hair.

—

Paul left the wake quite late, and headed home. He'd decided to walk; it wasn't very far. He'd pick up his car later. In the end, he'd only spoken to Jill Duncan very briefly. Standing with her, he'd felt too encumbered by guilt; it shredded his conversation.

He tried to tackle that guilt as he walked. He thought about Max and everything he'd failed to do. In the days following Max's diagnosis, Paul had sent Max a text. *A text.* And then he'd flown to New York for business. On his return, he was overloaded with work, and during each working week that followed (and there were painfully few of them) he'd told himself he would visit Max on the weekend coming, on either the Saturday or the Sunday, but he never did. What happened on the weekends? What did he do? He got the shocking call from Dan to say Max was gone, and after that there was no longer any choice for him. His visit, at the very least his phone call, had to sit inside him, left eternally undone.

At home, he dropped his suit jacket on the lounge and pulled out his folded funeral booklet from its inside pocket. A fine dusting of cocaine still lay on its cover.

21

Clare stood by her car in the waning light, waiting for Louisa. She tilted her face towards the soft, dusky light. The evening was exquisite.

Louisa was fetching their last box from the house. During the wake, Louisa had again stayed in the kitchen, well away from the crowds. 'I'm sorry, I'm sorry,' she'd say as Clare flitted in and out of the kitchen. 'It's okay,' Clare replied, over and over.

Clare wanted to describe to Louisa how it was in the wake. The conversation and the people, the family reunions, the pure heartbreak on the face of Keith Duncan. How she kept hearing the same words: *courage* and *generosity*, *friendship* and *love*. How many times had she heard the words: *my friend*, *a good friend*, *the best friend*?

All afternoon she'd watched human connection manifested. And it produced in her a feeling that lingered still. A feeling of deep personal relief; a sensation of safety she'd very rarely known.

—

Clare started the car and pulled out from the kerb, and Louisa kept silent, as she always did, during the procedure.

As they moved off down the street, Louisa said, 'It's like you've been taught something completely different to the natural way of driving a car. It's in your speed and the way you handle the controls with so much purpose.' She paused. 'It's hard to explain.'

'My mother taught me to drive,' Clare said.

As she drove, she described the wake to Louisa; the sense of human connection. Then she told Louisa about Chris Lang.

'He was our very first guest at Greta's wake,' she said. 'He's the one who recommended us to the Duncans.'

'Good on him,' Louisa said.

'He's nice,' Clare said. 'Again, a bit awkward at the beginning, a little stand-offish – definitely a bit of Mr Darcy at the ball – but he warmed up.'

Louisa snorted at Mr Darcy, and Clare laughed loudly. She felt so full of *life*.

'He was with this other man, Paul.'

She explained how the two men had stood out from the crowd. How they were both unarguably attractive.

'Paul,' she said, 'was so engaging and very complimentary. And Chris is a doctor. That always impresses me.'

'Oh, me too.'

Not that he'd told her as much; it was just that, moving through the crowd while serving, she'd begun homing in on his name without specifically intending to. It came up surprisingly often. He was an emergency doctor, it transpired, highly skilled, and he'd done a lot for Max Duncan in his final days. It was particularly good of him, people said, given that his wife had recently left him. The more she heard about him, the more her eyes seemed to stray towards him even as she was serving other guests. She'd been disappointed when she could no longer find him, and assumed he had left.

But he hadn't, she discovered, when he'd sought her out to say goodbye. He made a point of it. He thanked her for everything they'd done.

She thanked him too and said she was sorry for his loss. He looked steeped in sadness, standing there. And then, unexpectedly, he had started to talk about Max. He described their friendship, and tried to put into words what the world had just lost.

He said, 'I've realised I didn't give enough to our friendship. Not nearly enough.' He seemed to surprise himself with the admission. He shrugged and attempted a smile.

His honesty surprised her too; there was something so intimate about it. She wanted to tell him she'd heard the opposite, but instead she simply said, 'I'm sure that's not true,' and the inadequacy of her answer turned her silent.

Thinking back on it now, she had to admit to feeling strangely smitten with him. Then she grimaced. *Smitten* – had she ever used that word before? Surely not out loud.

And as Clare drove on, she started to tell Louisa about her closest friendship. About falling in love, in a way. She told her about Hope.

She'd met Hope when she and David were living in the town of Orange, in country New South Wales.

(Did Clare know there were no oranges grown in Orange because it was too cold? Louisa asked. And that the town was named after Prince William of Orange, later the King of the Netherlands?

'I did know that,' Clare said.)

David had taken a teaching position there, and it was in Orange that they became engaged. They bought a cute little weatherboard house in the middle of the town, opposite a park, and they were happily settled and busy making plans. They planned to get married in Orange in a year or so – maybe a wedding in an apple orchard? – but they'd eventually head home to Sydney.

Hope arrived in autumn when the trees had turned golden. Her father-in-law had an apple and cherry orchard a little out of town. He'd had a stroke, and Hope and her husband Bill left their jobs in Sydney – they were both lawyers – and moved to the farm to help him. Hope took a part-time job in the library, just across the street from the pharmacy where Clare worked.

Clare popped into the library during her lunch break one day, and there was Hope, standing behind the borrowing desk on her second day of work.

'She was a gorgeous person,' Clare said. 'There was so much light in her.' And those words were enough; tears pushed in her eyes.

Clare had slid *Middlemarch* across the borrowing counter and they chatted, agreeing the book was remarkably thick. 'There's *a lot* of reading required,' Hope had said with a grimace. But it was one of her favourites. She was hoping to read it again – when she found the time! 'Its last sentence is perfection,' she had said. 'And enjoy Rosamond,' she'd added, with an expanding smile. They'd talked until another borrower arrived and stood right behind Clare.

Clare had fallen for Hope on the spot. She just knew, in those first moments of meeting her, that Hope was going to make her *laugh*. Clare held a picture of the two of them stopped mid-walk on the main street of Orange; both of them doubled over with their legs pressed together. She could even remember the comments that led to the event.

'Something special goes into making you laugh like that,' Clare said to Louisa. 'There has to be a connection, a sense of *deep understanding*, to make you laugh that much.'

And it was true. Never before in her life had Clare felt so known, so completely understood.

She wasn't sure how to tell Louisa what happened to them. How to start, and whether it would make any sense. She felt a strange nervousness as she began.

'About a year into our friendship,' she said, 'we were at the farm, sitting in the sunroom.'

It was a Saturday, and Clare had driven to the farm straight from a morning shift at the pharmacy. A week earlier they'd all been to a party for a girlfriend's birthday – Clare and David, and Hope and Bill. Clare had printed the photos of the party as she was finishing up at work.

They sat on the lounge side by side, flicking through them. Clare would look at a photo and pass it to Hope, and they'd make comments about the photo, or the party, as they went.

Clare noticed it several photos in. She stayed a fraction longer with the photo, feeling a faint tremor start up in her hands, and then she told herself she was wrong as she handed it to Hope. After that, she looked for it, finding it again here and there, and gradually she said less and less, and so did Hope, as each photo was passed.

But there came a point when all she wanted to do was stop. Her heart was pounding and she thought she could hear Hope's heart too.

She could remember a couple of the photos as if she'd seen them only yesterday: the ones where love was clear, where David was looking across the room at Hope and love was written so plainly on his face. How had Clare not seen it at the time? How had the camera, not her, managed to close in and find it? In the other photos, it was more subtle: a face turned in Hope's direction, a soft expression seemingly produced for her. And in all those photos, Hope was looking elsewhere, busy, oblivious to his attentive, loving gaze.

Clare had quickly gathered up her photos and shoved them back into their packet, saying nothing, and Hope had cleared their teacups. She walked into the kitchen, saying something vague as she went, but all Clare heard in her voice was what they'd both seen.

'It's horrifyingly easy to kill a friendship,' she told Louisa. 'You just pull back, say no to a walk or a dinner, and it unravels from there. I told David I was ready to leave Orange, and he got a placement in Sydney not long after that. We put the house on the market and we were gone.' She paused. 'And I think Hope thought it was the kind thing to do, to let me sort through it on my own. But I never talked to her again.'

'And you never told David what you saw in those photos?'

'No.' Was it shame that she felt the most strongly? More than regret? Shame that she'd gone ahead and married David, despite what she knew. That she didn't ask him one single question about it.

Clare turned into their street. Part of her didn't want to look at Louisa, to catch her expression which was always so transparent.

Would it show disappointment? Would it hold some sense of the shame that Clare had always felt?

But when she did finally glance over, there was nothing like that on Louisa's face. There was just kindness and understanding.

'Well,' Louisa said after a few moments, 'obviously I'm no expert on the subject, but that all sounds pretty human to me, pretty reasonable.'

Clare looked at her and switched off the engine.

'Okay,' Clare said. 'Right.' She'd told her story, and someone else had listened; someone else understood.

They got out of the car and collected some boxes, and took them into Louisa's house. The day's light had gone. For several minutes they sat on the lounges in Louisa's back room with Gilbert sprawled between them. They chatted about the wake, and there was a sense of achievement in their conversation. Of something inimitable shared.

—

Two days later, in the evening, Clare went to see David. She walked down the driveway at the side of Mike and Caro's house and knocked on the small building sitting at its rear.

She'd sent David a text to tell him she was coming, and she was still knocking on the door when he opened it. He greeted her with an unguarded pleasure on his face. She walked in, giving him a brisk, purposeful hello, and then stopped: she'd forgotten how *stunning* the place was on the inside. How *inviting*. Caro had absurdly good taste, and for a few seconds it threw her off her path. David told her he'd opened a pinot with his dinner and asked if she'd like a glass, and she replied, 'Yes thanks, but just a small one, I'm not staying long.' Alex and Grace were at home. He poured the wine while she settled herself on an extremely soft lounge.

When he sat down opposite her and asked her how she was, she told him (fairly abruptly) that she had something in particular she wanted to say to him. She felt a new, sharp nervousness after that, but she forged ahead. With minimal introduction, she told him about Hope and the photos, about everything she knew, about not being brave enough and wishing, so wishing, she had handled it all differently.

He gave her an incredulous look. 'What are you saying?'

'I'm telling you I knew back then that you loved Hope.' She tried to keep her voice steady. 'That you loved Hope more than me. More *naturally*, anyway.'

He stared at her with a wild indignation. 'You got that from some photos? Taken at a party when I was probably drunk?'

Was he going to make her feel silly?

'And you never put it to me?' he went on. 'Is this why you wanted to leave Orange earlier than we'd planned? Because of those *photos*?'

'It wasn't just the photos.' She felt something like anger rising in her now. 'It was what I *knew*. I wanted to follow the path we'd laid out, just like you did. I wanted the comfort and safety of it, and the happiness, but now there was this fact I knew. After I saw those photos, I just knew it.' She looked him in the eye. 'And you knew it too, David. Admit it.'

The indignation left his expression. He pulled back from her, and his face slackened. And for several long moments they just stared at each other.

Finally he said in a low voice, 'All right, yes, I did have some feelings for Hope. I never wanted to, Clare,' he said shaking his head, 'and I never did anything about it. You know that's true. The feelings were just there. And I wished Hope had never entered our lives. That she'd never walked in our door.'

She and David had spent more than half their lives together. They'd slept every night of those years lying half an arm's length from each other, and woke in the same position to start every day. Together, they'd bought cars and houses, laughed at the same things, had children and raised them, planted gardens, despaired over money, holidayed and helped out with homework, supported each other. They had been the closest of friends; that was undeniable. But when had they ever sat facing each other like this, one soul talking to another soul, willing to be open, to tell the whole truth?

Not even on that night in winter had he told her the whole truth. He gave her a pleading look. 'But is that really relevant now?'

She didn't have an answer. She felt like saying, *Look at us, David, with the truth – this is new*, but she sensed the opening in that. Instead, she said, 'I think our time is done, David. We're done.'

And just like that, it was – they were finished. David told her again how sorry he was about the night he left; all the things he'd said about love. Maybe it was a mistake to try to name things, he thought.

She smiled. And then she told him she'd always wanted a life with a lovely feeling at the centre of it. She'd lost that feeling when her father died, but she'd found it again in the life she'd built with David.

'If you look at it that way,' she said, 'it must have been love.'

22

Chris explained to the family how it happened, how Keith had died of a broken heart. 'Broken-heart syndrome,' he said, 'otherwise known as takotsubo cardiomyopathy.' He told them how an unusually strong emotion – a grief as immense as Keith's – could sometimes change the shape of a heart and affect its ability to pump blood. It started in the brain, which reacted to the intensity of emotion by signalling to the body to produce stress hormones in quantities large enough to cause the heart to swell, essentially stunning the heart muscle. 'It's rare,' he said, 'and it mostly affects women.' And then his voice trailed away. He told them all of this in the hospital family room after Keith's death, but he knew all they really heard was *a broken heart*.

Keith had died three days after Max's funeral.

—

Chris arrived at the crematorium early and sat looking at Keith's coffin for a long time. Staring and imagining hearts beating. His own, Keith's. He didn't believe in God, and now he wished he did. Max came into his head and he felt the soft threat of tears. He was tired, and easily moved.

He saw Paul Swan enter the church about ten minutes after he had. He'd turned away from the coffin and swivelled in his seat for no particular reason – maybe looking for a familiar face, for the comfort he might find in one – and saw Paul taking a seat right down the back. The sight of Paul made him feel even wearier. He'd slowly turned back to face the front and held himself rigid, determined not to look around again.

He was sick of having Paul Swan – all the Swans, really – in his head. He'd become particularly obsessed by thoughts of Dan, Beth, and their son. He was too tired to rein his mind in, and it invented scenarios, emphasised his loneliness. He imagined the other life he might have chosen, and in it there was a small family surrounding him. And sometimes at night, he counted; he counted months and calculated the period of time that might have occurred between himself and Dan. Those nights, it seemed to him perfectly plausible that Beth's son could be his, that his old dream of having a child of his own was, after all, possible. He would wonder about the fact that Dan and Beth hadn't had any other children – maybe they couldn't have children of their own? – and that might explain why Beth, as honest and honourable as she was, had never told Chris about their son.

The idea was a comfort in his new solitude. Sarah was well and truly gone now. She'd taken three months off work and a few weeks earlier had headed off to Borneo with a girlfriend, a scientist. Once, he'd gone onto Sarah's Instagram page and seen spectacular photos inundated with green – even the light looked green. There was a photo of Sarah beside an orangutan and it looked like the two of them were sharing a joke. There was another photo of her deep in the forest, pointing at a storm's stork and grinning, and the life-affirming joy on her face had him vowing never to return to her Instagram page again. It was torture. *Here I am everybody*, it said, *engaging meaningfully in this verdant world. My life's better now that I'm freed of him.* But for all that, they had talked to each other daily right up to her leaving, and now her absence felt profound.

He slipped a glance in Paul's direction. He'd phoned Paul two days after Max's funeral and suggested they go for that drink. It was a little too soon, but Paul's card sat in his wallet with significance and he couldn't resist it. It was a mistake. They talked like strangers. Chris was received without rudeness, exactly, but with no great show of enthusiasm on Paul's part. Paul had offered a date three weeks in the future, citing an unusually busy social schedule and a conference interstate.

What had he hoped for? That Paul would be open and kind? That he'd have the courage to begin the last, absurd line of questioning: *When was Elizabeth's son born? The timing must be awfully close. Is there any chance, any, that her son could be mine?*

Of course, he could have simply rung Beth. Now that he knew her full name, he'd been able to look her up in the online telephone directory; he knew her home phone number and her address. But calling her directly felt beyond him. How would he start that call?

—

He flicked through the funeral booklet. Keith had been a good-looking man, fit and invariably smiling. On the second-last page was a photo from Keith's school days, and as Chris's eyes landed on it, he thought, *Now here is what I wanted to talk to Paul about! This! The wonderful spirit in this photo!* Their school days were magnificent, really. You met up with your friends daily; what an unusually beautiful time. And what other time in your life offered up so many moments of mini-triumph that were so well applauded? He remembered how they felt: the thumping debate wins in front of a room full of his peers; the unexpected rugby wins with a packed grandstand going berserk; crossing the stage on speech day to accept award after award, as a supportive murmur moved through the audience. Now he saved lives, but nobody *clapped*. For the most part, they didn't even know his name.

On any day, for any person, Keith's funeral service would be moving. The layers of tragedy in it. Chris was crying from the outset, not surprising himself at all this time. And when five courageous grandchildren each delivered a brief beautiful eulogy, each one a celebration of Keith's unconditional love, his generous attention, his limitless kindness (kindness was the thing that dominated the eulogies), Chris sat back in his seat with his shoulders sagging.

—

Keith's wake was held in a purpose-built function room within the crematorium grounds. Chris walked up a small winding path and entered a low-ceilinged, beige-carpeted room flooded with light. There were two rooms, in fact; three stairs took you down to the second room, which had doors opening onto a large patch of lawn.

He found Paul in the corner of this second room, standing on his own, propped against a wall and holding a half-full glass of wine. Despite deciding he was sick of Paul, he'd consciously looked for him; he couldn't help himself.

'Hi, Paul,' he said. 'You're on your own?' He was surprised by it.

Paul pushed himself off the wall. 'Hello, Chris. Yes, I'm hiding here because I haven't got the energy for conversations with semi-strangers, but I can't leave because I've already seen the food.' He smiled. 'And it's much quieter over here. Have you noticed how loud old people can get?'

Chris nodded. Really just acknowledging the quietness.

Paul sighed. 'Sorry, I had a shocking night's sleep. And speaking of shocks.' He held out his hands, palms up.

'I couldn't believe it was Keith when they brought him in,' Chris said.

'I heard how hard you worked on him.'

'Yes,' Chris said, feeling the memory of it. The desperation.

'There was something special about Keith, wasn't there? I had a soft spot for him from my very first play date with Max.'

Any small mention – or thought – of Max could still tug at Chris's heart. He smiled weakly at Paul.

'Anyway, Clare Shepard is here,' Paul said. 'The same caterers. We've struck gold on that front.'

In anyone else's hands that last sentence would have been outrageous. Surely Paul had a *gift* – to inject reasonableness into a remark like that?

Paul's head tilted, and Chris turned to follow his gaze. Clare was walking towards them. Chris was surprised by how much his heart reacted to the sight of her; its beat lightened and quickened. This was a much smaller funeral than Max's and it hadn't occurred to him she'd be here. He'd presumed he would never see her again. And now here she was, saying hello and announcing thin slices of toasted rye topped with ham and vintage cheddar, and a peach relish. He might have been wrong, but it did seem as if she'd made a beeline for him. She gave him a warm wistful acknowledgement: *yes, sadly, here we are again: our third funeral together.*

But then she turned to Paul and appeared to show him an equal warmth. And in Paul's enviable, sociable way, he drew even more warmth from her; a compliment, a funny comment at a wake: they seemed to come so easily to him.

Chris felt something rising in him. Not competitiveness exactly, but something in that realm. He offered up the first anecdote he could think of: how on his way in he'd overheard someone say, *This lunch is heaven.* (Though he was unsure whether he was repeating it as a joke or as an off-colour compliment, or just simply repeating it.) Clare smiled and Paul snorted – a highly good-humoured snort – and said, 'Thank goodness, a mention of heaven at last!' And so there he was, appreciating Paul again, silently barracking for him. Paul did seem tired.

Then Clare smiled again and moved on with her plate.

'Well,' Paul said as they watched her go. 'She's very lovely. She has beautiful eyes.' He brought the canapé to his mouth, took a bite and, with his eyes widening, exclaimed, '*Fuck! These flavours! They're geniuses!*' Then, with barely a pause, added, 'And how about those grandchildren? I walked in today feeling a tiny bit disappointed in myself, and they hit me with all that: one, two, three, four, five. Five!' The last bit of toast went into his mouth. 'What is that *cheese*?'

That's what Paul got from the eulogies?

'I hadn't factored my funeral into the children debate,' Paul went on.

'I haven't had any children either,' Chris said. 'And Sarah and I have separated.'

'That's a shame. I liked Sarah. She was so smart.' Paul took a mouthful of wine. 'I want to apologise for our phone call, by the way. I think I was abrupt. I've had a lot of stress at work, and if I'm going to be really honest, seeing you after all those years set off some hard stuff in me. So, I'm sorry.'

Chris had set *him* off?

'Well, thanks for the apology,' Chris said, 'but it's not necessary. I'm not good on the phone, so I probably made it awkward. And I should apologise for all the questions about Beth at Max's funeral.'

'I don't exactly *blame* you,' Paul continued, taking another mouthful of wine, 'but you set this chain of events in motion for me. Asking Beth out. And now she's married to my brother. She's —'

Paul's eyes had abruptly left the conversation. Clare was in the vicinity and Paul's attention appeared fixed on her movements. Was she coming their way again? Chris couldn't help feeling the same, and yet he badly wanted the conversation to be resumed. He wanted to talk about Beth.

Clare was now approaching them. She had the morning buns with her.

'*The morning buns!*' They pulled Paul out of his slump. There was some morning bun madness for a while (the caramel tones! the orange zest! the cinnamon!), during which Chris receded. There was such a mixed energy coming from Paul; it was tricky, standing beside him.

And then Clare was gone again. Chris held a warm morning bun in his hand, and as he lifted it to his mouth and took a bite of it, something in him shifted. The bun was outstanding, particularly the texture. It had a shiny crackly exterior and the softest, most delicious interior. Its simple generosity made him feel warm and expansive.

'I'm sorry about London and Beth,' he said to Paul. 'I imagine it was hard for you. I can see now, maybe better than I did back then, that you had strong feelings for her too. And I can appreciate how hard it would be now with Dan, too.'

His words appeared to shock Paul. His face had frozen into blankness; he looked lost for words.

'I handled things badly,' Chris went on. 'With you, and with Beth. Beth and I never said a real goodbye. Our relationship just dwindled into non-existence. I've had this thought lately that I should close things properly with her. Knock on her door, say hello, apologise, and say goodbye.' It did sound a little silly spoken out loud. He'd forgotten something.

Paul visibly started. 'Do *what*?'

'It's not only that. I've got some things of hers I need to return. I feel guilty about –'

'What things?'

'Some belongings of hers she left behind with me in London.'

'What could be so important after all these years?'

Chris sighed. His new energy for the conversation had lasted five minutes. He'd drunk too much wine on a hot afternoon and Paul was hard work.

'A winter coat and three large books. The books are early editions and valuable. There's *Ulysses* –'

'*Ulysses*? That's a monster of a book.'

'And there's *Middlemarch*, which is even longer. And a third one I've forgotten. And the coat is lovely.'

'The coat is fucking eighteen years old!'

Chris decided it was time to stop talking. Their voices were rising, and the conversation had become ridiculous. And into his mind had come Sarah's words: *I was never convinced Paul really liked you.*

But something in him couldn't stop. This could well be his last chance.

'There's one last thing, Paul. I'm sorry to ask you, but I have to. Is there any chance Beth's son could be mine?'

And for perhaps the first time, he looked straight into Paul's eyes as he spoke. And then, as he took in Paul's eyes – his pupils. Paul was using cocaine.

Paul shot him a vehement, 'Of course not! Jack is sixteen and London was eighteen years ago! Fuck, you don't get *everything*.'

Paul's words sat tight and hot between them. And in the next moment there was Clare, sliding through the tense atmosphere with one of her engaging smiles and a plate of lemon tarts.

They'd shocked each other into silence. Even Paul, so adept socially, said nothing. They took a tart each and nodded their gratitude. Chris looked at Clare, and he could see her confusion, her deep discomfort in the silence. She nodded back at both of them and turned and left without speaking.

Paul bit into his tart, mumbled something about piquancy and then looked at Chris and said: 'Do you want me to tell you how quickly she fell in love with Dan?' And then he paused. 'I'm sorry. I think maybe that's you and me done.' He put the last mouthful of tart into his mouth, chewed, swallowed, and added: 'I hope everything works out for you.' And then he held out his hand to shake Chris's. He placed his wineglass on a small table nearby, said a friendly enough goodbye, and headed off in the direction of the bathroom. As he disappeared through a doorway, Chris knew he'd probably never see Paul again.

He stood alone with the turmoil still in him, then decided to leave. He found Jill and the boys and expressed his sympathies again, and said goodbye. He strode through the car park, and it was only as he reached his car that he realised he hadn't spoken to Clare; he hadn't said goodbye to her this one last time. He drove away thinking about Clare and Paul and Beth, and a great expanse of emptiness surrounded him.

23

Paul stood on the very edge of the gathering, deciding. His eyes slipped to the spot where he and Chris had been standing and he saw it was now deserted. He took several steps to the right and looked out to the lawn. There was no sign of Chris. The crowd at the wake was thinning. Paul sighed, thinking. He liked positivity. He always felt the need to have some sort of light in his day, something good, but this day had started badly and travelled due south since then. Lately, he was having a bit of trouble turning a bad day around.

Earlier that morning, he'd sat at his desk in a North Sydney office block scrolling through a document and trying to focus over the noise in his head. It was at its metallic worst. The ringing, deep in his skull, was almost a permanent fixture now. At a minimum, on a good day, it was like a soft cicada thrum that was simply annoying, but at other times – when he was stressed or overtired, say – it was closer to the noise of a small piece of machinery, and that could come close to debilitating. For eight years now he'd put up with this resident cicada in his head. He'd told nobody, and therefore it existed only to him. There seemed something inherently demeaning, embarrassing, even unmanly in the word: *tinnitus*. What a terrible name. He had little doubt it was self-inflicted, a woeful product of his twenties, a decade spent listening to hard rock in small pubs and playing too-loud music in an impossibly small bedroom. What he'd give to turn back time and turn all that bloody music down.

He was left with no *silence*. He lived in a parallel world in which there was an utter absence of silence. He couldn't read in silence, couldn't think in silence, couldn't wake up or go to sleep in silence. It was hard to be completely calm without silence. And, as a bonus, in a crowded noisy room he might even struggle to hear what was being said.

That morning, the day of the funeral, the machinery started up. So about two hours before Keith Duncan's funeral he'd taken a fifty-dollar note from his top drawer and snorted a line of cocaine at his desk. He regretted it in the fraction of a second after he'd done it, there was a flash of disappointment, but he shrugged and smiled and carried on working.

The renewed cocaine use was a recent thing for him: the result of an unfortunate conflation of events. The end of a six-year relationship – the one he thought would be it, the one that would lead to a family – in the same month they'd employed a new accounts manager in the firm. It had been a simple enough offer over welcome drinks: 'I've got some nice cocaine, if you're interested?' Liam had suggested generously. To that point, Paul hadn't used cocaine for almost twenty years. Not since London. Perhaps, he thought, it might help with the ringing.

—

In hindsight, it wasn't a great plan, attending a funeral while coming down from cocaine. God, when he walked in, he felt so low, so *flattened*. And god, they were going to do it again without God! That particular fact hit him as he took his seat in the very last row of the crematorium. He was agnostic, a hedger-of-bets, quite open to hearing about heaven. But not one funeral he'd been to in the past few years – not Max's, or several others before him – had been held in a church, and here he was again. He knew how it would go: there'd be not one mention of God, no comfort of heaven. No making their slow, mournful way through Psalm 23. They were all doing away with God, but they'd brought nothing in to replace him. What a torturous vacuum. *People!* he wanted to scream. *Why are we going it alone?!*

He sighed dramatically then picked up his funeral booklet and slowly flicked through its pages. The funeral celebrant spoke and he lifted his head, listening for a little while, and then he scanned the room until he found Chris Lang. He'd known Chris would be here. He'd been told Keith was taken to Chris's ED, and now a question sat in the mean depths of him: *So why couldn't you save him?* From a distance of half-a-dozen rows back, he watched Chris Lang with the relentless hum of machinery in his head (he was beginning to suspect the cocaine made it worse). The back of someone's head could be a very provoking thing; he focused on it so intently that for a few glorious moments the sound in his head was forgotten. It occurred to him that Chris Lang made him feel *lesser*. Was that the right word? With Chris Lang in the vicinity, he felt secondary, inferior, all those words. Everything felt harder and not worth the effort. And when you look inside yourself and accept something like that, what on earth justifies a friendship? Half a lifetime of friendship built on competition and discomfort; Chris Lang always there in the corner of his eye, good at everything, always winning. What about a small world to live in where Chris Lang didn't feature? What would that have been like?

He drew in a deep breath and pressed his shoulders against the seat. He'd probably hung around with Chris because Chris was so clever. He'd always been drawn to clever people. He was only close to clever; he was quirkily and uselessly bright: his mind easily stored film scripts and very good lines and occasionally, *occasionally*, he was capable of bringing two highly unalike things together to make a powerful point. A couple of award-winning ads had come from the latter. But he wasn't naturally or genuinely intelligent; wasn't capable of building bridges or saving bloody lives.

His mind wandered. Here was an excellent line he remembered: Virginia Woolf, eminently clever person, writing: *The past is beautiful because one never realises an emotion at the time. It expands later,* (there was, of course, more after the comma, but it seemed his crowd-pleasing mind hadn't chosen to keep it). Virginia Woolf may have been a little too insightful for the good of mankind. But he stayed with it; maybe, according to Virginia, that past early discomfort with Chris wasn't fully realised at the time and so a friendship could form; but he was realising it *now*, and he could almost feel it: the irritation and resentment expanding. What she was wrong about was the *beautiful* part.

Here was another line he remembered verbatim: Chris Lang, eighteen years ago, saying: *I was hoping you wouldn't mind too much.* Delivered as if a sentence like that could fix everything. And then Dan saying much the same thing less than a year later. Maybe it was his lot in life, introducing Beth to people she found more attractive.

He sat on his pew, stewing in mean thought. Watching himself stewing in mean thought. He didn't believe people were born mean, and he tried to believe he was fundamentally good. He'd once thought about how it might happen: that maybe one small, mean, but relatively harmless thought – early, in childhood – sparks another mean thought, a bit of envy, or a mean act, on and on, through the years, one sparking another, until it happens enough times that a mean streak is formed. Something deep, something permanent. Something that's with you, waiting. And it leaves you forever defending yourself to yourself, forever forgiving, forever restoring *you* to yourself.

He sat upright again, rolling his shoulders, and it was in that moment, as his eyes bored once again into Chris, that Keith's five grandchildren stood up. They walked together to the lectern, so young and good-looking, and one by one, with more skill than he had ever possessed, they delivered their mini eulogies on Keith. On Keith's unforgettable kindness.

And later, at the wake, he did something very unlike him. He separated himself from people. Found a corner and stood there, dispirited, housing cicadas, staying on at the wake purely because the anticipation of the food was so great he couldn't leave. But Chris found him. There was no God.

He mostly kept his distance from Dan and Beth, mentally and physically. He attended family gatherings only when he felt he had to; he succumbed to Christmas. The last thing he needed was Chris in his life again, highlighting where the whole thing had started. What if his head had been turned the other way on that morning in Westminster? What if his attention had been on something banal, something on the Thames, and someone else had come to her rescue? What of love then?

When he'd finally got away from Chris, he'd gone into the bathroom and snorted another line of cocaine. Did it in sheer bereavement for himself and the life he'd had to settle for.

—

Now, only minutes out of the bathroom, he stood alone at the edge of the crowd, trying to remove Chris and their conversation from his mind. He thought about Clare. Thank goodness she'd been here; she was like a beacon in the weary landscape of that afternoon! He was attracted to her. He realised he had been from the beginning, but it wasn't in an easy way. She was gentle and measured – quite the opposite to him – and in her presence he did feel a little slapdash, not quite his best self. He found her lovely, but if he were to be completely honest (which the mini eulogies did seem to now compel), watching Chris look at her, seeing the way he looked at her, may have made her a little lovelier.

He turned, decided, and headed for the kitchen, towards his fellow food lovers. He filled with a renewed vigour as he walked. He tapped lightly on the open kitchen door and went in, feeling immediately welcomed, and he stayed there for a relatively long time. He helped them clean up. He was in entertainment mode with the world's most talented funeral caterers as his audience. He felt his day shift. Unstoppable, he even asked Clare out as they were all finishing up. He made it hard for her to say no, and then he left quickly so she couldn't change her mind. 'Great, see you tomorrow night,' he said, and slipped out the door.

24

Louisa asked Clare if she was okay. She'd pulled out of her parking spot with an unusual speed and sense of authority. It was unsettling.

'Honestly, Louisa,' Clare replied, 'I'm already riddled with anxiety.'

Louisa went close to suggesting she slow down a bit, but when she looked at the dashboard, she saw they were still well under the speed limit.

'Why would you ask someone out *at a wake*?' Clare swivelled to face Louisa, giving her the most agonised of looks, then she flicked her head back to the road.

Despite Clare's agitation, Louisa decided road safety sat solid in the depths of her. She relaxed back in her seat.

'Maybe it was his version of seizing the day,' Louisa said. '*Carpe diem*. Life can end unexpectedly, so I'll ask out the bereavement caterer.'

'I don't even know him.'

'A *date*,' Louisa mused. 'It's a funny word, isn't it, with all its different meanings? *Date*. And a very short word.'

'Oh, let's hope it's short. But it's not really a date. It's just *dinner*.'

'I've had some dreadful first dates,' Louisa said. 'They were about as much fun as a mammogram or a pap smear.' Then she hesitated, trawling for the worst experience daily life had to offer. 'I'd rather fill out a visa application form than go on a date. And I mean that. It's not just a throwaway line.'

'Don't worry, I believe you. But it's a dinner.' Clare drew in a long breath. 'My heart almost hurts it's beating so weirdly. This is too soon for me. And I'm still *married*.'

'Are you? David's been gone for ages.'

Clare rounded a tight bend. She was now on the approach to the Sydney Harbour Tunnel with its tricky (in Clare's opinion) lanes. They were both silent for a few minutes while she negotiated all that.

'When he asked you out,' Louisa said eventually, 'in the kitchen *with me there*, did you notice how I stopped moving altogether? How I tried to blend in with the cupboards?'

'Yes, I was aware of that in my periphery. It didn't help.'

'I got the shock of my life when you said yes. I thought David would have destroyed your interest in men for the time being. Like those antibiotics that wipe out your tastebuds.'

'And it's so soon!' Clare almost wailed. 'Tomorrow night. Why so soon?'

'Because tomorrow's Friday. It's date night.'

Clare groaned and clutched the steering wheel, leaning over it. Again, unusual behaviour: the latitude with the steering wheel.

'I'll give you this, though,' Louisa said. 'He was *funny*.'

Paul Swan had come into the kitchen and introduced himself to her. He was one of those people who would be at ease anywhere, and he was particularly buoyant for a wake.

'You might have to rethink your position on dates,' Clare said. 'I wouldn't be surprised if Amir gets around to asking you on one.'

'*Amir?*' She said his name as if the prospect was a shock, and absurd, while feeling none of that. '*No.*'

Amir had called in fairly often while they were preparing for Keith's wake. He came at odd hours of the day, but he stayed for the right amount of time. Long enough to give them a meaningful amount of help (he could cook, though he was prone to over-stirring) but not so long that he interfered with the overall flow of their day. There was something attractive in his sense of what was right. And his crisp white t-shirt with the tiny Tommy Hilfiger logo. And his musicals.

The preparation for Keith's wake had been relatively easy. They were working with low numbers, they had Amir's help, and they had a little more experience. That said, they'd still left too many things to the final few days. 'Something we might need to iron out in the future,' she'd said to Clare without thinking, and the expression on Clare's face was clear. *The future?* All the wakes so far had been very much in the present, a floundering reaction. They'd been asked to do Keith's wake and agreed without discussion. It was the right thing to do.

'I popped out of the kitchen for a few minutes during the wake,' Louisa said. 'Very brave of me.' She'd taken in the room. Spotted Jill Duncan and the boys.

Clare took her eyes off the road long enough for them to exchange a look of deep understanding.

Sitting there with Clare, Louisa was filled with a sensation of trust and comfort. And with it, her old defences crumbled.

She told Clare about her opened-up memories, how her mum and Janie had appeared suddenly in her dream, about the tightness in her chest the morning after that. 'The tightness comes and goes,' she said, 'but I'm allowing myself to think about them. Now and then, I'm letting them in.'

And as they were pulling up in front of her house, she told Clare about the trees her grandfather had planted when her mother and Janie were born. On the day of each birth, her grandfather drove into the state forest near where they lived and planted a flooded gum tree seedling in his new daughter's honour. The flooded gum was his favourite tree. He put a plaque next to each tree commemorating the birth. The trees stood side by side and were now more than seventy years old, and probably more than fifty metres tall.

She told Clare she'd been to see the trees once, in her teens, with Janie. After Janie was gone, she couldn't bear to go back.

—

The next morning, Louisa took Tim through the Royal Botanic Garden. She showed him the ancient Wollemi pine, the sacred fig by Lion Gate Lodge, the black bean tree behind Macquarie's Wall. They walked to the lower garden, near Farm Cove, and stood under the oldest specimen of jacaranda in Australia, a great aged tree in full bloom. It was the best month of the year to see it. The gnarled grey trunk was like entwined fingers reaching and its brilliant purple flowers cluttered the sky.

Between the trees, Louisa said: 'I've been thinking about Mum and Janie a bit lately. How well do you remember them? Can you remember them at all clearly?'

He jerked his head and looked at her. She'd given him no warning. She'd gone straight from telling him about the medicinal seed pods of the black bean tree to her questions.

'Yes, I remember them,' he said. 'Pretty clearly. I remember how similar they were.'

When they were young, her mum and Janie were often taken for twins. And they laughed exactly the same way. If you weren't looking, it could be hard to tell who was laughing.

'And I remember your mum's cooking,' Tim said. 'That super-high yellow sponge cake with the mock cream in the middle?'

'That sponge cake.' Louisa moaned. 'That was fresh country eggs. You can't make a sponge like that without great eggs.'

'It was so *spongey* and so delicious. I can picture myself eating it right now. Holding a huge yellow-and-white wedge of it up to my mouth. That cake is the main reason I hung around at your house. Your mum used to give me a container of it to take home.'

Louisa stopped, right in the sun, and turned to Tim. It gushed out of her, all the conflict inside her.

How she was worried that she'd never grieved enough for them, not like the word seemed to mean. She was so young and scared when her mother died – did she grieve enough, or was she too worried about herself? Did she sob? She can't remember sobbing. And Janie. What was it really like for Janie when it was only the two of them? She'd once heard her mum and Janie say to each other: *I can't imagine living in a world without you in it.*

Her voice cracked on that sentence. When she'd heard them say it, she'd thought, *No, I can't imagine that either. How would they do it?* But she didn't think they'd ever have to. And where was she in that sentence?

She looked at Tim hopelessly.

And there was a kid at school who'd asked her once: How could she be sure her mother had died in an accident? Her mother could be so sad at times.

Tim gaped at her. 'God, why would a kid ask you that? How old were you?'

She shrugged. 'Thirteen or fourteen. I think I was pretty hard work at school.'

'No, you weren't. All these things? You've been carrying all that? I wish you'd talked to me about this before.'

He told her he'd heard her sob. He'd heard her when she was twelve, when he'd stayed over; he'd heard her sobbing herself to sleep in her bedroom. He'd heard her sob at seventeen; sobbing herself to sleep at his house.

'You heard me?'

'Definitely. It was sobbing. And you question whether you mattered enough?' He paused. 'You were *loved*,' he said softly, emphatically.

She took in his expression and his words and realised, in that instant, it was enough. She trusted him, and he knew, he was there; it was enough. She went to hug him then, but she wasn't anything close to a hugger, never had been. Personal space was too important to her. When the exchange was over, she immediately said, with her eyebrows hitched, 'Well, that was weird. Sorry.'

'What *was* that? I saw you coming for me and I had no idea what to do with my arms.'

They had tea at the cafe by the pond. They watched seven ducklings follow their mother.

Tim said, 'Mum could tell you just about anything you want to know. You should go and see her.'

Louisa smiled. 'I'm going to do that. I'd love to see your mum again.' And then she told Tim she'd like to do another wake. She wanted to try harder to work through the crowd thing. But she'd have to talk to Clare first.

'Maybe not today, though,' she said. 'Clare's going on a date.'

They made their way through the gardens together, heading towards Tim's car. And the sorrow and beauty of their shared past still lay in the space between them. How wonderful it was to have Tim with her, Louisa thought, to know him! She smiled at him as they walked.

25

It was a beautiful afternoon and Clare and Louisa stood side by side in Clare's family room, watching four bees. What crucial endeavours!

The bees foraged on a giant flower. The flower sat on the tip of a branch that splayed generously across the family room window. The branch was less than half a metre from the glass. As flowers went, it was a prize, a perfect setting. A creamy-white magnolia, large and unfurled, open like a bowl.

Louisa pointed out the bee's tiny pollen sac on its hind leg; it was bright yellow and bursting with pollen.

'That bee's basket looks pretty full to me,' Louisa said. 'It needs to head home and drop off its shopping.'

'I didn't know they had a basket,' Clare said.

'Well, the baskets are tiny. And when there's nothing in them you wouldn't know they were there. The basket is actually a small concave area on their hind leg and it has fine hairs around it that pin the pollen in place. Bees are covered in fine hairs.'

They were filling in time. Clare felt very nervous.

'I love honey,' Louisa said. 'It's such a magical substance.'

A light breeze arrived, ruffling the dark glossy leaves and bouncing the branch. One by one the bees flew away. Sunlight hit random leaves, turning them lime.

Clare sighed heavily. 'I am in no mood for this silly date. I slept so badly.'

She'd had a nightmare she had to yank herself out of, and didn't get any sleep after that.

'What was the nightmare?' Louisa asked.

'I can't remember the detail, but the crux of it was that I was trying to get dressed while people were waiting for me in a car outside. I'm naked and they're waiting to go somewhere very important, and time is passing so quickly, and I can't seem to find the right thing to wear. I'm completely panicked, and I just can't get my act together to pull something out of the cupboard and put it on.'

'You call that a nightmare? Getting dressed?'

'I was naked the whole time! It had the sensation of a nightmare. You know that terrible unsettling urgency they have?'

—

Later that afternoon, the unsettling potential of a wardrobe became a reality. She stood before her open wardrobe, staring into it, illogically despondent. What was left? Just empty hangers and forlorn impossible pieces. She twisted to look back towards her bed, which was now covered in clothes, thinking maybe there was something there she hadn't worked with properly. A top that just needed jewellery to lift it? Her wardrobe was smallish by any decent shopper's standard, and yet she'd been there for well over an hour, almost two, selecting from it, changing, then presenting herself for inspection before her full-length mirror, often in outfits so wrong they made her heart bolt. She'd thrown grimace after grimace at her reflection. Vanity hit the alarm button. On the back of far too much failure, she'd begun to put together very odd combinations, things that were never going to work, and in one moment, looking at herself in a flouncy white skirt and a high-necked spotted blouse (why did she ever think spots were a good idea?), it seemed to her there was not one fashionable or beautiful outfit in her entire wardrobe – and just how had she managed to achieve that in a lifetime of shopping?

She'd found numerous things to dislike about herself that afternoon. For one, she could lie quite easily. She'd called up the stairs to her children – better that her lying face not be seen – to tell them she was going out for dinner with Helen. Helen wouldn't be coming in as she was short on time. She'd babbled on a bit about Helen, guiltily and unnecessarily, until she caught the full whiff of their lack of interest all the way down the stairs. 'Not sure what time I'll be home,' she'd said, and returned to her wardrobe.

She stared into it and thoughts of calling Paul with tales of absurd dramas ran through her mind. She was convinced he'd realise he'd made a mistake the moment she opened the door. Wearing some deplorable outfit.

—

He knocked a little before eight, and behind him shot the yellow-white glare of a soon-to-disappear sun. He said hello and smiled at her, with his eyes creasing nicely at their edges, and she stood on her doorstep, half-blinded and smiling too broadly. She mumbled something oddly formal in greeting, which she sincerely hoped he'd missed, and then fumbled with her door.

But he kept smiling and talking, certainly appearing oblivious to her idiocy. He threw out sentence after sentence with apparent ease: there was something about her garden and all its flowers and its free-flowing forms – he'd heard a comment by Prince Charles on the unnaturalness of hedges and, although he'd never thought about it before, he was inclined to agree. Where in nature did you find perfect straight lines and ninety-degree angles? He said something about the state of the sky.

His car was low-slung and European and it jangled her nerves, but as she took her seat and he slipped in beside her, he turned and said she looked beautiful. *So beautiful* were his exact words, and although she was generally uncomfortable with compliments – in fact, her first instinct was to laugh – his words affected her deeply. They were warm and giving and delivered so naturally that her tight shoulders eased a little; her heartbeat might have slowed. She buckled her seatbelt.

They were heading into the city. There was a restaurant he'd been wanting to try and he was quite excited to try it with her; he suspected she was as obsessed with food as he was. The restaurant had opened six months earlier and was now virtually impossible to get into. A colleague had a long-held booking he now couldn't make and had passed it on to Paul. They were officially the Basil-Joneses for the night.

'Not the Tripplehorns?' she'd asked. She had no explanation (other than her thrashing nerves) for the courageous oddness of her question. Why on earth hadn't she simply said, *How nice of them?*

His eyes flicked from the road to her. 'The Tripplehorns?'

'From *Date Night?* The movie?' *She'd brought up the word date!*

'Of course, *Date Night!* The Tripplehorns! I can't believe I missed that.'

'It was a bit of an obscure –'

'No, no, it was excellent. I've got to tell you, stored in my head are a million movie lines so obscure I can barely hope to use them in context once in my lifetime, and there I've gone and missed my Tripplehorn moment.' A small thump on the steering wheel.

She found herself grinning back, surprised.

'For instance,' he went on, 'I reckon I have the entire script of *When Harry Met Sally* – close to useless except for *I would be proud to partake of your pecan pie*, which I have used, relevantly, a couple of times, mainly in the nineties. In my limited-storage brain I have that whole movie and none of the science behind climate change. Beyond embarrassing.'

'I probably have the whole movie too. Not that I've tested myself.' She refrained from offering to tell him what she'd been reading recently on climate science.

'It's a near-perfect script, don't you think?' he asked, and she smiled and nodded. 'I'll test you,' he added. 'Scene one. Can you give me a reasonably obscure line?'

It was quite pathetic how little thought it required. '*I have it all figured out,*' she said. '*It's an eighteen-hour trip, which breaks down into six shifts of three hours each, or alternatively we could break it down by mileage.*'

'Fantastic!' He gave her an appreciative nod.

From there, the conversation flowed with Tripplehorn ease, and they arrived at the restaurant almost too quickly, the Basil-Joneses with their much-coveted booking.

Their waiter, Cameron, appeared at their table exactly when he should have – a generous yet not-too-lengthy amount of time after they'd been seated in chairs so comfortable they required a determined effort not to slouch. Cameron had a boyish face and a neat little ponytail. He was instantly likeable: he had an infectious joie de vivre and enthusiasm for his role, an impressive and well-received show of commitment to task. How were they tonight? How had their day been? Great! Would they like water? And off the three of them went, playing out that short, often ironic drama: the restaurant water decision. Tap, filtered, still, sparkling? Paul's eyes had beamed at her and later, quietly, he commented on how very important it was to settle the issue of hydration before anything else. Heaven forbid they sat down too parched to think straight.

'Let's be a bit fancy,' Paul had said to Cameron. 'Sparkling!' And Cameron left immediately to collect their fancy water.

The truth is, Paul told her, he used to think the whole water-choice thing had gone way overboard – it's only water! And he was in advertising and well aware of all the spin. But, in fact, it was not *only water*. He'd done Draugust – he'd missed dry July and taken his alcohol abstinence into August – and to save himself from the absolute mind-numbing tedium of not drinking when he was out, he indulged in high-end mineral waters. 'Those things are *pristine*,' he said. He went on to develop what could rightly be called a fiscally irresponsible water habit. *There are some waters so good you can pay up to four hundred dollars a bottle!* He had an addictive personality, and once he'd tasted some of the European varieties, he could see he was getting into very tricky water (she silently noted his fondness for a pun). The European varieties were sensational, the mineral content so high they were fruity and salty and complex – he'd drunk one (if he could believe the bottle) from a 15,000-year-old glacier in Canada. The really good ones had such distinctive flavours, rainwater that took on the flavours of the earth as it filtered down through all its layers.

'Gosh,' she said, 'you're making me thirsty.'

Their waiter returned with their water. This one had been sourced from the unspoilt eastern border of the Snowy Mountains; the Australian Alps, Cameron called them. Her first sip of water ran pure and cool down her throat, exceptionally thirst-quenching, but she couldn't quite articulate its particular taste of the earth. *Minerally* was all that would come to mind. Cameron, who'd by now picked up on Paul's inclination for facts of this nature, said it was worth recalling, as you drank it, that it had been filtered through a geological strata that was many millions of years old. She drank more of it, and felt singularly refreshed.

They were handed a small, beautiful piece of paper on which were printed the details of their eight-course degustation. It was a thoroughly modern menu, each dish described with a teasing succinctness – clusters of lowercase words creating a tantalising prospect: *chocolate, raspberry, tonka bean, meringue* (she went straight to the desserts).

After two tiny, delectable amuse-bouches, their first dish arrived: *puftaloon, smoked trout, finger lime.*

On his first reading of the menu, Paul had asked Cameron, 'What the hell is a puftaloon?' with his eyebrows flaring. He said he had truly believed he knew every food term in existence.

'Imagine a cross between a damper and a scone that's fried in butter until crisp,' Cameron replied. 'Our version of the puftaloon is petite.'

'Fabulous,' Paul said, as if he couldn't imagine anything better.

And who could have imagined *oyster, passionfruit, chive* would work so well?

Paul hesitated briefly over the oyster. He wasn't a lover of oysters – he suspected he had a mollusc intolerance – but he hated missing out on *anything*. And oyster eaters tended to swoon.

'A mollusc intolerance?' she'd asked. 'I haven't heard of that before.'

'Yep. Covers oysters, mussels, scallops – the list goes on.'

She frowned. 'But I think you might have the wrong collective noun? They're all bivalves. A subclass of molluscs.'

'Bivalves? I can't admit to a bivalve intolerance. That sounds awful.'

He ate the oyster, determined to ignore his intolerance: 'I'm so intolerant of my intolerance,' he said, smirking.

By the time the outstanding *snapper, warrigal greens, potato, beurre blanc* was served, they'd talked briefly about Clare's children and extensively about both their jobs. He was born to talk people into things. She told him she'd gone into drug regulation because she loved science and wanted to help people, but there was the fact of the detail, the feeling that the helping part was a bit lost in the forest.

And it was shortly after they'd devoured *beef, black garlic, buckwheat, shallot* that she asked him about Chris Lang. She was curious about their friendship and quite intrigued by Chris. Emergency medicine? How brave he must be, how calm under pressure, to do such a job. She'd once considered studying medicine, she admitted, but she worried about how she'd handle the stress; her mother had advised her to lower her sights. 'She wasn't exactly motivational,' Clare said with a wry grin.

She was slow to pick up on his irritation when she asked about Chris. Cameron came by with more water, a tiny palate cleanser arrived – *cucumber, lovage flower, Davidson plum* – and although she'd begun to notice the change (the stiffening, the tightness of his mouth), she stupidly made one last statement on the subject and watched it detonate in him: 'You have to admire him,' she said, so slapdash. 'Handling that level of responsibility, the emotional pressure of saving lives.'

'But do I?' he almost demanded. 'Do I *have to* admire him?' He spoke with a disturbing aggression. 'What if he's only doing it for how it makes *him* feel? What if it's basically about his ego?'

She stared at him in shock. Did he actually *dislike* Chris Lang?

'It's not unusual,' Paul said. 'There are a lot of narcissistic doctors. It often goes with the territory.'

'You think he's narcissistic?'

'Yes, possibly. A suggestion of a God complex maybe? The tiniest hint of Trump?'

'*A hint of Trump?*'

Why would he say that? She couldn't tell if he was joking. He didn't seem to be; she sensed some meanness in his responses that was unnerving. She felt a strong urge to leave. She was sitting with a stranger.

But suddenly he was smiling and raising both palms in the air. 'I was joking,' he said, 'but I've gone way too far. I'm sorry.' He leant towards her. 'I'm sorry,' he said again. 'Chris and I have history, and I tend to ramp things up a bit in his case. Let's leave it with him having a solid self-belief.'

And then Cameron was back with a dessert wine, breaking the tension. They changed the subject, and the warm, likeable version of Paul was restored, the one she could almost believe she knew.

Placed before them next was *aniseed myrtle, crème pâtissière, rosella fruit* – a scene-stealing dessert, tartly delicious on a character-restoring level – and when Paul told her a story about talking to Ryan Gosling in a Paris patisserie, standing right beside him at the big glass cabinet and giving him advice on the various macarons, she was again laughing with delight. He could be so irresistibly entertaining. And she could see how hard he was trying to make this easy for her. Maybe there really was something wrong with Chris Lang, she thought. Maybe she'd had him all wrong. They were brought fine cups of tea with *mandarin, madeleine, clove.*

And there was the manner of their leaving. Another highlight. As they walked out the door of the restaurant he tripped down the stairs, a flying stumble that took him right to the gutter where, to save himself, he was forced to grab on to the open door of a car from which a woman was emerging. 'Allow me, madam,' he said, as Clare stood watching from the top of the stairs, laughing far more than she would ever have expected to that night. He looked up and saw her face and gave her a rueful sort of grin, something with so much grace and good humour it left her confused.

But the prospect of the night's ending soon took any laughter away; it consumed her all the way home. In the car, she became hyperaware of his every movement and the closeness of their arms; how incredibly small a car could feel. She talked quite a lot, saying nothing of substance, and the moment he parked the car she flung open the door as if the car were on fire. To his credit, he still managed to make it around the car in time to help her out of her seat. A circumnavigation record, surely.

They walked down her path. She shielded her jittery glances and wild worries, and he walked beside her, calm and congenial and so easy to like.

And at her door, he told her he'd had a wonderful evening. He'd love to see her again. Would it be okay if he called?

She arranged on her face the look she thought she should give him and said yes, but it was a lie – she was convinced she'd never be doing this again. And then she had no time to think, as there came a kiss on her cheek, a gentle hand landing briefly on her shoulder, a soft, quite lovely goodbye, and he was gone.

She waved him off, flooded with relief, then slipped in through the front door and closed it behind her. She stood still for a while, smiling into the darkness. It was done, and it wasn't nearly as bad as she'd feared. But she vowed to have an excuse ready for when he next called. She wasn't ready to date; and, maybe, she wasn't ready for him.

26

Paul started the day with cocaine. It was unusually early for him, but it was a Saturday, and Saturdays could be bleak when you began them alone. He'd woken up, and his first clear thoughts were about the night before and his date with Clare. How he'd asked her at her door if he could call her, and then he'd seen on her face that the answer was no, even though she'd said yes. He lay in bed for a few minutes, trying to decide whether he'd misread her expression or not, and his gut feeling was no.

He got out of bed, fetched the paper from the front lawn, then shuffled about his house, fiddling and aimless, and eminently bored. Through the rear French doors, he could see clearly how the day would be. The coming of summer. So beautifully fucking summery. And there was something in that he really couldn't bear. The burden of potential. Knowing he'd struggle to make one good thing out of this day.

He stared out the doors at the day, thinking about how he just never *fit*. He didn't fit into the life he'd been given; didn't fit into the family he'd been given. He was the one who often got left out, on the edge; the one who didn't get the good family genes; the not-really-the-one-you'd-choose if a choice had to be made. He loved Dan, yet he could envy Dan with a debilitating force. He tried to believe in an afterlife because maybe that was where he was destined to shine, for it sure as fuck wasn't *here*.

It was only eight o'clock when he found himself kneeling at his coffee table, snorting cocaine. Why not? (He still didn't regard it as a habit.) And he stayed there with his mind ratcheting upwards, poring over the *Sydney Morning Herald* he'd brought in from the front lawn and placed there half an hour earlier. He did the *Good Weekend* quiz without cheating once, scoring twenty-one out of twenty-five, which gave him a boost. *I really am quite smart*, he thought. *Definitely underutilised.* He finished with the paper and went out his French doors and took the leaf blower to the back deck – the jacaranda and all its falling foliage could be so annoying – and rendered the whole thing entirely leafless in less than five minutes. The thrill of productivity glowed in him. But when he turned the machine off and the deck fell silent, across the fence came the noise and mania of the Hudson boys practising basketball shots for their game, and he was stunned and disturbed again. Saturday sport: the story-laden, pride-abounding sport of parents. God, he would have loved that.

He went back into his house, turned on his coffee machine, and fixed far too many of his thoughts on Chris Lang.

He snorted another line of cocaine.

And then he rang Beth.

He rang her while enduring a swirl of thoughts, not one of which was pleasant. He rang her for reasons he couldn't explain, except to say it felt *instinctual*. And the moment he heard her voice, it struck him how much he loved its sound: it had a lilt, closer to singing than speaking. He felt better already.

'Hey, Paul,' she said, and she couldn't really hide her surprise. He caught the faint note of bewilderment in her voice.

He never rang Beth. Never ringing her was one of his many small acts of survival, honed over two decades.

He knew Dan was at the Opera House. Dan's dream gig was coming up – a David Bowie tribute concert with the Sydney Symphony Orchestra and a handful of stars – and he'd be rehearsing all day. (They'd talked a few nights before, and Dan had told him all about it, and oh, it did shit him a bit. That his brother got to spend his days playing guitar for money! At the Opera House with the Sydney Symphony Orchestra! All that applause! And then the despair, that Bowie was dead! Almost three years now!) Beth was home on her own. She told him she'd woken that morning feeling a bit fluey – achy joints and a sore throat and a swimming head – so Jack had arranged a lift to his game with a teammate. 'Dan is already at the Opera House,' she said, with a happy sound in her voice. He could tell she was walking around while she talked, and he asked what on earth she was doing out of bed if she had the flu.

'I just didn't feel like lying there,' she said. 'I tried, but I was too restless. My head feels a bit better now I'm upright.'

She'd made herself a cup of tea and sat on the lounge in the sun for a while and felt marginally improved. Enough that she regretted, just a little, that she was missing Jack's game.

He heard her still moving about as she talked – 'Just pottering,' she said. She worked five days a week, and weekends were her best opportunity to re-establish something vaguely resembling order to the house. She asked him about his work, and they chatted along quite easily, though he could still hear the question in her voice: *Why are you ringing, Paul?* He rabbited on, ignoring it, but soon he got the impression she was in fact cleaning while they talked. She might not be giving him her full attention, he realised, and a nugget of annoyance lodged in him.

'My phone battery's very low,' she was saying now, 'so please don't be offended if the line suddenly goes dead.'

'Sure,' he said, and then he heard a soft grunt. 'What are you doing now?' he asked.

She laughed. 'Sorry! This is going to sound a bit stupid.'

She'd just climbed up onto the kitchen bench. She'd been listening to him – 'I was always listening!' she insisted – but at the same time she'd looked up and noticed how dirty the rangehood was. She was concentrating on his voice and not really thinking her actions through when she climbed up.

'You're *where?*' he asked.

'I am listening,' she assured him.

He would blame cocaine for what he did next: he embarked on a rant. He heard himself, and he was excessive and sometimes his tone was aggressive. It was as if filters he'd held in place for decades just dissolved, one after the other. He took her back in time, he broached subjects never before raised between them. He heard the shock in her voice and still he ploughed on. He told her he'd recently crossed paths with Chris Lang. Chris had set all this off in him.

'You've seen Chris?' she asked after his first barrage. There was a tremor in her voice.

'Yes,' he said. He told her about Chris wanting to see her and how much that annoyed him. Then he told her why he was annoyed.

He told her he'd loved her at the beginning. From the very first moment. That he'd loved her his whole life and it seemed beyond him to stop. How in those first moments of meeting her he'd thought, *This is it. Here comes life.* He talked about the jealousy and regret he felt when she ended up with Chris, and then Dan. He alluded to the great breadth of unhappiness he'd known *because of her.*

'Gosh,' she whispered. 'I had no idea.' There was so much shaking in her voice.

And next came the moments in time he would go on to explore, surely, for eternity.

She said something like, 'Wait a moment, Paul, I need to get down.' She was still on the bench, standing with the phone in one hand, a cloth in the other. She'd been up there the whole time.

Later, he'd picture her, standing tall on the bench with the bright day beaming at her from the windows, with his voice in her ear. On and on, pitching high with anxiety, persistent.

And then he heard a muffled scream. Or did he?

He was still mid-rant when he heard it and it was mixed in with his own voice.

There was a loud noise of some description. Had she dropped the phone? Lowered herself with a thump and a loud yell to the floor?

He said her name and there was silence. He hung up and re-dialled her number and it went to voicemail. *She's calling me back,* he thought. *Or maybe the phone battery's dead and she's busy recharging it.*

He couldn't say how long he waited. It was a while. He paced about his back room. He stared out his French doors with his heart racing. He told himself everything was fine, that she was probably fine. She'd dropped the phone and given a yelp as she did it. And now her phone was broken, or dead. There was a plausible explanation.

He dialled her number three or four times. He put his phone down and actually wrung his hands, looking down at them intently as he did it. He was coming down from the high and feeling terrible. Panic and paranoia bloomed in his chest, and his thoughts were erratic. He couldn't imagine her; he couldn't imagine where she was.

He was close to her, the closest of anyone, and much closer than Dan. She was only ten or so blocks away. He refused to take the car – she would be all right, and he couldn't risk driving in this condition. *Be sensible*, he thought. *Just check on her.*

And so, he ran.

He ran out his front door, not stopping to close it behind himself. He ran down his street, through air too hot to be running in. He barely paused at intersections to check for passing cars; had a car been coming, he would have been in serious trouble as he never really slowed his pace.

He ran panting, heart pounding, breath-robbed, with a bloody taste forming at the back of his throat. Plans and intense worries pitched through his mind, through desperate visions of Beth.

He wound his way across the suburb with his feet now pounding in a slower, exhausted rhythm, and gradually, as fear and panic lowered enough for thought, he saw the utter stupidity of what he was doing. Running like a madman. The run was taking forever. He was too slow and unfit. His heart felt huge, its beat too hard, too fast, unhuman. Each breath was a loud, violent gasp. Did running make any sense? An idiotic impulse that surely – but this thought was cut short as he rounded the corner of her street and simply had to stop for a few seconds to drag in lungfuls of air.

How he'd fucked up!

A car slowed near him but kept going. Its movement stirred his intent, and he drew himself upright and started moving again, up the long, taxing incline of her street.

—

He made it to her front door and knocked. He knocked several times and nothing happened, no one came. But something in the simple act of knocking without an answer calmed him. He breathed deeply, and more slowly. This very thing happened more often than not. Beth and Dan's doorbell had been broken for a decade or more; a faded cross of tape announced its inaction, it stood as a testament to their combined un-handiness. Visitors frequently knocked with no answer. Beth or Dan would get a phone call: *I'm on your doorstep, can you please come to the door?* They were a noisy household and lived mostly in the back rooms of the house; at any time, there could be loud music playing, the television on, boisterous talking. A faraway knock didn't stand a chance.

How many times in twenty years had he knocked into a void? This was normal, he said to himself, and it settled him. This felt normal.

Now he walked. He walked around to the side of the house and through the gate. He would try the back door. Check Beth was okay and apologise for the rant.

He turned the back corner of the house, and for some reason now he was almost creeping. Discomfort and doubt were bleeding through his actions, to the point that he hesitated for a few seconds before peering through the glass doors.

He could see her, and he registered that fact with an over-whelming relief. She lay on a lounge, turned at a slight angle from his gaze. She lay outstretched, with one arm raised and a hand placed by her head. The other arm lay straight by her side. You could easily tell yourself she was sleeping. That she must be resting. She was okay.

He knocked quietly, but she didn't move. He tried the door handle. It was locked.

He stared at her through the glass. Strained to hear through the noise in his ears. Did he see her arm move? He watched her chest, focused on where her heart must be, but from this distance nothing was clear or certain; he'd left the house without his glasses and his vision wasn't great, and she was a fair distance away.

Then he caught a flicker of movement from somewhere behind her, down the hallway. *Someone else is home*, he thought. *Oh, thank god.*

He turned and walked back down the side of the house, through the gate, taking care to latch it behind him. And then he headed towards home at a layman's pace. Everything would be okay; she was resting, that was all. He felt the relief again, coursing through him.

He would text Dan later that day. He'd ask how the Bowie practice had gone, what songs they were doing, and Dan would send some sort of normal reply, something ordinary, something everyday, and he'd know she was fine. Life would carry on, exactly the same, because she was fine.

But for all that, the shrill in his ears wouldn't settle. Wouldn't lower one notch.

27

She hits her head coming down from the bench, and time alters course in that instant.

First, it pauses as if thinking, *Which way?* Pulse beats pass, one after the other after the other, while she waits in a place that's silent and blank. There's a moment when her eyes fly open unseeing – there's only a wisp of confusion – and they close just as quickly unaware. The pause lasts only seconds, not minutes, and then time turns back with its path close to decided. It briefly loosens its hold on her, like a gift, and she dreams.

But is it a dream? It's a strange sort of state; is she thinking or dreaming, or is it something else altogether? She knows she's not asleep, but she's certainly not awake. She sees Dan and Jack coming towards her, but soon it's unsettling. A bright urgency rises at its edges. She realises she's not at all well.

—

There'd been a sequence of bad decisions. Given the chance (which she suspects she won't be) that's what she'd say to people, rueful smile attached. Paul had rung in the middle of a quick clean. She kept on cleaning, little jobs here and there, while she listened. It was Verbose Paul, worse than she'd ever known him to be; to keep up with the conversation she only needed to register one word in three. What she was really doing was waiting for the reason he called; he never called. But one moment she was listening, scrubbing the sink, and the next, there she was, standing high on the stone benchtop in her flimsy slippers. A scenario with limited grip-possibilities, she'd readily admit. She just seemed to arrive there, cleaning cloth in hand, the dirty rangehood somehow snagging her attention and demanding some action.

She was inclined to blame the flu for her airy, easily led, head. On any ordinary day, she was no avid cleaner.

And then he'd mentioned London, periods of heartbreak, everything she'd done to him, and it had stunned her and upset her so much she knew she needed to climb down. That he'd hidden all that for so long! Back then, she'd thought she'd offended him when she started going out with Chris, and that he hadn't liked her very much ever since. She was shaking from deep within herself, but she'd been careful, or so she thought: trying to get down with a slow mindful squat, her slippered feet negotiating the bench with Paul's voice still coming through her phone. But there was a flurry of slippage, a cry from her, and her phone went flying, disappearing in the vicinity of the lounge.

She'd fallen, and her head hit the island bench. In the very last moment of her fall, in a too-fast infinitesimal span of time, she'd thought to move her head, to save it, and so she'd been struck on the temple.

And now she's on the floor, dreaming. Trying to hang on to that vision of Dan and Jack.

But she pulls herself out of it and looks around. She stands up, careful and untrusting, and takes slow, uncertain steps to the lounge. Then she squats – maybe the phone is just under the lounge and she knows she needs it to make a call – but as she lowers her head it goes into a wild swim and she's forced to sink onto the lounge. *I'll just stay here*, she thinks. *Let my head settle a bit first*. She lies back and becomes aware, vaguely, of their cat coming into the room and pressing its body against the lounge, and she drops her hand down to it for a moment. Then she brings her hand back up to her head, to the throbbing pain at her temple, and falls again into that dreamlike state.

The sense of urgency is no longer there. Dan and Jack have gone. Now she stands outside, somewhere green and lovely, and the air is sparkling and exquisitely soft. She doesn't mind the solitude. She raises one hand and turns it gently in the air, as if she could scoop and hold this most precious of substances.

But in the next moment she wakes, yanked from the dream. She feels very sick. She thinks to go to the bathroom and hauls herself into a sitting position, takes one breath and another, and stands. And that's when she truly suspects: it's done. There's no step to be taken, no forward movement, nothing else. There's just this, time leaving. And is it only in her mind that she turns? To the left, to the right, to the kitchen table, backwards to the garden, taking one last look at it all – at life? Now, she lies down again in a slow, gentle falling and closes her eyes. A strip of sunlight crosses her legs. Blood slips from her ear.

28

Chris only made it to the beginning of Beth's street. He turned the corner with a horrible jerk in his heartbeat and had to pull into the first spot at the kerb. He switched off the engine, frowning. What part of him thought this was possible? When had he last knocked on a door unannounced?

He'd driven straight from the hospital. At four that morning he'd been called in to work for a multi-trauma – five people in a car accident on Mona Vale Road – and so maybe it was sheer weariness that allowed him to follow through with his plan, to ignore the voice of reason that usually dominated his decisions. Beth's three books and her coat lay on the back seat of the car. He left the hospital car park and didn't take the route that led to his empty house. Instead, he drove towards the address scrawled in black pen on a piece of paper lying on the passenger seat beside him.

He drove towards Beth's house under an early bright sun and with Bob Dylan singing, his life's soundtrack since the day Max had died. And so maybe a lyrical Bob Dylan and a beautiful sky propelled his wayward plan too – the feeling that anything was possible in such a light, with such a song. Even picking up a too-old past and reminding yourself exactly what it looked like.

Paul Swan had made him a little crazy. Curdled a memory he'd been so sure of, that had felt so clear and straight. And now he didn't know whether he'd headed to Beth's house hoping to redress his wrongs and put regret to bed, to say sorry for not ringing more or writing better letters, sorry for not saying goodbye properly and delivering her things earlier – or whether he was there simply to ask: *How much did you love me?* What a tragedy it would be if there hadn't been love.

He certainly wasn't there to ask about her son. He'd settled that in his mind. Beth would have told him, he knew that. Her sense of grace and her kindness wouldn't have allowed her to do otherwise.

But once there, once he'd turned into her street, he couldn't go any further. The reality was confronting; this act wasn't him. He'd think about it tomorrow, or the next day. Or maybe, by some wonder of fate, their paths would cross again, or one day Beth might instead call on him.

The morning was literally twinkling. He wound down the windows, breathing in air that had turned beautifully warm. Dylan was singing about diamonds and the sea and his thoughts were now on Max – how he missed him! – and then his eyes went to a large flowering gum tree across the road, a canopy full of fiery red flowers. He was reading a book on trees – *The Overstory*. Sarah had pressed it on him and he knew Max had loved it. (He'd put his book about Putin in the charity bin.) It could well be that he'd never really *looked* at a tree, which seemed ludicrous. He stared into the tree, seeing the tone of its leaves, the swirls in the bark, the soft movement of the wind through its branches – and then his eye caught sight of a man who was going to fucking fall off a ladder!

Just behind the tree, to the left, a thin elderly man was making his way up a ladder that leant against the side of a house. He didn't look to be slowing down. He was going right to the top – to the gutter, no doubt. Chris's heart sank. How he hated ladders. They kept ladder statistics in emergency; they were the second-highest cause of accidental death. Men over fifty were most at risk, and men over sixty-five, like this fellow, shouldn't even be on a ladder in the first place. His sense of balance wouldn't be nearly sufficient.

Chris got out of his car. He couldn't sit and watch. And now he could see that the ladder sat on uneven ground. Fuck. He walked briskly to the house and let himself in the front gate. He arrived at the foot of the ladder and held on to it tightly. Then he spoke to the man, keeping his voice calm and soft so as not to give him a fright.

'Hello? Could I possibly sort that gutter out for you?'

There was an understandable element of surprise in the man's quick upper-body turning, in his *What the hell?* expression, and Chris had to rush to explain his point of view. A doctor who just couldn't bear to watch. He'd seen far too many do-it-yourself deaths. Sorry to be morbid, but he'd much prefer to be safe than sorry.

The man, definitely in his seventies, was going up to clear out a gutter filled with leaves and wouldn't be dissuaded from his task. 'Done it a million times,' he said.

Chris sighed. 'I'll stay and hold the ladder then.'

'Righto,' the man said, and he continued climbing until he stood on the last rung, and he stayed there, overreaching and flinging out leaves, while Chris watched this stubborn insanity with a galloping heart. Just this month he'd seen a subdural haematoma and fractured back from precisely this act. Yes, the man had survived, but he would never be the same again.

He was still gripping the ladder when he saw Paul Swan running. The sight made his breath catch. Paul was on the other side of the street and his exertion was clear. Chris was on the brink of calling out, but the fear of surprising the ladder man stopped him, and on thinking about it, what would he say? As Paul had said, they appeared to be very much done with each other. It was a long, winding street and Chris watched him intently, twisting his body to stay with him, until Paul was gone. Chris looked up again at his elderly adventurer, wondering about Paul and where he was going – was he headed to Beth's? – and then the man reached out one more time and slipped, and all hell broke loose. The ladder teetered to the side and the man half went with it and then it was a total collapse, the ladder, the two of them, with Chris doing his best to catch the man or at least cushion his fall. He managed a frantic fumbling combination of the two, a flailing-limb manoeuvre that ended, thankfully, with the man lying on top of Chris, apart from one arm that he'd flung out to his side for support. It was from this arm, unfortunately, that they both heard a crack.

And so it was that Chris returned to his car with a patient, and with his own back aching. His hand didn't feel quite right either. He drove off with the sun behind him. With Bob Dylan asking him question after question, telling him the answer was somewhere in the wind.

29

Louisa took the call from Clare in the Royal Botanic Garden, standing in the sun by a towering flooded gum tree. She'd just finished with a tour group and a few stragglers were now disappearing into the distance. She hadn't been scheduled to do the tour, having stepped back with all the funerals, but she'd agreed to take this one when Emma Humphreys called in sick.

She'd changed her style. Hadn't even attempted any of her usual light comedy. She'd felt a bit too wistful; a weak smile short of melancholic. It wasn't like her not to want to draw out a laugh. Humour always felt like an important line to hold; the instinct, always there, that things would go better if she packaged herself with humour. Being *largely serious* didn't usually seem a viable option. But today, instead of comedy, she'd shared some highly personal facts with her tour group.

She told the group about *her* trees. The ones her grandfather had planted. She explained they were now more than seventy years old, and stood more than fifty metres tall. ('That's almost one hundred and seventy feet,' she added for some members of the party.) The tree's botanical name was *Eucalyptus grandis*, she told them. There was a flooded gum tree in the Myall Lakes National Park, north of Newcastle, that was thought to be the tallest tree in New South Wales. It was four hundred years old and seventy-six metres in height. Locals called it 'the Grandis'.

She described the particular place in the forest where her family's trees stood. The road took you into a gully and past stand after stand of flooded gum trees; hundreds of them, with their powdery-white trunks rising skywards. On a sunny day, when pale light streaked through the stands, it was like a drive through a cathedral. Her grandfather planted his trees a little further on, separate from those majestic stands. He chose a place near a creek where the forest workers filled their billies and stopped for tea.

—

Louisa could now describe the drive, and the trees, because she'd seen some photos and talked to Tim's mother Anne. The day after she'd spoken to Tim in the gardens, she put Gilbert in the car and drove north to Hawks Nest. The trip took her close to three hours and Gilbert was an uncomplaining passenger. Sometimes, he sat tall in the back seat, with his head held high at the window like visiting royalty.

Anne lived in a small weatherboard house two streets back from the beach. There was a Norfolk pine in her front yard and a small white car in her driveway. Louisa had called the day before and Anne was expecting her. The screen door was flung open the second Louisa stepped from the car, and within a couple of seconds she was hit by a warm gush of welcome. In that moment, as early as that, she regretted not making the trip sooner.

'And who, may I ask, is this?' Anne asked, as Gilbert sprung from the car.

'This is Gilbert, my young charge,' Louisa said.

Anne ruffled his ears. 'What a superb-looking dog,' she said to him, and he cocked his head back at her with interest. 'He's a real character,' Anne added.

'He's actually Ed Sheeran reincarnated.'

'*Ed Sheeran is dead?*'

'No, no, no, he's alive! Sorry, it was a joke. I just think Gilbert looks like Ed Sheeran.'

'I'm not sure I remember what Ed Sheeran looks like.'

'Like this!' Louisa said, gesturing to Gilbert.

Anne frowned, seeming completely flummoxed by that. To her, apparently, he looked entirely like a dog.

Louisa and Gilbert followed as Anne led them into the house and down the hall to the kitchen, saying, 'Gosh I can see your mother in you,' over her shoulder as she walked.

Louisa laughed. 'I don't look much like her.'

'It's your eyes,' Anne said.

Louisa towered over Anne. Anne was short and nuggety; she looked fit for a woman who'd just turned seventy. With her beige tailored shorts, bright red top and solid sandals, she had an air of absolutely no fuss about her.

But that said, Anne had gone to some trouble with their morning tea. It was waiting for them on the small kitchen table: a veritable mountain of Sao biscuits – each one topped with fat slices of tomato and cheese – and next to it a small French teacake, freshly baked, with tempting hints of cinnamon wafting from it. The table was already set too, with teacups and saucers.

'I've been thinking about it,' Anne said as she hit the button on the kettle. 'I haven't seen you for eleven years.'

'Eleven?' Guilt flushed through Louisa.

'You've lived so far away for so much of it,' Anne said.

In the year after her mother died, Janie and Louisa left the town they'd always lived in, the town where Anne lived at the time. In the years that followed, they moved regularly, and Louisa went from school to school. It was as if Janie couldn't properly attach herself to the world anymore.

'But I've kept up on most of your news from Tim,' Anne said. 'A summary, anyway. He's always looked out for you.'

Anne poured the boiling water into a large teapot wearing a chicken cosy and brought it to the table. They sat facing each other, pouring their tea with Gilbert lying at Louisa's feet. Louisa picked up a Sao and placed it on her little cake plate. She'd have to eat at least three of them to make a polite dent in the mountain. The sweet-smelling French teacake would just have to wait.

Anne asked about the past eleven years, wanting to fill in the gaps in Tim's accounts. So Louisa took a small mouthful of tea, and started on the last decade of her life. She told Anne about the job in a garden centre she'd held for a number of years, which sadly ended when the centre went broke; about cooking in cafes and for a catering company; about a long relationship that was, by its end, rather average (there was very little to say about it really; his name was Hugh). She listed the different towns she'd lived in before Sydney. Then she took a bite of a Sao, swallowed, and skipped a few years, telling Anne about her new house and Gilbert, about her garden tours and the lawnmowing, and the wakes. In total, wrapping it all up, it didn't sound like nearly enough to fill eleven years. A couple of times she had to stop and think: *What have I been doing?* And it occurred to her that she sounded like Janie. She sounded like a wanderer.

After Hugh, it was the wakes that interested Anne the most. She thought they sounded intriguing.

'Tim mentioned them to me,' Anne said. 'What an unusual way to help people. And it does warm my heart to know you're working with Tim,' she added. She paused. 'Now,' she said, with a firm hand placed on the table, 'you wanted to talk to me about your mum and Janie.'

Anne had been friends with Louisa's mum, Ally, since kindergarten. Janie was one year younger than them. The three of them were tight, but Anne would never be as close to them as Ally and Janie were to each other. Ally and Janie looked alike and laughed the same way. They recognised themselves in the other.

Louisa picked up another Sao, listening intently. The biscuits were decidedly dry. She swallowed a couple of times and took a big gulp of tea.

'Ally and Janie were so close,' Anne said, 'they were given presents on each other's birthdays when they were young. And it wasn't that they demanded them, it simply had to happen. And they *happily* wore matching handmade clothes until Ally was twelve. Your grandmother was an excellent seamstress.'

'Twelve? That's old to still be doing that.'

'There'd be a variation,' Anne said. 'Same dress but in a different colour. Maybe a frill on one and not on the other.'

'That makes it a bit better.'

'Most of the time they carried it off, they really did. They were popular.'

'I think I've heard about the sewing before,' Louisa said.

'Would you like a slice of teacake?' Anne asked.

'I'd love one.'

Louisa could have sat talking to Anne for days. Gilbert lay with his face pressed against the leg of the chair, snoring.

'I know in the last few years you didn't see enough of the fun side of your mum,' Anne said. 'That was a shame. She changed when you were about eight. It was as if this huge sadness was waiting around the corner for her. Like it just landed on her. I don't think it was ever properly explained to her. She was put on some kind of medication, and that helped a little bit. Some days she was good. And she tried her best to hide it when things were bad. She once said to me that on the bad days it felt like her personality had been taken away. She was left with a blankness that made everyday life hard to wade through.' Anne sighed. 'Janie saw it all, though. And Janie helped her.'

'What do you think happened with the car?' Louisa asked. They'd never talked about this before. Not specifically, not about reasons or actualities. Louisa had never asked the question out loud.

Anne looked at her as if to check how far she could go.

'Tim mentioned that you were worried about it,' she said. 'A few people had their opinions at the time, but I know it was an accident. It was a terrible accident. In my head, this is what I picture: I see her driving and I see her with that blankness she talked about. That awful blankness stopping her from seeing the road clearly, stopping her from concentrating. And it had been raining, it was slippery. She loved you too much. She wouldn't have left you and Janie. She just wouldn't have. And definitely not without some sort of goodbye.'

An aching feeling, a good feeling, rose in Louisa. It started in her chest – *She loved you too much* – lodged in her throat – *She wouldn't have left you* – pressed behind her eyes. Tears slipped down her face. 'Sorry,' she said, 'sorry,' brushing them away.

'No, *I'm* sorry! Have I said too much?'

'No, it's not too much. Not at all too much.' And Louisa smiled and grimaced through her tears, still wiping them away. 'It's good to hear it.'

'I still miss them. I'll always miss them,' Anne said, and she got up to grab a box of tissues. 'But their trees!' she said, brightening as she placed the box on the table. 'They're so beautiful.' She reached for a pile of photos, and a map sitting at the end of the table. Over the years, when the need struck her, Anne had visited the trees, and she had taken a lot of photos.

—

Louisa stood before her group, and for once that's exactly what they were: a group.

Trees in a forest communicate with each other and consider each other, she told them. They are social and careful in how they share their space. Her mum's tree and Janie's tree had stood so close together for seventy-two years they would share a root system by now; they were old friends, sisters, who shared sunlight and nutrients and understood survival. They were now so close, so dependent on each other, that when one died the other might follow.

Louisa had only seen the trees once and found it too hard to return. She'd made a conscious choice not to talk about them.

But now she saw them in a different light; she understood. The trees were hers. They were life, and death, and love. They talked to each other and they talked to her.

Her story was very well received. There was a consensus that her grandfather's acts were extremely heartwarming. One lady became particularly teary, saying she held a vision of them, a sense of a cloud-piercing eternity.

When the group had disbanded, Louisa stayed on for a while. A soft afternoon light bathed the gardens. There was a cloudless sky, and the surface of the harbour was spread with small dancing jewels.

Her phone rang and she fished it out of her bag. It was Clare. She'd just had a phone call from Paul Swan and he'd asked them to cater for a wake. His sister-in-law had died tragically three days earlier.

Clare paused. 'It's going to be quite big,' she said.

30

The morning of Elizabeth's funeral was beautiful and still.

Clare and Louisa arrived on the doorstep of the impressively large home of Elizabeth's cousin Rachel. The front door itself was an unusual size. 'Could one person open this?' Louisa asked, leaning back to take it all in. What a stupidly big door.

The house sat on an equally daunting street that ran along the harbour, with only a small public path separating the two. Louisa had admitted to a growing sense of unease as they'd parked.

Compelled by nerves, they'd arrived well before the time they had agreed with Paul. It was better to get settled and started, Clare thought. And Louisa genuinely thought tomorrow couldn't come soon enough.

—

There'd been blood everywhere. It was a deep, terrible cut. Blood was in the onions and on the cutting board, on the bench and in the sink, and Louisa had reacted very badly. First, she'd yelled out in shock, before turning ominously quiet and pale. She couldn't look at her finger or have her finger anywhere near her. She thrust it towards Clare: *I can't look at it. Can you fix it?*

Clare ran a little water over it, patted it dry, and wrapped it up in a small clean cloth. And then she thought of Chris Lang.

They went straight to the car and were at the hospital within fifteen minutes. Clare took Louisa in and dropped Chris's name with the triage nurse – a quite proud *I know this important person* was apparent in her tone. *I don't really care*, was apparent in the nurse's response.

Louisa returned to Clare's house around two hours later. The triage nurse had, in the end, given her the slightest boost in the queue. Louisa let herself in, walked straight into the kitchen, and stood at the bench.

'Right,' she said with her bandaged finger held high. 'Where was I?'

And Clare knew, in that moment, that she loved her.

—

Louisa pressed Rachel's doorbell and they waited. Bulging bags and boxes lay in clumps by their feet. Nobody came. Clare checked the house number against a piece of paper in her pocket and then Louisa pressed the doorbell again, and again they waited, looking at each other with a little apprehension now. They looked up and down the street; there was nobody about.

'Everybody in the house must be thinking someone else is going to answer the door,' Louisa said.

Clare pulled her phone out of her bag. 'I'll text Paul.'

'Is there any chance we've got the wrong day?' Louisa asked, and they exchanged immediate, horrified looks.

For a second, just a second, anxiety had them believing the question wasn't absurd.

'Why would you even say that?' Clare demanded, with her hand clasped to her heart.

'It's the painkillers.'

'Stop it,' Clare said. She'd started to grin. 'Now I'm grinning. The grinning thing is back!'

'You're going to set me off.'

Clare looked away from Louisa and checked her phone, still smiling inanely. 'Paul hasn't answered.'

'I'm not ringing the doorbell again,' Louisa said. Instead, she reached out and turned the big doorknob and pushed.

The door swung open to reveal an impossibly grand foyer, and no sign of human life. Just a magnificent bunch of flowers on a slim antique table.

They shuffled into the house, struggling with the weight of their cargo, and followed a long hallway to a high-ceilinged living room. Sky and water floated in its tall windows and there were flowers everywhere, filling the air with their competing fragrances. This room, too, was deserted.

'Did Paul say where to meet?' Louisa asked.

'He said he'd see us at the house. We're half an hour early, remember.'

'Right.'

'Should we just try to find the kitchen?'

Louisa nodded.

They made their way through another doorway and down a shallow flight of stairs, breathing heavily with the exertion, telling each other they would need to hunt down some helpers to retrieve the rest of their gear. They looked up, and before them lay a vast open room, lined with French doors.

And in this room, temporarily evacuated of its usual furnishings, sat a pale closed coffin.

They stopped.

White chairs, at least a hundred of them, were arranged in neat rows, and a small aisle was fashioned between them with the coffin at its apex. Beyond the French doors another hundred or more chairs lined a flat expanse of bright-green lawn, stopping only where the lawn sloped suddenly towards the water.

'Oh, look at that,' Clare said, indicating the coffin. 'There she is.'

The only person in the room was a lady who sat on a chair placed next to the coffin. Her gaze was fixed on the glittering harbour beyond the wide-open doors. Her legs were crossed and her hands were clasped in her lap. She had a measured elegance – skirt-suited and all pearl and white, apart from a large navy hat on her head.

They both looked at her as she sat there, stone-still.

'I'm undecided about those hats,' Louisa said softly.

The lady must have sensed them staring. Her head turned and she saw them, signalling that she had with a brief wave and a smile. Then she tilted her head towards a doorway in the corner of the room to her left. Her expressions and movements were discreet and gentle, and it crossed Clare's mind that it was a demeanour they should perhaps try to emulate.

Louisa gave the lady a small *right you are* nod, and they went as directed. They were staggering past the rows of chairs when they saw the small white table with the two photos of Elizabeth.

Clare heard Louisa's quick intake of breath. They stopped and stood still again.

In her features and her colouring, she wasn't at all what they'd imagined. Not a hint of Rosamund Pike. She looked like no one they knew. But the affinity was there in the sense she projected: the brightness and warmth they'd imagined, the aura of kindness, the beautiful smile. She was perfect. They stood smiling at her photo and were slow to walk away.

—

They finally made it into a large, stunning kitchen, which, at first glance, appeared to have capabilities well beyond its circumstances. 'This thing looks *commercial*,' Louisa said in awe, 'and yet it still looks so inviting.' She walked around, pulling out blue-painted drawers, opening cupboards, whispering, '*Who are these people?*' with every astonishing find. The generosity of the room gave their spirits an immediate boost. Anything, surely, could be achieved in that room.

Paul appeared half an hour later. He came in looking leaden-limbed and bleary-eyed, apologising for not meeting them at the door or seeing them in, apologising for his mishandling of the numbers, apologising for himself and his behaviour in general. Clare couldn't stay annoyed with him when she saw the state he was in.

'How are you, Paul?' she asked, feeling a rush of sympathy, but he didn't even form a reply. There was such an awful change in him; talking appeared to cost him some effort.

He was holding a platter. 'Someone just handed me this,' he said. 'Caramel slice, I think. Looks nice.' But he handed it over with an expression close to nausea.

'And expect a vast quantity of scones,' he said, as he was leaving. He'd rung an aunty, he explained, a scone maker of some repute, and told her about their numbers problem. She'd left the house for the shops while he was still on the phone.

—

The scone aunty slipped in about fifteen minutes later, and she'd been, without question, undersold. Her scones were perfect; appropriately petite yet still light and lofty, and their tops were crusty and golden.

'It's already mayhem out there,' the scone aunty said as she left.

Clare and Louisa shared a scone the second her heels crossed the threshold, marvelling at its crumbly interior.

'Any chance we can pretend they're ours?' Louisa asked, lifting a last morsel to her mouth. 'Sorry,' she added, 'of course we can't.'

—

The house was already near full. The chairs were all taken and most of the standing room too. And the lawn was filling up. Paul weaved his way through tight groups of people, past an impossibly huge gang of plaid-skirted students. He scanned the room, and found the two men he was looking for more easily than he'd imagined. He pressed past people to get to them.

'Graham,' he said on approach, 'I was told you wanted to see me?' Graham was Rachel's husband.

'Paul! Yes.' He pointed to the other man. 'This is Ethan.'

Ethan was Graham's neighbour, and together the two men had produced the funeral video. Ethan was a professional film editor; he'd once won a Logie for a documentary. Dan had selected the photos they used and Graham had liaised with Ethan. From the start, Paul hadn't liked the sound of it. Was he going to have to watch a produced movie about Beth? He was trying to keep his boundaries as small as possible in these overwhelming circumstances.

'It's not a movie,' Graham had said a few days ago when Paul had tentatively aired his reservations. 'It's a montage.'

But now, it seemed, in the hands of an accomplished editor, it was far more than a montage.

'I watched it last night,' Graham said. He gave a small grimace. 'I get your point now, Paul. Funeral videos aren't usually done by professionals. It was' – Graham paused – 'well, it's very sad.'

'But the sadness in it is real,' Ethan objected. 'It's true.'

Graham thought it capable of sending already teetering emotions to the very edge of reason. It had been beautifully and seamlessly put together, set against the most stirring of soundtracks. Graham mentioned a particular section in the middle when 'Moon River' played. It was a version of the song he'd never heard before, sung by Neil Finn and Paul Kelly, and it accompanied photos of Elizabeth in her twenties. He was broken well before the plaintive harmonica started playing.

'We have to go with it,' Paul said. 'What choice do we have now?'

And he left the men. He intended to watch the service alone. A chair in the front row of seats had been reserved for him, but he didn't take it. He found a spot off to the side, standing among strangers.

The service soon began. The guests, the multitude of them, were silent. A small group of students sang 'Blue Skies'. When Dan spoke, Paul lowered his head and fixed his eyes on the floor.

Tears dripped. He heard Dan's words along with the knowledge that no day in his life would be free of this: this guilt, this loss, this grief. But still, he couldn't decide on the worst of what he'd done; he couldn't properly name it.

—

Clare slipped out of the kitchen. For the past two hours they'd listened to the wake through the kitchen's walls. They'd heard the rising thrum of voices as the house filled with mourners. And then they'd heard the faint sounds of the service: a lone voice speaking, some people singing. But a few minutes ago, all that noise had stopped. They could hear almost nothing. 'It must be close to finishing,' Clare whispered to Louisa, with the impulse to see. Sophie and Josh, their university students, had arrived to help them, so things were relatively calm. She placed her knife on the board and told Louisa she'd only be gone a few minutes.

Clare walked quietly down the short hallway and stopped before the closed door to the living room. Someone was speaking. She turned the doorknob and opened the door a fraction then sighed; her way was blocked by people, packed in right to the room's outer limits.

Two tall, bulky men stood in front of her. They became aware of her presence and moved slightly, but all it did was allow her to open the door one fraction more; she remained largely in the hallway. She craned her neck and all she could see was a high wedge of the room, some heads, some sky, the tips of flower bunches. She couldn't see the man who was speaking. She only heard a few cracked words; he was finishing up. She couldn't see or understand why everything went silent. *I've missed it all*, she thought. *I've missed it all.*

She waited. Stole a few seconds more. Slipped herself a fraction further into the room. But still there was silence. Not one person around her spoke. The reverence in their attitudes overwhelmed her.

Her heart beat in her ears for no reason. *We're the same age*, she thought suddenly. *I could be her. I could be her.*

She tried to make herself taller, stretching and straining, but she saw nothing more. She could hear, though: she heard 'Fields of Gold' start. A group of young girls were singing in heartbreakingly sweet voices. She heard the exquisite song all the way through with tears welling. Then, with her blood pumping hard, she turned and slipped back out of the room.

—

There was a photo of Beth and Chris among the 'Moon River' photos. The editor lingered on it long enough that you could read a hundred things in it, if you paid close attention. You could recognise this couple were in Hyde Park during an abundant spring. You could see they were intensely happy in that moment and you could believe they'd always felt that way, whenever they were together. You could understand the moment was special enough that they'd asked someone, a passing stranger, to help them document it. You could realise, now, that Beth must have kept the photo and that it had some sort of significance for her – enough for Dan to generously select it for this important forum. You could know it was love.

—

The video played. Paul believed he was in some way prepared for it, given Graham's warning, but he wasn't. He thought he'd understood what they'd lost – you're not even close, this video said. The 'Moon River' photos were destroying. There was one in London with Beth and Chris Lang. Paul Kelly singing about seeing the world and there was Chris. Just the one photo though; a flash of a time and a scene you could easily miss. Paul featured in a couple, but for the remainder of the film it was all about Elizabeth and Dan and Jack.

When the film was done and the screen went blank, when it made its terrible final statement – this stunning life is finite, it said, this one life is over – something broke in him. Protecting himself no longer seemed important. She was everything and he was nothing. How she deserved – and others deserved – that the truth of her death be known. And how could that happen while *he* stayed silent?

He turned towards the back left corner of the room; towards Chris. He had caught a glimpse of Chris standing there, seconds before the service had started, and now he headed for Chris through all the densely packed bodies. He walked without questioning his instinct. Chris had come to him as a relatively safe harbour for his first confession. As a possible source of understanding that might act as a buffer when his words finally exploded in Dan. (Chris knew what it was like not to have Beth's love, the devastation of that.) And Chris dealt with the daily disasters of life: he witnessed death, understood human frailty, even the havoc wrought by the flu.

Chris saw him coming, and their eyes locked as Paul made his way to the corner. As he approached Chris, he started to say, *I need to talk to you*, but Chris got in first.

'I need to talk to you,' Chris said, with a keen sense of urgency in his voice. 'I've been looking for you, Paul. I saw you the day Beth died. I saw you running up her street. What were you doing there?'

Paul's heart thumped in his chest. He hadn't yet prepared himself for accusations.

'You saw me?'

'I was intending on talking to her but I couldn't, I stopped at the bottom of her street.' Chris spoke quickly, brushing the question aside. 'What were you doing there?' he repeated.

'I'd been talking to her on the phone,' he said, and there it was: the truth beginning to leave him. 'I upset her. And I think I heard her fall. She was standing on the bench while we were talking.'

'You heard her fall and *you were running*?'

'I *thought* I heard her fall. I wasn't sure.'

'But you didn't call someone? Dan? An ambulance? Why did you run?' Chris's voice was rising.

Paul hesitated. 'I was high,' he said, and his voice was shaky. How abhorrent the truth could be.

He watched Chris's face collapse.

He went on, with his heart now pounding in his throat. 'I went to her house and I think I saw her as she lay dying! As she lay dying! Do you know what that's like? To hold on to that image?' He took in a deep breath and it shook again through his chest. 'But the door was locked, and I couldn't know what was happening at the time. From where I was looking, I thought she was sleeping. I thought she was fine. That she didn't need me.'

Paul looked straight at Chris, feeling so desperate. 'I told her you were coming to see her. I told her everything. About how I'd loved her. I may have even told her that she'd ruined my life.

But could the flu have been a factor too? Could the flu have made her fall?'

'The flu,' Chris went to say, but then he stopped talking abruptly. His face turned away from Paul, and Paul followed his gaze. Louisa Shaw stood nearby, staring at them, holding a plate. And Dan was with her, clutching a scone.

—

Near the end of the wake, Clare went looking for Chris. She found him sitting alone on an ornate wooden bench positioned for a prime view of the harbour. Almost all of the guests had now gone.

'I'm sorry,' she said when she reached him. She knew some of the story from Louisa. She'd heard that Paul and Dan Swan were caught up in a terrible discussion in some other room of the house. She could see Chris's distress.

She offered him the small plate she was carrying. On it sat one triangle of chicken sandwich. His shoulders went back a little, and a faint smile came to his face.

'I saved this for you,' she said. 'We had so few of them, compared to the number of people, they were a bit like gold.'

He moved so she could sit down beside him. She smiled. 'I wanted to say thank you, for helping Louisa. And I really didn't want you to eat the frittata.'

He leant back against the seat. He told her he now knew what Paul had done, and he was struggling with his own part in it. He longed to take back some of the things he'd said to Paul. He was there in it, part of the chain of events that had led to Beth's death.

From what she knew, she thought he was being unreasonably hard on himself.

'Couldn't that be said about a lot of things in life? Aren't we often part of a chain of events? It doesn't mean you see something wrong through to the end. And wasn't it an accident, really, in the end?'

He nodded slowly, but she could see he didn't quite accept that.

She stood up to go, saying they had a fair amount of packing up left to do; though she felt reluctant to leave him. When she looked at him, she thought about what Paul had said about Chris at their dinner, and Louisa's report of the scene she witnessed. Between the men, there seemed to be a relationship charged with emotion, loaded with history. How human, she thought, and her heart ached for the two of them.

31

Chris had three rostered days off after Beth's funeral. He spent the days at home. He sat, walked, read, watched television and listened to music and it was all done with sadness. Sadness was in him, on him. It was as if he'd never allowed himself to feel it before.

He felt the huge sadness of Max gone. Of Beth gone. Of their magnificent voices now silent.

On the third day, he sat on his back deck in the hot morning sunshine. Magpies warbled next door. He'd made himself a coffee, and he drank it while looking out at the day. Clear summer mornings could look so perfect. And the humidity, for once, was humane. At the back of his garden stood a large jacaranda still in bloom, an almost implausible purple, and in the middle of his sadness the colour was piercing. And then his eyes went to his far neighbour's tall cypress hedge. It had been pruned for the first time in its life. A funny sort of job had been done. Its lack of anything truly linear, its overall haphazardness, brought a soft smile to his face. Someone had tried.

On the fourth day he returned to work and to one of those surprisingly calm days. A midweek day when you could believe the world was predominantly well. And in the minutes before he left the hospital, he phoned Louisa Shaw. Before that, he'd rung the number of the funeral home he'd called when tracking down the caterers for Jill Duncan, and spoke to a Tim Buchanan. He'd explained who he was and asked for Louisa's number. He spoke to Louisa briefly and asked for Clare's address. She lived in Willoughby, a few suburbs from him, and around twenty minutes later, in the early afternoon, he knocked on her door.

It had come to him midway through his shift that he wanted to see her. That it was possible. At the time, he was attending to a man who'd been shot in the face with a paintball. The man had retained a surprising amount of good humour about it, despite one of his eyes being at risk. Right then, standing before that man and his impressively upbeat attitude, he thought, *I could just knock on her door.*

—

As he waited, he heard a scuttling noise in the hallway. Someone, at the very least a small frantic dog, was at home.

Clare opened the door.

'Hello,' he said, smiling.

She smiled back. 'Hello.' There was a nice look of surprise on her face.

He hesitated. He'd been so caught up in the logistics of getting her address, and arriving at her door, that he hadn't really thought beyond this point. About what might happen when she opened the door.

'I was wondering,' he said (and he had to go with the truth, it was all he had), 'whether you'd like to have dinner with me some time, or lunch, or a cup of coffee even.'

And her smile widened.

A small brown dog sat beside her, staring up at him intently. He was being judged.

She answered straight away. 'That would be lovely. Yes, I would. I could make us a cup of tea right now, if you're free?'

'That would be great,' he said, and she stood back to let him in, and then he followed her down the hallway. She took him into a small sunlit room off the kitchen; neatly squeezed into it were two pale couches and a coffee table. 'My daughter Grace calls this our snug,' she said. 'Louisa calls it our office.'

His long legs negotiated a space. The house had a sense of comfort he liked. Books lay on tables and windowsills.

He stayed past three cups of tea. And he wasn't, historically, a tea drinker.

He felt a mixture of feelings, sitting there with her. There was a definite nervousness – an acknowledgement that this was important – but alongside it existed a warmth, and a feeling close to relief; that life could again feel this right, this exquisite.

An easy intimacy was quickly established between them. Chris told her he was recently separated from his wife, Sarah, who was now living in Borneo for an indefinite period of time. They had no children. Clare told him she had separated from her husband, David, about four months earlier. They had two children, Alex and Grace, who were fifteen and twelve. Then she went a little further. She described, briefly, the night her husband had left her, and told him about her accident and how Louisa had saved her.

Clare also told him she was in the middle of a big decision. She held a sheet of paper up in front of her. There were two roughly drawn columns: one headed 'Pros', the other headed 'Cons'.

He gave her a quizzical smile. 'I didn't know people actually put that sort of thing to paper.'

'I never have before. But I read somewhere it was helpful to write it down and see it in black and white. A bit like saying an affirmation out loud.'

He sank back into an extremely comfortable lounge cushion. 'Can I ask what the big decision is?'

'Yes, you can. I need to decide whether I do another wake with Louisa. Whether I keep doing more.'

That surprised him. 'I assumed you would be. You're extraordinarily good at it.'

She smiled. 'Thank you. But it's not what I normally do. It's not what I've spent my life studying. It's so far from what I've been trained for.'

'What do you normally do?'

'I work for a large pharmaceutical in the drug regulatory affairs department. You probably know what we do. I'm a manager and I have a lot of technical knowledge and experience.' She gave him a comical grimace. 'That sounded more conceited than I intended it to.'

'I'm sure it's a fact,' he said. 'But that does sound very different.'

'Louisa called in a few hours before you. Her friend Tim from the funeral home has another funeral for us. A small one.' It was what Louisa had talked about in the beginning: an elderly lady who'd apparently died peacefully in her sleep.

He leant in to look more closely at her sheet. She handed it to him.

After a first glance he said, 'You have quite a few cons.'

She pursed her lips and nodded.

She had written: *unstable income, stress of large numbers, on my feet all day, potential for sadness, some mind-numbing tasks, L's bad admin, have an established career.*

In the other column, she'd written one pro: *I feel more alive.*

He smiled at her. The decision looked fairly clear to him.

She asked him to stay for dinner, but after a short discussion they decided to go out instead. Her children, she said, were with their father for dinner. Clare said she'd shoot into her bedroom and get changed, it wouldn't take her a minute, but she was actually gone quite a while. He saw *Middlemarch* sitting on the end of the kitchen bench – the same edition he'd been intending to return to Beth – and sad memories stirred through him. He reached over, picked up the weighty book and started to read.

Miss Brooke had that kind of beauty which seems to be thrown into relief by poor dress.

—

Clare's heart pounded at an unhelpful rate. Her breathing was rapid. What on earth should she wear? Nothing looked right. She'd already tried so many things on and she knew well, from recent experience, the limited potential in her wardrobe. She grabbed something plain in the end, not wanting to look like she'd been gone for so long because she was trying too hard. But the air of casualness she'd hoped for was obviously lost.

She couldn't entirely believe he was here. That he'd walked out of his hospital and knocked on her door. His presence in her house had sent all her senses flying.

He stood up quickly when he heard her returning, and the look he gave her did nothing for her fluttering heart. He said she looked lovely, and would it be okay if he changed too? He lived only fifteen minutes away.

They drove to his house together. He said he'd be very quick, and she said she'd wait in the car. He strode to his front door and she waited, looking through the windscreen at the late afternoon. She opened her car door and got out. She stood in a corridor of brilliant soft air. A gentle breeze brushed her face.

He was quick. He came out wearing a pale-blue shirt, the delicate blue of a perfect morning sky. She liked absolutely everything about him in that moment: his crisp beautiful shirt, his eyes, his smile. The feeling felt new.

32

Clare and Louisa drove through the forest. On Clare's lap sat a handwritten sheet with detailed directions. It was a treasured, fragile thing, yellowed with age. Louisa's grandfather's cursive handwriting carried enough flourishes to make it a challenge in itself to read.

'I think,' Clare said with a great deal of uncertainty, 'we take the next left.' She squinted at the sheet. 'It says here "Spankers Flat Road". Can that be right?'

'It's right, but we were on Spankers Flat Road ages ago.'

They turned left anyway. Found themselves on Smailes Road instead.

'Take the next right onto Slacks Road,' Clare said. 'And then we need Rabbits Ridge Road,' she added, trying to enlarge the map on her phone, and Louisa said she'd watch out for it. Louisa liked to think they weren't completely lost.

They'd driven five hours north to see Ally and Janie Shaw's trees. A week had passed since Elizabeth's funeral.

Louisa's phone rang and Clare answered it for her.

'Hello, Tim,' she said, holding the phone out between them.

He was ringing to check how their trip was going and Louisa said, 'Great so far. Though there's a chance we're a little bit lost.'

'Just travelling down Slacks Road, Tim,' Clare said. 'There's some excellent road-naming going on in this forest.'

'How's Gilbert?' Louisa asked.

'He's great. In fact, he's just said he likes me more than you. He wants to live here permanently.'

'Tim gives Gilbert too many treats,' Louisa said after they'd hung up.

—

They were getting close. They now knew where they were on the old map. They drove along a ridge and then headed down into a gully. 'Flooded gums grow mostly in gullies,' Louisa told Clare. 'In a gully they feel safe and nourished, and they're protected when they're young. They reach for the full sun and the wind once they're older and stronger.'

As they descended, they felt the drop in temperature and noticed the change in the light. Here, the light was filtered; shafts of pale sunlight streamed into the forest. They drove around a bend and there, in the near distance, was the forest cathedral Anne had described to Louisa. Before them rose stand after stand of creamy-white gum trees, so grand and ethereal, almost closing the gap between a green earth and sky. Louisa slowed the car and they tilted their heads out the windows.

They drove on, turning, lastly, onto a less-travelled road much narrower than the ones before it; the forest came right to its edges;

leaf litter scattered its surface. Louisa slowed again and stopped the car in the middle of the road and they got out.

They'd found the trees. Two things of beauty.

The trees had been planted not far from the road's edge. They had socks of brown bark and smooth pale trunks. Louisa and Clare stood beneath them, craning their necks, with angled sunlight bathing their faces. They stared into two extraordinarily high canopies. And beyond the canopies lay a deep blue sky, a blue so perfect it looked imagined and painted.

Louisa smiled and went to each of the trees and pressed herself against each one in a wide-armed embrace. Clare followed her and did the same.

And when they stood back again, eyes looking skywards, they heard the wind rise in the canopy high above them; and with that, a single leaf left Janie's tree and headed for the ground in slow, fluttering arcs. They both saw it, and Louisa leapt into action as the breeze took it and began to carry it away from them, towards the thick forest. She scrambled over the undergrowth and flung out her arm and caught it before it could touch the ground.

They both looked down at the gum leaf in her palm. Looked up at each other. Well.

'Now I'll need to get one from Mum's tree, too,' Louisa said. 'Before it touches the ground.'

'I totally agree.'

And so there they stood under Ally Shaw's tree, heads tilted back, watching and waiting for a gust of wind to come along to stir the head of the tree. Waiting for a leaf. They were there for quite a while. Eventually, the canopy was ruffled again by the wind and a leaf fell, but it rode the wind too well and no amount of excited, snake-worried scrambling through the undergrowth could get them to it before it disappeared into the forest.

So back they went, under the tree, watching and waiting, knowing they couldn't leave without it.

'There's another one!' Louisa cried finally, seeing a leaf fluttering high above, and they were off, lurching and tripping through the undergrowth, until, yes, success was Clare's, a leaf in her hand! She felt such unbridled delight. She handed it to Louisa.

They had a picnic lunch in the boot and set it out on a rug right in the middle of the dirt road. They ate figs and prosciutto and chicken sandwiches with the two leaves placed carefully on the rug beside them.

Later, when they left the forest, Louisa put David Bowie on in the car. They pulled out onto the main road and she turned the volume up. 'What a ridiculously wonderful gift David Bowie was,' she said loudly over the music. 'How lucky are we to live in his wake?' The car filled with 'Starman' and they wound down the windows, singing loudly and badly to the air. They were filled with joy from the simplest of things: a song, a friend, two trees. *How beautiful this life is!* their hearts cried in unison. *How precious!*

When the song finished Louisa played it again, and again, until they were word-perfect.

Acknowledgements

Thank you, Sally Inglis. Your question in the dog park that morning when we crossed paths for the first time in years – 'How's that novel you've been writing going?' – kicked everything off.

Thank you, author Suzanne Daniel, for offering to be my first reader and for extending to me nothing but generosity and support. And to Dianne Blacklock, an amazing editor and mentor. Suzanne's suggestion that I engage a professional editor for a reader's report led me to you, and what a wonderful association it's been.

To Catherine Drayton, my literary agent: thank you for finding the best publishing homes for my manuscript, for steering me so expertly through the publishing process, and for working tirelessly to expand on a dream.

To my publishers – Rebecca Saunders from Hachette Australia, and Francesca Main from Phoenix, UK – two incredibly talented, warm women who have been an absolute joy to work with. Rebecca, from the very beginning you have treated my novel as something precious, which I will be eternally grateful for. And

Francesca, your passion and belief in my novel has been a delight, and a constant, driving force for me.

Thank you, Ali Lavau, the copy editor of my dreams. *The Wakes* is so much better and richer for your close involvement. And thank you to Christa Moffitt for the book's beautiful and uplifting cover.

Thank you to the brilliant teams at Hachette and Phoenix who have championed my novel through the editing and sales processes and continue to do so; especially to my project editor, Karen Ward, for seeing me through the deadlines, for your expert, thoughtful advice, for standing beside me so kindly and patiently while I learnt to let go, and also: Louise Stark, Fiona Hazard, Kelly Gaudry, Chris Sims, Lee Moir, Kate Taperell, Lillian Kovats, Madison Garratt, Sarah Brooks, Emma Dorph, Kirstin Corcoran and Alysha Farry.

Thank you to those whose time and expertise have greatly helped with some of the finer details of *The Wakes*: Robyn Hunter (my sister and kind, inspirational navigator through life) for being a sounding board, a giver of impeccable advice, for always being there at the end of the phone; Dr Liz Swinburn, for your medical advice and for so thoroughly, and happily, answering my many questions (though any errors in translation are entirely mine); Alex Hunter (talented chef and wordsmith) for the delectable-sounding food served at Clare and Paul's dinner; and Catriona Glover for being there at short notice when I unprofessionally flung legal questions in your direction.

A special thank you to Karen Saddington (Assistant Number Two) for supporting me in so many ways, and to Margie Hartley for cheering me on from the moment I first voiced the intention of writing a novel. And thank you to all my dear girlfriends (you know who you are) for the conversations and laughter, for giving me an understanding of friendship that lies deep in my soul and is the backbone of my novel.

Thank you to Mum and Dad for teaching me what it means to love life and value human connection. To Mum, for bringing such an abundant love into our home, for the pure joy, the singing, the sheer closeness; how we adored you. To Dad, for filling my upbringing with great books, a strong sense of justice, for all those trips to the bush and the beach. To my sisters, Robyn and Julie, and my brother, Peter: truly, what magnificent, funny people I got to grow up with! Thank you for being a family with me, for the loyal support and unconditional love, for the stories and laughter, for the unbreakable bond we formed early on. And to my extended family, the Stephensons, a big, close, loving family that I'm so fortunate to be a part of.

To the memory of my beautiful fifteen-year-old Groodle, Charli, who died the day before I had my first interview with publishers: gorgeous girl, you were often there, sprawled by my feet, during all those years of writing.

To my children, James, Tom and Emma, and their partners, Viv, Georgia and Ben. You are the lights in my life. You make it all better, shinier, and lovelier. What a joy it's been sharing my book with you.

And to my husband, Tony, thank you for everything; for an enduring love, for your kindness, for encouraging me when I talked about a dream. This novel wouldn't exist if it wasn't for you, and so I could go on and on: thank you, thank you, thank you.